The Postern

A "Postern" is a private or retired door or gate. It implies an inconspicuous or even hidden means of entrance.

Robert Woolfolk

Wynnton Publishing Company
Houston, Texas

Wynnton Publishing Company
11315 Smithdale Road
Houston, Texas 77024
www.wynntonpublishing.com

Library of Congress Control Number: 2017917447

Publisher's Cataloging-in-Publication data
Woolfolk, Robert.
The Postern / Robert Woolfolk
ISBN: 978-0-9716358-1-4
Published November 2017

Cover/Book design & artwork by Katharine Marie Gordon
Brain image (Sebastian Kaulitzki) and head silhouette (Essl)
Image Rights purchased from shutterstock.com

The paper used in this publication meets the requirements of the
American National Standard for Permanence of Paper for Printed
Library Materials Z39.48-1984.

Printed in the United States of America

To my beloved wife, Betty.

Thank you to my readers:
Sherry O'Hearn
Mindy Benefield

INTRODUCTION

The Postern is the first of a series of books that continue the stories of the principle characters. A postern is a back door or gate, a small private entrance, sometimes used to gain entrance into a castle.

There are thousands of documented cases of people knowing events in a precise fashion before they happen, although we do not know where this universal knowledge comes from, whether it is simply around us or given to us by a Supreme Being. In nearly all these cases the individuals get a vision of coming events, much the same way television sets receive electronic signals for translation into pictures. Our brain has the ability to translate electronic signals from within into pictures; therefore, it is easily believable that the right external electronic signals could be translated into mental pictures, as well.

I believe that most cases of ESP or clairvoyance are no special enchanted abilities of individuals but rather a flaw in or malfunction of the brains of those possessing the gift or curse. There is strong theory that closed brain injuries increase ESP ability. There should be a specific minute location in the brain that prevents universal knowledge signals from entering into the processing functions of the brain that translate electric impulses from brain cells into images. My contention is that these people apparently have a flawed filter that allows some supernatural transmission to leak through and be translated into conscious images.
That flawed filter is a postern.

CHAPTER
I

At 7:00 a.m. Wednesday morning, Bud Hinton's company Ford joined the fancy gas-guzzlers heading north on I-45 from his office in Texas City to Houston's business district. A stream of pickups was going in the opposite direction into the haze of Pasadena, Baytown and Texas City. The endless mesh fence dividing the north- and southbound lanes was a huge sieve that separated white collars from the blue, Brooks Brothers from Levi Strauss, dispatching them in opposite directions.

Settling down into his maroon F150, he inserted a CD, found his favorite Charlie Rich ballad and hummed along to "The Most Beautiful Girl in the World." After a few minutes on the highway between Galveston and Houston, Bud began to regret leaving his refinery this morning. He didn't like not being able to see the horizon. It confused him. He didn't like the Easter-egg colors and irregular shapes of the towering glass buildings comprising Houston's downtown. He didn't like stretching a tie around his seventeen-inch neck, and he didn't like taking a chance on provoking Dan London, executive vice-president of Global Oil and Refinery Corporation, one of the largest energy complexes in the country. But what he did like leaving behind was the gas odors belched out by the refineries of the many oil companies that lined the coast of Galveston Bay. He did not realize how bad it was until he left.

What worried him the most was carrying bad news to his president, Richard, even though there was also some good news. He had plenty of time to rehearse what he would say. He was cruising at bumper-to-bumper thirty-five miles an hour.

After an hour's drive, Bud saw the Houston skyline, a group of towering pastel glass and mirrored buildings, reflecting on each other from the morning sun, a view that always caused a strong sensation in his heart. This was the oil capital of the world, the hub of the oil industry. Bud was pleased to be an integral part of it.

Traffic into Houston was nearly out of control this dreary November morning. The fast-growing city had doubled its population regularly for the last one hundred fifty years and was still growing in 2010. Not to mention the influx of residents that flooded the city from New Orleans after Hurricane Katrina. Six thousand miles of streets and more than two hundred miles of freeways crisscrossing and ringing the city were inadequate to accommodate the new residents who continued to pour into his Bayou City.

Bud felt more at home along the Ship Channel area of the city, where over one-half of the nation's petrochemicals and one-quarter of the refined products originated, where its heartbeat was the relentless gurgle of oil being rearranged into gasoline, lube, plastics and rubber. Its pulse could be felt from the multilayered maze of underground pipelines that connected the two hundred chemical plants and refineries with each other and to the thirsty tankers and barges waiting to fill their bellies.

At the Scott Street exit, Bud's pickup melted into another crowd of early risers going into downtown Houston. Although the company's main building was not far from the freeway, the traffic made the trip seem interminable. Finally, he slid between two cars in the reserved section of Global's parking garage at 8:45 a.m.

Global Oil and Refining Corporation, housed in their seventy-five-story hive on the south end of skyscraper row, made a notable contribution to the national energy program. Bud was proud to be part of the company. He was extra proud that their president, Richard Winrock, thought enough of him to put him in charge of the Park Refinery in Texas City. He still wondered why it took a seventy-five-story building full of people to keep track of what Bud's operators were doing in the refinery and petrochemical plants throughout the state and his men who were drilling for oil. It was hard to imagine the boss sitting up there on the top floor saying grace over all these people and all that money.

Few people knew that Bud had served in the engine room on the same destroyer as Richard during the Vietnam War. Wrong conclusions might be drawn. Bud hoped that the bond they developed during those navy years would withstand what he was planning to tell his boss. But he had confidence in Richard, having seen his leadership in the war.

While they were on patrol off the North Korean coast, their ship had sustained a direct hit on the forward five-inch gun turret, killing the gun crew outright. A typhoon overran them while they were limping home. For three days the ship pitched, yawed and rolled in twenty-foot seas until everyone's inner ear was pounded into submission, and their insides felt like a two-inch hose had been jammed down their throat and sucked out everything inside, including the lining. Bud never forgot how Richard, sick as he was, had served many double shifts on the conn to replace his officers who couldn't stand. He remembered how he had circulated relentlessly through the ship, inspecting the watertight integrity of the hull and the emotional integrity of the men. He set an example of pure guts and courage that eliminated self-pity from the crew's vocabulary and minds. No one ever said it just right after they were safe in a friendly port, but they had been to hell, and Richard had helped them make it back.

On the way up the elevator to Richard's office, Bud began humming, trying to dampen the effect of anxiety. He hadn't seen Richard's new office since Global Tower was completed a year ago. Most of their visits happened at the plant in Texas City. He had been amazed at how plain Richard's old office was—just a few dark brown leather chairs, a large walnut slab desk and lots of filled bookcases with glass doors. Not at all what Dan London would have chosen if he was the big boss. But then, Richard wasn't much for frills. He didn't need fancy trappings. Anyone who worked for or around Richard soon learned that he was usually one or two hundred yards ahead of them, not just steps, but what counted: the company, the employees and the future. He gained respect by being damn smart and dedicated, not by throwing his weight around. Bud bragged about Richard in refinery circles, said Richard was wise enough to know that he didn't know his ass about refining. What Bud was really saying was that Richard let him run his own shop without interference. Even Dan London, executive vice-president, left him alone. Bud loped toward Richard's corner office with the peculiar gait that cowboy boots give a man. And out of courtesy to his boss, he held his large Texan hat in his hands. The austere Global look he remembered had given way to the environment of an antique store showroom. Round-back antique sofas lined the wide hall that was carpeted so deeply Bud had trouble negotiating it without swinging his arms. Large modern oil paintings with splashes of bright colors lined the walls; delicate brass tables with glass tops held ornate lamps and marble ashtrays. Was he in the wrong building? Was this Richard's?

A blonde woman greeted him suspiciously outside Richard's office. Before he could answer her questions, he looked up and saw Richard waiting. He had cancelled a business breakfast to be certain Bud would not have to wait. Bud was jumping several channels coming directly to Richard, and Dan London would be on Bud's back if he found out.

Entering the resident's new office, Bud's apprehension disappeared when he shook Richard's hand and looked into those intense blue eyes. "Thought I might have trouble seeing you, Boss." Bud's East Texas drawl rang clear. "Who the hell is that woman?"

Richard smiled, hesitated, then, with an apologetic tone

said, "Linda Blake is my new assistant. Brilliant young lady ... tremendous help to me. Does get a bit overprotective at times. But she's surely eliminating a lot of interruptions."

"She your decorator, too?" As he asked the question, Bud reflected on the brief image he had gotten of Linda as she rose from her desk and walked erect and stately to retrieve some papers from the file cabinet. He had noticed Linda's loosely draped silk dress that indicated her firm body and the gently feminine taper to her legs. Then Bud cut his deep-set eyes around Richard's new office. His hardened, weathered lips pursed as he found it difficult to believe that Richard was sitting in an office crowded with French provincial antique furniture, Vygotsky rugs and no bookcases. How different from his old office! "Where the hell are all your books?" Bud asked.

"Everything's on the computer," Richard replied with some sadness in his voice.

Trying to change the mood, Bud said impulsively, "Damn, it's good to see you, Richard. It's been a while. You know, I push my guys at the plant by tellin' 'em that Mr. Winrock sits here in the tower ringing up their profits on the giant cash register sittin' right on his desk, just like the one my daddy had in his hardware store. That's something they can understand."

Richard couldn't resist that "Bud-ism." He laughed and then led Bud to the far corner of his office where both men shared the recent successes and failures of their children. Richard seemed hungry to talk about old times—back in the Navy, at Mid-America Oil and Gas where they had both worked, and a few favorite hunting trips. There was something lonely and detached about Richard, but nothing Bud could quite put his finger on. He seemed to be trying hard to keep his mind on their conversation. Bud had complimented Richard on his appearance. He was still a young-looking sixty-two years with his full head of rich brown hair and his high, smooth forehead, but there were changes in Richard that worried Bud. Richard shifted himself frequently in his chair when they talked. He used his hands more than Bud remembered. As they talked, Bud could see stress cracks in Richard's face, around the eyes and a few around the mouth. His nose didn't seem as sharp, and the bones of his jaw were slightly padded. His suit seemed to be too young a cut for the president of Global—just not Richard's style.

Bud realized he could delay his message no longer. He put his boots together in front of the oversized wing chair that seemed ready to swallow him, slapped his hands on his knees and began, watching Richard's eyes as he started speaking. "Lemme start with this: I don't have anything concrete for you ... just gut feelings."

Richard couldn't resist saying, "That gut is reputed to be cast iron lined with tantalum. Its sensitivity is suspect."

"Not tantalum, tequila," Bud boasted. "That's why it tells me things when there's something worth telling."

"Come on, Bud. What's on your mind? I don't mind telling you I'm more than curious since you called me."

Bud gathered his courage. "Richard, somebody's tryin'

to sabotage the refinery." Richard didn't respond. He slowly took off his rimless glasses and placed them on top of the latest copy of *Fortune* on the coffee table. He waited for Bud to continue. However, Bud was waiting for a response. They both looked at each other, diverse thoughts being rapidly processed. Bud wondered if he had erred in carrying such a story to headquarters. Richard wondered if there was a connection between this and other strange events lately.

"I don't get your weekly report anymore, Bud. What specifically has happened?"

"Look, in just the past two weeks, we've had two run tanks of naphtha turn up with mega amounts of organic chlorides. I don't need to tell you that stuff makes the reformer run away and cokes up the catalyst. There's no way a tank that's been checked the way we check things turns up with chlorides unless somebody's slipped 'em in. It'll take months to blend it off. There've been other things, one right after the other."

"For instance," Richard inquired, his voice revealing more emotion than his face.

"Well, a valve on our desalter got itself opened last week, and the damn thing salted up our big heater. We were down thirty-six hours correcting that problem."

"Could it have been a simple operator error?" Richard didn't want to believe what he was hearing.

"No way. This valve's hard to get at, and it's open/shut when the plant is on stream." Bud became aware that his tie was suddenly too tight. He loosened it, then checked it up squarely between his long collar flutes and placed his wide hands back on his knees.

"What else?"

"Get this." Bud thrust his index finger at Richard. "We had a valve close off the jacket water cooling to our main compressor plant. Then, when the engines were red hot, it got itself opened and cracked a number of power cylinder heads. That one'll cost us over a hundred thousand in repairs alone."

"Hasn't that ever happened before?"

"Not like this. Richard, you don't sound like you believe me. Listen, have I ever come to you with a story like this?"

"No, not that I can remember."

"I'm no alarmist. You know me. I usually wait too long before saying anything. This time, I'm sure as shit that we have someone trying to damage us." His voice was emphatic.

"Who would want to do something like that? Could the union be behind it?"

The worst was over. Bud had dumped the whole smelly mess right on the table. Now he felt more at ease. It was not *if,* but *who.* "I don't think the union's got a damn thing to do with this. We aren't negotiating with them right now. Our contract has another thirteen months to run."

"Do we have morale problems down there?"

"No, Richard, we don't—just the opposite. The men seem to be happy with their jobs and with working conditions."

"I'm trying hard."

"I know, Boss. You told them in the newsletter last month," Bud reminded Richard.

"So I did."

The good news is that research reports good numbers for the catalyst. In fact, not only good numbers but exceptional ones."

Richard's eyes brightened, and he said, "That is not only excellent news but timely. We are having the security analysts at the reception tonight. I can speak with greater assurance. Back to the alleged sabotage. Do you have any idea who or why?"

"No, but the grapevine around the plant is that some company's trying to take over Global. Is there anything to it?"

"Who knows, Bud? I have heard the same news from sources on Wall Street. You know, the rumor mill in both places is usually pretty good."

Richard stood and for a full two minutes paced up and down in front of the large glass windows facing northwest Houston. He now believed Bud, yet somehow was saddened at Bud's report that his people were not only disloyal but destructive. It hurt deeply. He could feel tension building in his temples. How would he mobilize against a phantom enemy, one that slipped around his refinery doing his malicious mischief?

Richard and Bud had been trained to fight enemies on other ships, on shores, on submarines—enemies who shot at you, bombed you and torpedoed you. Once you identified them as enemies, you developed hatred for them so you could try to kill them before they killed you.

This sabotage was different. It corroded your trust in everyone. Everyone was suspect until the culprit was rooted out. The company Richard and Bud loved had a cancer. It must be removed. But first it had to be located and the full extent of its encroachment into the company machinery identified. In humans, the knife could carve out the cancer, not allowing it to kill its host. This enemy was set on the destruction of Global for whatever reason. Richard was determined to put an end to what was going on. No one would destroy his ... his ...

Richard suddenly turned to Bud. "I'm going to take some action in the plant. It's better you don't know anything about what we'll be doing. Just keep an eye out and keep quiet about this visit. If it comes out, say I asked you to come up to brief me on refinery activities so I could prepare a better talk for the safety award dinner."

"Good idea. That's my story."

After Bud left, Richard reviewed their conversation. Then he said to himself, "What if the pilot tests in Texas City were a failure?" Most of the risks

Richard had taken in the past were primarily his own. Now he was preparing to risk Global's future and two hundred million dollars of new shareholders' money of the stock offering for the commercialization of his research if successful. The decision weighed heavily on his mind.

CHAPTER
II

As soon as Bud had disappeared around the corner of the wide, elegant hall of executive row, Linda knocked on Richard's door and entered with her appointment book.

"I rescheduled several meetings that were on the calendar for this morning, which complicates the rest of the week."

Richard slowly leaned back in his chair to disguise his anxiety level. The only clue was his heavier breathing. He let his throat relax before he said, "Linda, don't try so hard. I wanted to visit with Bud. We had important business. I did spend more time with him than I expected, but we're friends from way back. Bud is the best refinery man in the business. Please have a note sent to file stating that Bud came up at my request to give me background for my safety awards speech. No more, OK?"

"But, I have already prepared the final draft of your presentation."

"I know. But I'll have a number of informal comments after my talk." His expression indicated the debate was over.

"Very well." Linda grew more confused.

"I believe I was to see Arnie Anderson this morning.   Could you let him know I'm ready?" Impatience was encroaching on his usual gentle voice.

"We have a problem. I have rescheduled him for Friday."

"Well, Linda, you'll have to reschedule him back again for today. I need to see him right away, at least by 11:30 if possible."

Linda unconsciously bit her upper lip then said flatly, "As you wish."

"Also, ask Clyde Warner to join us if he's available."

"Yes, Mr. Winrock, I'll do my best."

Linda had looked forward to this morning with great anticipation. Her boss had given her an assignment the previous day that would require all her talents, all her education, all her energy and all of today. She was poised to present her work to him when the refinery man arrived unannounced. She was sure she had offended Bud, but she was not concerned. Just so Richard believed in her. After notifying Anderson and Warner to meet with Richard in thirty minutes, she took one last look at her work then buzzed her boss.

"Mr. Winrock, I've finished the press release for your meeting this evening."

"Linda, you must've spent the night here."

"I did run up a little overtime, but it went together

nicely." Linda had held over four of her staff until midnight to complete the work.

She proudly carried in the documents and placed them on Richard's desk. He picked up the report and, thumbing through it quickly, said, "Incredible. You did the charts yourself?"

"Yes, I did, sir."

"Beautiful. I like the way you laid them out." His gaze shifted from the printed page to Linda. "Tell me, Linda, do you think we accomplish our purpose with this release?"

She spoke with a ring of authority. "I do. We disclose just enough to give the analysts something to analyze. But, we don't preempt the information you'll present at your annual stockholders' meeting next month." Linda liked her answer.

"What I was asking is, Does the report make you want to go out and buy Global stock or, more importantly, sell it to your customers?"

Linda hesitated before she answered. If she was going to be valuable to Richard, she knew she would have to tell it like she saw it. Richard detested patronization. He could always tell when he was getting a calculated answer.

"Mr. Winrock, I'm not sure about people rushing out to buy Global stock now, but if they're holding Global shares, they should want to hold onto them. Your report should cancel any bad press they may be getting."

Richard's expression changed. Trying to be casual, he asked, "Are we getting bad press these days?"

Linda detected his mood change. "I have picked up a few nonharmonic vibrations about Global lately." Linda shifted her weight and looked out the large glass expanse behind Richard.

"Do you remember the source?"

"No, sir, I didn't pay much attention."

"What exactly did you hear?" Richard wasn't going to let the subject drop.

Linda stalled for words then said, "Oh, something stupid like we're overextended—can't meet our drilling commitments. You know, that kind of talk."

"Was this inside or outside the company?"

"Definitely outside," she said without hesitation. Her hand gesture was exaggerated, and the pitch of her voice was elevated.

Richard tapped his fingers on the report as he looked squarely at Linda then dropped his voice and said, "Try a little harder, Linda. I would be surprised if you didn't remember who made such a statement. You don't forget anything that I know of."

Richard's expression was new to Linda. There was no smile around the eyes. The jaw was set. In near panic she said, "As well as I can remember, someone in the elevator going to the Texas Club was talking about Global. I believe one of the men in the group was with General

Petroleum. I didn't know the others." Linda stopped and waited.

Richard rubbed his chin as he tried unsuccessfully to make eye contact with Linda. "OK. I'll look this over. Market analysts don't tolerate mistakes or ambiguities. Thanks."

After Linda left, Richard walked to the window and stood there silently. He realized he had overreacted, but he was disappointed in Linda's answer. He had heard much more serious rumors that were unfounded and could become damaging to Global's immediate position in the stock market. Global had problems, but being overextended was not one of them. Where was this information coming from? Was there a connection? Well, if anyone knew what was going on behind the scenes in the oil patch, Bob McLean would know. He would arrange to talk to Bob right away.

Linda was close to tears. In the twenty months Linda had worked at Global, Richard had never been critical. Yet today, he chastised her for "trying too hard" and had been obviously upset by her answer to the bad press. She must be more careful. Considering Richard's background, she reassured herself that she was fortunate not to have experienced his sharper edge often.

Linda realized that in many ways Richard was still a military man. He didn't run Global like a navy ship, but he did go by the book. He was strong-willed and inflexible on many issues, yet he seemed to care deeply about people, "his people," as he often referred to the six thousand employees of Global. For Linda, being one of his people—"his right hand" as he often referred to her—was exactly where she wanted to be.

She hoped she was not imagining things. It seemed that Richard had begun to stare at her when she was busy taking shorthand from across his enormous desk. He was beginning to confide very sensitive company matters to her. Linda was thrilled by the progressive change in their relationship since she first arrived in Houston almost two years ago to interview for a job. She had guessed it would be an excellent opportunity when she first heard from the search firm. Why would they fly her all the way from Boston otherwise? she had thought. Linda had made what many of her friends back home had considered a comedown from an important, influential position.

The old guard secretaries criticized Richard for hiring an inexperienced tall blonde with a BA from Yale and a master's from Harvard Business School. Richard's changing of her title to assistant to the president didn't help matters. However, most everyone on the floor had accepted Linda. All, that is, except Global's executive vice-president, Dan London. She had heard that Dan was ticked off because his girl Rena had been queen bee of executive row until Linda arrived. But that was not Dan's problem. She knew he would resent anyone who worked directly for Richard. She would smooth over the problems she had created today. She would never underestimate Richard's insight again.

Back in Richard's office, Richard was left wondering whether Global's problems were internal, external or both. He knew he was going to have to keep a tighter watch on the happenings of the company as well as outside information that filtered in. "Hmm," Richard said to no one in particular, "I might have some rough times ahead." He was anxious to get this meeting with his security staff, Arnie and Clyde, under way. He hoped this was the first step in unearthing what had really been going on in the company.

CHAPTER
III

At nine o'clock sharp that morning, Bob McLean had entered his office in a garçonnière over his four-car garage on Lazy Bend. He was still wearing a bright yellow warm-up suit after a brisk six-mile run through his neighborhood. Bob considered it a good day if he worked in a run.

Picking up his *Wall Street Journal*, he flopped down in a leather reclining chair and began consuming it as though it was the last issue to be published. Often, something he read sparked an idea that launched him on the pursuit of a new deal. Bob's interests varied widely, an educational publishing venture one month and a crude oil trade in the Middle East the next.

He had completed the "Summary of the News" and was changing clothes when his phone rang. I guess that's Rich, calling me to arms, he thought to himself.

"Mr. McLean, this is Lenora French with Lenora French Real Estate. I understand that you own the Antebellum Apartments on Sagewood."

"I am one of the owners, yes." Bob was not pleased with the call, and he made no attempt to hide his feelings. He didn't like unsolicited calls involving his businesses.

"Oh … I understood you were the sole owner."

"Incorrect, Miss French. Sam Butler is my partner in this endeavor," Bob replied testily.

Lenora made a note of the other buyer and said sharply, "I'm Mrs. French. Do you have authority to speak for the both of you, Mr. McLean?" She did not want to offend a prospective client, but she wouldn't pretend to like his manner.

"Why do you ask, Mrs. French?" This time Bob's voice had less of an edge.

"I have a buyer group who is interested in your property."

"I get a lot of calls, Mrs. French. I'm not interested in selling."

"I would like to visit with you, Mr. McLean. May I make an appointment to discuss the project?" Lenora asked, politely and businesslike, her instinctive approach.

"Who are your buyers?" Bob decided to settle the matter quickly.

"I can't disclose their names, but they're two Italian gentlemen. They have already acquired considerable property in Houston."

"Aha. Two Italian gentlemen, buying us up. Isn't that interesting," Bob said with obvious sarcasm. Bob had gotten numerous calls from agents representing deals with mysterious foreign investors that never materialized, never got past the big talk. "Frankly, Mrs. French, I think you would be wasting both my time and yours. I am happy with this project; it's doing well. I couldn't replace it."

"Mr. McLean, my clients want the site for a very specific purpose."

Bob McLean had owned the five-hundred-unit ten-building complex and a piece of adjacent land with his friend Sam Butler for nearly five years. The architecture was reminiscent of New Orleans, the city that held his heart and origins. He had spent considerable money renovating the apartments. The project was considered in the trade to be one of the nicest in close proximity to The Galleria. The thought of someone tearing down five years of effort was offensive.

"Mrs. French, I'm very fond of this project."

"I understand, Mr. McLean. But my clients are very fond of your land," she responded immediately.

"Just how fond are they?" Bob began enjoying the battle of wits.

"Mr. McLean, I would rather not discuss specifics on the phone. Would you give me thirty minutes of your time to visit you?"

"I would throw my best pitch if I were you. I have tried to convey that I'm not interested. Haven't I made that clear?"

Lenora paused and gathered her composure. "Yes,

you have. Very well. My clients would be willing to offer fifty dollars per square foot for your nearly ten acres. That comes to over twenty million dollars."

Bob McLean was silent for a full twenty seconds as he mentally computed the capital gain he and his partner would make if he sold at twenty million. Lenora waited for a response, without a word.

Bob broke the silence. "Is that liras or dollars?"

"Mr. McLean, my clients are serious buyers. Could I meet with you if I brought an executed twenty-one-million-dollar earnest money contract?"

Not really caring to pursue the possibility of a sale further, Bob almost chuckled. "If it includes a check for ten percent of the contract, which is nonrefundable if they fail to perform."

Lenora French immediately responded, "I'll have it by Friday morning. What time can we meet?"

Bob realized he had been outsmarted by a very assertive, quick young lady. Stalling for time, he said, "Well, let me see. OK. What about ten o'clock?"

"That would be splendid."

"Do you know where my office is, Mrs. French?"

"No, I don't, but I'll find it."

"I'm not sure you will. My office is in a white two-story building serving as the garage next to my home. I presume you know my address. I suggest you use the north entrance facing Lazy Bend. I'll see that the gate is open."

"Thank you. I will see you at ten on Friday."

Bob's mental computer had evaluations to run before he would meet with Lenora French. Though most of the calls he received were of no consequence, this lady may represent a real buyer. She was playing for high stakes. Her commission for such a purchase should exceed eight hundred thousand dollars if he decided to part with the project.

At eleven, Bob McLean was still thinking about the deal when his phone rang again. This time it was Linda Blake calling for Richard Winrock.

Richard came on saying, "Bob, I want to ask you a favor. Would you mind coming in early today before our meeting with the security analysts?"

"I guess not. What's up?"

"I'd rather not discuss it on the phone. I am extremely concerned about something and need to talk to someone I can trust. Someone who is also a director."

"You're going to make me earn my director's fee yet, Mr. Winrock," Bob said in jest.

"Bob, that's ridiculous! You've made many invaluable contributions to Global."

"It's nice to be appreciated," Bob chuckled. "What time do you want me?"

"Let me check." Richard asked Linda about his other commitments for the afternoon. He returned to the line. "Three thirty will work."

Rich's call puzzled Bob. Richard had confided his intimate company problems to Bob recently, yet somehow this was different. Why couldn't he discuss the problem or at least the nature of the problem on the phone? Was he worried about the phone being tapped? Was Richard getting paranoid?

Although he was only an outside director of the corporation, Bob had devoted much of his time to various executive committee activities and had done several extensive economic analyses for Richard.

Over the past few years, his friendship with Richard and his concern for Global had grown. Actually, Bob was an old friend of Rivers Kern, the now semiretired founder and chairman of Global. When he brought Richard in as president, Kern insisted that Bob serve on the board. Bob always believed that he was the watchdog for Rivers, who originally had not been a hundred percent sure of his new president. But it didn't take long to convince him that Richard Winrock knew how to run an oil company and increase the earnings. Richard's style was dramatically different than River's, but the results were outstanding. Bob put his musings aside and decided to have a cup of tea and return to his *Journal*.

CHAPTER
IV

Bob was sitting back in his recliner when his phone rang for the third time that morning. This time it was his wife, Helen.

"Darling, I ran into Sam at St. Matthews this morning."

"What's going on with Sambo?"

"I'm not sure. He was evasive when I asked questions. I don't know if anything is wrong or not. Why don't you call him and ask him to dinner?"

"Good idea," Bob agreed. "I'll try and get him at the hospital, although it won't be easy," he added. "They guard their premier neurosurgeon like the crown jewels."

"Please do. I feel bad that we haven't done anything for him since he moved out of the Inwood house."

"Helen, Sam's a big boy. He should know how to take care of himself by now."

26

"He should, but I'm afraid he doesn't. I hear he's doing at least three and sometimes four major surgeries a day. On top of that, you know how much time he spends with his patients."

"I never thought he was happy with Gladys. But the divorce still seems hard on him. Maybe it's the kids."

"Maybe," Helen answered, ready to change the subject. "Dear, I'm sorry to interrupt you. I guess I felt guilty, somehow, when I saw him. Would you prefer I call him?"

"No, of course not. I'll get him. When would be a good evening?"

"Let's make it anytime he can. We'll adjust."

"You have a big heart, Helen."

Bob hung up the phone and began to reflect on the years he had known Sam Butler. Sam had reached the top of his profession and was considered the most skillful neurosurgeon in his part of the world, yet the jolt of the divorce had apparently made him a compulsive worker.

Bob's thoughts drifted back to the early days when he first met Sam. They were both in chemical engineering at the university. Bob had done everything he knew to help Sam through his sophomore year, but Sam was beyond help in those courses that required a solid mathematics background. Bob had risked their friendship by suggesting Sam change the direction of his life away from engineering. Surprisingly, Sam was receptive and shifted to a liberal arts curriculum, quickly becoming a strong student in subjects that required recall. Ultimately, he was able to get into medical school. He interned at the Charity Hospital in New Orleans and stayed on for his residency in neurosurgery.

When Sam moved to Houston, he already had earned a wide reputation and had developed a new neurological procedure called the "Butler Bridge."

The large, handsome surgeon gained immediate social acceptance in Houston, where family lineage wasn't as important as it was in New Orleans. In a short time, "Big" Gladys Elliott had arranged for "the prize of Houston," as she referred to Sam, to escort her daughter to the various debutante parties. After Sam and "Little" Gladys were married, the Butlers entertained the right people, joined the right clubs and had two attractive daughters. Yet they must have drifted apart over the years, Sam losing himself in his surgery and Gladys becoming submerged in her Junior League activities and her River Oaks Garden Club.

Bob called St. Matthew's Hospital and left an emergency message for Dr. Sam Butler to call him as soon as possible, knowing any other message might not elicit a response for several weeks. Bob was surprised when Sam returned his call within twenty minutes.

"I called as soon as I could, Bob. Anything wrong?"

"Forgive me for leaving an emergency message. That's the only kind they give you."

"Well, not quite, but it did get my attention. What

can I do for you, Bobby?"

"I don't hear too many 'Bobbys' anymore, Sam. I didn't have anything urgent ... just started thinking about my old friend and wanted to get together with you. Why don't you have dinner with Helen and me soon, like tomorrow night?"

Sam chuckled. "You've got to be kidding. I'm booked."

"When are you going to slow down? You can't keep up that pace."

"I've been at this pace for over twenty years, Roberto, though I am tired lately."

"Sam, you surely don't need the money. Our real estate project is doing famously. Why don't you treat yourself to a quiet evening with us?"

"I can't think of anything I would enjoy more, but I have to start planning a night out at least a week in advance, maybe two."

"Look, Sambo, you're talking to old Bob. Don't give me all that malarkey."

"Seriously, my office has me booked solid." Sam continued to hedge.

"Isn't there someone who can stand in for you—just one evening? Suppose you caught a cold or slammed your finger in a door?"

"I'll see what I can do ... if you don't mind a late supper. Sometimes I don't get away at all from this sweatshop."

"Sam, Helen, our own neuropsychologist, says you need a home-cooked meal and some understanding conversation. We care about you, you big walrus. Don't want to see you destroying your health. Don't give me any more excuses. Just say you'll come to dinner in the next few days ... at midnight if you like."

"OK, I'll do my best. Got to run. I'm holding up ten people right now."

"I'm going to hold you to this, Sambo."

CHAPTER
V

Arnie Anderson and Clyde Warner arrived promptly at eleven thirty. They eyed each other without a word as they sat waiting for Richard to finish a handwritten memo.

Richard spoke up. "Read this and give me your comments on paper." He handed them each a yellow pad and pencil. They read the memo then looked back at Richard with troubled faces.

Arnie started to speak, but Richard put his index finger to his lips then pointed to the pad. Arnie scribbled down something then sat back and waited for Clyde Warner to respond to Richard's request. Clyde thought through his answer before writing it and handing the tablet back to Richard. Since Clyde was head of security and worked directly for Winrock, Richard's comments stunned him. Obviously, Richard thought his office was bugged, yet Richard had not previously advised them of this fear. Also, Richard rarely discussed covert actions with anyone outside of security. Clyde knew that, as head of personnel, Arnie was in the inner circle of Richard's confidants, yet Clyde's philosophy was, "Don't trust anyone, and you'll never be disappointed."

Clyde's comments were direct and to the point. After carefully reading them, Richard handed the comments back to each. They all nodded their heads in agreement.

Richard broke the silence with, "How soon can you arrange what Clyde suggested?"

Arnie and Clyde agreed that two to three weeks were sufficient.

"Good. Now, one other point. As you know, we've important meetings—tonight with the security analysists and next Tuesday with high-ranking Saudi officials. Linda has the final details available for you."

He walked around his desk and faced the two men. "I would like Global's maximum effort to protect them. Let's use all our people we can spare. Clyde, see if HPD will furnish some officers to give round-the-clock surveillance. Their entourage should include about ten. We will hire off-duty officers if we have to. And don't forget to tell Daryl that I'm relying on him to take care of the reception, greet the early guests and oversee the caterers."

Clyde nodded approval. They both stood to leave.

Richard asked, "Arnie, please stay behind. I've some personnel business to discuss." Richard rose, thrust out his hand and gave Clyde a firm handshake, looking him squarely in the eye. Clyde could see grave things in Richard's face.

"OK, Arnie. Fill me in on Hunter Kern." Richard felt secure discussing this problem in his office. Hunter was the son of Rivers Kern, board chairman and chief supporter of Richard. Hunter's problem at Global had begun to be worrisome.

Arnie began, "As you know, I cleared Hunter's transfer with you before discussing it with his boss. Bernard, as head of the department, would be delighted to get rid of Hunter. Says he's a disturbing influence in his department and doesn't produce anything of value. Frankly, Bernie would fire Hunter if he thought he could get away with it. Of course, he can't. Rivers, being your predecessor and present company chairman, would come down on him like a broken awning."

"Go on."

"I got Bernie's permission to present the Denver transfer directly to Hunter. Bernie was really concerned about his job if he tried to make the transfer himself. Last I saw him, Hunter flat-out declined. Said he didn't like Denver—it bothered his asthma. He shrugged the whole idea off as something he wouldn't even consider."

"He did, did he?" Richard's curiosity was piqued.

"Yes, he did," Arnie assured.

Richard shifted his weight in his chair. "I'll have to take this matter up with Rivers. I can't see any other alternative. If Hunter was anyone else but Rivers's son, I wouldn't expect you even to let me know you had tried to fire him."

"When do you think you can discuss this with Rivers?" Arnie pressed.

"I'll make it a high priority. I wanted Rivers to

attend the reception we are having this evening with a group of investment security analysts at the Spindletop Club. He declined. He may not be in the office for a few days."

"What do you expect Rivers will do with Hunter?"

"Hard to tell, Arnie. Sometimes he acts like Hunter is his progeny; other times he seems ready to disown him and throw him out in the street."

Global's personnel director was now looking out the window at the people below. "It's a real shame that Hunter has been allowed to challenge every authority he's ever had. He has no respect for anyone who backs down, and most people do when he comes at them with a billion-dollar family fortune behind him. Damn."

Realizing he must finally bring the question of Hunter's poor company performance and disrespect for authority to a head, Richard said sadly, "Arnie, I don't relish this cup you have passed to me. On the other hand, I'm the only one Rivers Kern would want to discuss the problem with. I'll get it straight one way or another. We can't put it off any longer. Our whole morale could go down the drain."

"He's already caused more problems than I care to enumerate," Arnie added.

Arnie knew the meeting was over when Richard's eyes turned to the papers on his desk. He quickly left a troubled chief executive.

"Linda, bring in my confidential file on Hunter

Kern," Richard said into his intercom. The file was kept in Linda's safe.

As Linda left the office, Richard flipped through the file, shaking his head. He would edit the file and let Rivers read it. Perhaps Rivers would finally let action be taken. Hopefully, this problem would not cause serious trouble at Global.

Richard cancelled his lunch engagement with a group raising money for a new Episcopal school. He and Linda worked through lunch to get back on schedule.

Finishing up, Linda said, "Don't forget that Slizer called yesterday to set up a meeting of some board members at one thirty. He said it was an emergency."

Winrock was more concerned with presenting Global's new expansion plans at the five o'clock reception at the Spindletop Club and said half to himself, "I wish Slizer would pay more attention to his trucking business than to Global."

CHAPTER
VI

Elliot Slizer, H.J. Finley and Hillard Tinhauser entered the office waiting room promptly at one thirty and, without saying a word to Linda, proceeded into the president's office. It was obvious to Richard that there had been a meeting prior to this meeting. The three directors had set scowls on their faces as if they were facing an errant comrade.

"We'd like to speak with you about the reception tonight," began Elliot Slizer. "It is our opinion that you are preempting other possible actions of the board of directors." Offering a file folder with both hands, Slizer stated with the authority of a drill sergeant, "I've got a deal here that you need to poll the board on."

Winrock motioned for the group to seat themselves around his leather sofa and chairs at one end of his office. He said, "Well now, Elliot, let's see what kind of deal you have," then sat and slowly reviewed the three-page document in silence.

Slizer was noticeably nervous and thumped his small fingers on his crossed knee. Tinhauser and Finley watched Slizer but sat quietly.

With a careful, soft tone, Richard responded, "Preempting? In what way? There is time for board discussions. Tonight's meeting is for the purpose of encouraging interest in our company so that if we want to make a stock offering later, we have laid the groundwork."

"But, how much are you going to tell them? The board doesn't even know everything that's going on," H.J. Finley retorted.

When Winrock had reviewed the contents of Slizer's deal again, he placed the document on the mahogany coffee table, rose slowly and walked to the windows. He turned back to the directors and said in a studied, deliberate tone, "Gentlemen, you have wasted your time. I have no intentions of polling the board on your proposal. Frankly, I think it wise you destroy these copies."

Richard continued, "You see, some of our findings are still speculative. We are anticipating the new field, El Gato, to be enormous, but the final stats are not in yet. Drilling in the deep water of the Gulf will also be a reality only if we can get the concession from the Mexican government."

At this point Richard stopped, afraid to disclose the research findings about the use of a new chemical process that would allow the recovery of one-and-a-half times more cleansed hydrocarbons per barrel of crude. If the three individuals before him were aware of this process, they would be indignant about the prospects of inviting others to share the company. They would be more interested in the refinery capabilities than in El Gato or offshore drilling.

"Look here, Rich, we represent fourteen percent of this company. Who the hell do you think you are? The board runs this company. We can easily get board support for this deal." Slizer's response showed he had been stumping for his position. "I would like to cancel our public stock offering. We could offer a private placement with a group that is ready with up to five hundred million, even if they acquired only El Gato. You can have twenty percent of the deal."

There was a long silence before Richard asked Slizer, "What do your friends know about drilling—and about the El Gato field? We have been testing these for over two years."

Tinhauser said, "We know Elliot can raise the money."

H.J. added, "I don't see how he could raise a hundred dollars on the technical information you have given the directors."

"That puzzles me too. I have mentioned our R&D project in our annual reports for two years, but no specifics. I wouldn't weigh in on what we have made public," Rich said. "Slizer, you must have more than that."

"I smell a major leak." H.J.'s tone belied their union on the matter.

"H.J., you surprised me with your courier-delivered twenty-page document at noon." Richard turned to the others. "H.J. came in with a merger offer, an offer we turned down months ago. H.J. hasn't given up. He has raised the ante by twenty percent. He's offering us six shares of H.J. Finley Oil for each share of Global now."

"That smells leak, also," Tinhauser said.

"H.J. says he can furnish the capital we need to commercialize El Gato. He also wants us to wave off the offering." Richard paused a moment before he stated firmly, "I'm going to say this only once then hope we all forget this happened. Your proposal is probably the most flagrant violation of your fiduciary responsibilities to the company you serve as directors that I have seen in thirty years in business."

Tinhauser asked, "How do you figure that?"

"In the first place, all of you are insiders. You already know about the research." Winrock fixed his steel gray eyes on the three directors.

"We know damn little about the research," H.J. reiterated.

"You know all you are supposed to know." Richard was getting angry, and he continued, "If this type of proposal is executed with three directors, the shareholders will launch a class action suit that will be the mother of all class actions."

As Winrock handed the document back to Slizer, he said casually, "Ethics are one question; the second one is whether you have the money committed. I don't think you do."

"We have it all right. If we don't use it for this deal, we have other uses you won't like," Slizer said, getting noticeable concerned looks from Tinhauser and Finley.

Attempting to close the meeting, Richard said slowly, "Gentlemen, your mere proposal of a joint venture with Global in which the company would be a minority equity holder with you as insiders and directors could easily constitute a serious securities violation. I suggest we agree this meeting never happened. I won't accept a copy of your deal in order to protect us all."

Slizer stood and pointed his finger at Winrock. "We have a fairness letter being prepared as we speak that covers any insider problems. You will get a certified copy of the letter and the proposal before five. The research may not work, and your offering may not sell. We are ready to put at least two hundred million in a risky deal with no assurance we will get our money back."

Winrock responded, "This is quite a change of heart for all three of you. You have voted against every resolution for development funds for the project. What changed your mind?"

Neither Slizer, Tinhauser nor Finley chose to answer.

Slizer placed the proposal back in his folder, patted the folder with his left hand and said, with a smoldering rage, "We're not playing games, Rich. You will get a certified copy. You won't be able to say you didn't get it in time. If you refuse it and don't act to cancel the securities meeting tonight, you and Global will be facing the mother of all suits for your failure to act responsibly for the company. The Vinson & Elkins Attorney Firm is ready to file it. Don't do something foolish. You can still have twenty percent of the deal."

Slizer turned quickly and walked out with his two flunkies. Winrock chose to ignore Slizer's threat and proceeded with his plans.

CHAPTER
VII

Bob McLean arrived early at Richard's office and noticed that Linda let him wait for ten minutes before notifying Richard that he had arrived. Bob was an intense, driven man, but a man who had recently learned to control the pace of his life at a level that placed no tax on his emotions or on his body. In earlier years, he would have immediately confronted Linda with her lack of consideration. Now, instead, he sat quietly reading the latest *Barron's*, which had a comprehensive article on the U.S. oil industry. He decided not to tell Richard about the incident, but wondered why his friend would allow his assistant to treat people poorly.

"Thank you for coming in, Bob. Please close the door. Better still, let's go talk in the coffee lounge up the hall."

Bob looked quizzically at Richard as they shook hands. "You look troubled. Tell old Bob about it—he's a professional problem solver."

"That you are, Bob. That you are." They walked together silently.

When they were seated in one corner of the lounge, Richard opened up. He told Bob of his fears about a takeover plot, about the strange events at the refinery, the rumors circulating on Wall Street.

"Do you think your office is wired, Richard?"

"I don't know. I don't want to take any chances at this point. I got an uneasy feeling this morning that I was getting compromised."

"It's hard for me to believe all this. I'm sure you have good reason for these fears."

"Who knows? I have been trying to ignore some grim thoughts. When Bud spoke with me about the refinery situation, I decided to take things seriously."

"Who could be behind it, Richard?"

"God knows. But whoever it is, they're smart. I can say that much for them."

"Surely you'll enlighten the security analysts from Wall Street about Global's financial condition. That should cover that base. But the refinery might be hard to protect."

"Clyde is going to get to the bottom of things there."

Bob looked over the top of his paper cup of coffee. "Do you think there's anyone from Global involved?"

"Sounds like it at the refinery. I don't know about the home office."

"Well, it's not uncommon for the enemy to have a few Trojan horses in camp," Bob confided.

"Yes, I know. Money makes people do curious things."

Bob rubbed his hands briskly as he felt his anxiety increasing. "We may have the bad actor right in our midst this evening at the reception. Surely if some New York analysts are involved, they'll be drinking our whiskey."

"That's what I was thinking, Bob. I'd appreciate your getting to the club early and playing host till I get there. I've asked Daryl White to be there in case I put my foot in my mouth. Also, Bernard Stone has a few comments to make on our business development, and then Dan."

"Of course. By the way, how are things going with you and Dan? Has he gotten over being passed up for the presidency?"

"Dan has been keeping a low profile lately. That worries me."

"Maybe he's finally getting mellow."

"I don't think so. I've asked him to go with me to the reception tonight to dispel any rumors we're at odds. I also want to keep my eye on him at the reception, you know, see who he talks to."

"Sounds like you don't trust your executive any farther than you can throw him."

"Bob, I wouldn't say this to anyone else in the

world, but I really don't trust Dan."

"What is he doing?"

"I shouldn't have gotten started on that, Bob." Richard began to see his visitor back to the elevators. "We don't have time to really cover the subject. Maybe we can have dinner sometime soon, and I'll fill you in—away from the office."

"Very well, but you've really left me hanging."

"I'm sorry. That wasn't a nice thing to do."

"I'll survive," Bob chuckled. "You know, I get a really good feeling about the morale in Global just walking up the hall reading the faces. You've won the respect and admiration of just about everyone here. Don't let a few soreheads spoil it. If the boss indicates concern, it spreads like wildfire."

"You're right, Bob. I knew you'd set me straight. Thanks for coming in. I'll see you at the club."

CHAPTER
VIII

After meeting with Bob, Richard Winrock had a new resolve to rise above the adversity that seemed to be piling up against him. He seemed to be jousting with an enemy that as yet had no shape or form ... or face. He stood at one of the ten-foot picture windows that lined his corner office, rod straight, legs spread apart, hands clasped behind him, looking down on Houston's downtown business.

Then, Richard focused on the only photograph in his office. In a small gold frame were the smiling faces of his wife, Evelyn, and his grandson, Lenny. He recalled the grief his family had suffered after the diagnosis of Down syndrome until this loveable child with his limited intellect began reaching out with unlimited love. Little Lenny had brought his family closer together than it had ever been. Richard loved the child dearly and wished that his daughter, Lisa, lived in Houston. Perhaps he needed a break from the corporate pressures, which had sometimes been oppressive lately, to visit his daughter in Columbus, Georgia.

"Excuse me, Mr. Winrock, Mr. Moore is on the

phone. Do you want to take the call?" Linda Blake asked over the intercom.

"Of course, but call him back on my secure line." Winrock sat at his desk.

"I'm glad you called, Thad. We have been trying to reach you all day," Winrock said. He had more relief than frustration in his voice at reaching the board's vice-chairman who had stood by him many times in many years.

"My beeper went off while I was in the air, but I didn't want to call on the airline phone. I'm at Hobby. Just landed," Thad said, breathing hard.

"We've got problems, big problems," Winrock said quietly.

"What can I do?" Thad asked.

"Well, I wanted to meet you outside of the office, but there isn't time."

"We could meet in one of the private rooms at the Spindletop Club before the meeting," Thad suggested.

"No. Everyone would know we met." Winrock shook his head.

"Then spill it. What's happened since we talked last night?"

"You won't believe it." Richard relayed the details of Slizer's proposal. "They were dead serious. I rejected it—wouldn't even accept a copy."

"I knew Slizer was putting a deal together. One of the other directors asked me if I knew about it. The dissenters didn't ask me. I guess they know how I play the game."

"I wish you had told me. They surprised me completely." Winrock let a little edge creep into his voice.

"I thought you knew. I had no reason not to tell you," Moore answered, recognizing Winrock was disappointed in him. "How did Elliott take your rejection of the deal?"

"He was ready to explode. He said he will sue me if I turn him down. If I take the deal, we'll all get sued by the shareholders."

"What will you do when they deliver a copy?"

"I'll file it and put it on the agenda for the next board meeting. Just wanted you to know. We had better be prepared at the next meeting to shoot this proposal down," he added.

There was a long silence as Thad Moore processed this information. Finally, Thad said, "It's crazy. What do those worms know about any of this?"

"I have no idea. All they're claiming is they've raised money," Winrock responded.

"I don't see how he could raise any money with the technical information you have given the directors."

"That puzzles me, too. We have mentioned our R&D project in our annual reports, but no specifics. I wouldn't invest in what we have made public."

"He must have more than that. I smell a major leak." Thad's voice deepened.

"That's not as much a surprise as the second offer. Finley came in with a new merger offer: a twenty-page document." Winock checked his watch as he spoke.

"We turned his offer down flat, months ago," Thad answered.

"Old H.J. hasn't given up. He has raised the ante by twenty percent."

"That smells leak, also."

"Thad, you need to be there at five. I need your support. I'm not sure what's going to happen."

"I'm on my way. I'll be there if the traffic doesn't get me," Thad promised.

After Thad's phone call, Winrock rubbed his eyes with both hands and let out a long, deep sigh. He reached for the phone and dialed Bud Hinton in Texas City on his secure line.

"Yo, Hinton here," Bud answered in a sing-song tone.

"I don't have much time." Rich spoke softly. "Can you think of any way Slizer could have gotten his hands on our last test run results?"

"Hell no. I told you this morning, no one has seen those but you and me. My copy is in my safe." Bud was shocked at the suggestions.

"Finley may have gotten wind of what we have, also. H.J. is putting all his chips on the line to merge with us. Without more information than we have given out, this doesn't compute."

"Is your copy safe?" Bud knew his boss well enough to ask.

"I've had it with me or in my safe at all times. Doesn't your research crew know what we have with El Gato?" Winrock asked, knowing the answer.

"They have a pretty damn good idea. I took all the readings myself, but they couldn't miss what was going on," Bud answered.

"I think our ship has a leak, Bud. We'll need some damage control. Things are getting out of hand."

"Just hold course, Boss. Give those security analysts your best dog-and-pony show. We still need to get El Gato kicked if we're going to develop block 320, but your idea to shoot other areas seems to be working perfectly. It has thrown our competition off," Bud said.

"Thanks, Bud. Would you come up about eight? I'll be through with the meeting by then. I'll meet you in my office. Got to run." Winrock was getting anxious.

"Yes, sir." Bud's ten years in the Navy couldn't break an old habit.

Half a world away, Iran's minister of exports,

Abdahade Calib, was receiving a phone call from the States. It advised him that a fax would be coming to him immediately that described substantial information on Richard, data that could come only out of Global's secret files. Abdahade Calib was both excited and terrified. Iran frequently executed those who failed in their job. Calib would have to pay his informer in six figures for this information on Richard and ask for more.

The fax arrived on Calib's private machine, in Arabic. As he read, he punctuated each sentence with guttural curses, throwing the fax on his desk when he completed it. He grabbed the phone and called an emergency meeting of his top advisors and others from several departments.

CHAPTER
IX

Finally off the phone, Rich Winrock looked again at the oversized envelope from Elliott Slizer then picked up the two large packages of documents for the evening's reception and stuffed them in his briefcase. He stopped for a moment to look around the room to make sure he left nothing behind.

Linda Blake had been wringing her hands outside his office as five o'clock grew closer. She finally punched the button on her intercom. "Should I order the limousine now, Mr. Winrock?"

"No, Linda, I'm going to take my car. It's only two blocks," Winrock said.

"Better let Richard know we should be leaving right now," Daniel London called from the hallway in a sour tone, looking sternly down at Linda from a pair of bloodshot eyes set in his furrowed, leathery face.

Dan resented Linda because as executive vice-president of the company, he needed access to Richard Winrock frequently and on short notice. Linda Blake hovered over her boss like a mother hen, insulating him from everyone, so even Dan had to arrange to see Rich through her. He had complained to Richard about the arrangement, without results. Richard was a private person who preferred to administer by written directives, memos and bulletins rather than by numerous informal discussions and meetings—Dan's style.

Linda relayed the message to Rich on the intercom, and then with her head slightly tilted to the side, she turned to Dan and said, "He will be with you in a minute. He said that Daryl White has gone over early to see that everything is arranged at the Spindletop Club."

Dan grunted and began pacing up and down. At 4:46, Richard Winrock emerged from his office carrying his ostrich leather briefcase. Striding past Linda's desk, he said over his shoulder, "Did you cancel the limousine?" Then to Dan he said, "I am taking my car so I can leave from the Spindletop Club."

Linda nodded and said, "Yes, sir."

Her eyes followed Richard Winrock as he led Dan London down the hall to the private elevator. The contrast between these two men was striking, she observed, as they waited for the elevator. Richard stood erect, his broad shoulders squaring up a gray worsted pinstripe suit. Dan stretched a rumpled, tailor-made Indian silk suit over a badly maintained, stooped body, which was struggling to receive enough oxygen.

Richard confided, "I'm not sure how this meeting is going to go, but I'll do my best."

"Meetings with those vultures rarely go well," Dan answered, punctuating his response with repeated jabs at the elevator button.

Richard and Dan entered the carpeted elevator, headed for the parking garage.

"Just sit back and watch the eyeballs, Dan. You won't have to say a word unless they bring up some technical question I can't answer."

"I don't recall you ever restraining yourself from answering technical questions, Richard."

Richard noted that traces of resentment were becoming more evident in Dan's voice lately. Dan had unwittingly revealed one of his deep-seated hostilities about Richard's behavior. Richard had a financial background and understood the broad fundamentals of the technical side of Global's business. Dan was a petroleum engineer with considerable geology and operating experience, having come up through the ranks of the production department. He had briefed Richard extensively on Global's pertinent technical matters for this meeting, yet Dan was not confident that Richard would say the right thing if one of the security analysts zeroed in on a technical problem of Global's.

CHAPTER
X

The elevator stopped on the floor of the parking garage that was reserved for the executives of Global. Richard walked at a brisk pace toward his Mercedes sedan parked in the second spot on executive row, the first spot being reserved for Global's chairman, Kern. Dan struggled to keep up as Richard waved to Bill Martinez, a security guard, who was circulating around the parking area in a golf cart, unlocked his car from the driver's side and quickly entered it. Dan settled into the front passenger's seat.

As Richard prepared to back out, he turned his head and caught a flash of movement reflecting from the back seat of the car. He looked down and into an automatic pistol pointed at his head.

"Don't make any funny moves, or you're both dead men," said a nervous voice with a foreign accent from behind his seat. Slowly, two figures came up from crouched positions. "You do exactly what I tell you, Mr. Winrock," one man said.

Then the second asked, as he motioned his gun at Dan, "Who is this man?"

55

"One of my company officers. What do you want with us?" Richard's heart was pounding so hard he had difficulty speaking.

"You will know soon enough, Mr. Winrock. Now, don't look back. That might be fatal. We are going to drive out of here, understand?"

Dan remained silent, frozen in the seat, his hands pressing on his knees to keep them from shaking. Richard's car lurched forward. The irregular movement caught the eye of the security guard, Bill. As the car turned, Bill noticed the extra passengers in the back seat and radioed the security station on the first floor.

"Juan, block the exit ramp from the second-floor executive parking," said Bill. "Something is wrong. Two guys are in the back of Mr. Winrock's car. I don't know where they came from. Hurry—they're headed down." Bill Martinez quickly followed the Mercedes.

Juan, the ground-level guard, rushed over to the exit ramp and stopped a car that was about to turn onto the street.

The gold-colored Mercedes emerged slowly down the dark, circular ramp that ended at the blocked exit. As Richard came to a stop behind the sedan blocking the exit lane, the gunman behind him jammed his pistol against the right side of Richard's head and snarled, "Tell him to get his car out of the way, or you're dead."

Richard was now shaking all over. He was lowering his window when he saw a figure rush to the driver's back door and attempt to yank it open. The gunman turned as the car rocked. He appeared to be moving his gun from Richard's head to defend himself when the gun fired, striking Richard in the side of the head above the ear. Bill Martinez stared in disbelief as Richard slumped forward over the steering wheel.

The leader of the two gunmen barked out some orders in a language Dan did not recognize. Then they swung open the two back doors, catching Bill unaware and knocking him backward. His gun slipped from his hands as he fell. The gunman who had shot Richard was out of the car and standing over Martinez before the guard could regain his composure.

Immediately, the gunman kicked Bill in the head, knocking him unconscious. Then both gunmen ran onto the sidewalk, turning north on Foster. As they ran, a car pulled up alongside then slowed. They jumped into the car, which merged into the congested traffic.

People were beginning to gather around the car Richard and Dan were in as Juan called 911. By now, Richard had fallen over in Dan's direction. Dan spread out his hands and arms to catch Richard's head and felt the warm blood that had begun to soak Richard's thick brown hair. Dan almost pulled his hands away in horror, but managed to hold on. He looked out at the gathering crowd with a pitiful, pleading expression while he held Richard's head in his lap. His glance at Richard's head made him think that Richard was gone. There was a red hole that must be where the bullet had come out. Poor Richard, Dan thought. He didn't deserve to die like this.

CHAPTER
XI

Daryl White paced nervously around the Travis Room at the Spindletop Club, trying to avoid conversation with the twenty investment security analysts who had been invited by Global Oil and Exploration of Houston to discuss the company's future plans and earning prospects. Cocktails had begun at five o'clock, and Richard Winrock was to make a presentation at six. It was now 5:32, and neither Richard nor Dan had arrived. Daryl noticed a number of guests frequently looking at their watches. He checked his watch then pulled out his cell phone. "Linda, glad I caught you. Where is your boss? It's past 5:30. This crew is getting nervous."

"What do you mean, Daryl? They aren't there yet? Richard was going to drive over."

"Drive over? It's only two blocks."

"Well, he isn't here. What the hell could have happened?"

"I don't know. He left the office just about four forty-five. I will call downstairs and find out when he left the building. Hold on."

Linda direct dialed the security office on the ground floor. The phone rang ten times before being answered. "This is Mr. Winrock's assistant. What time did Mr. Winrock leave the building?"

"You mean you haven't heard? Mr. Winrock's been killed by some gunman. Shot him in the head."

Linda caught her breath. She got a terrible sick feeling in the pit of her stomach. She gripped the top of her desk. Slowly she asked in a whisper, "What did you say?"

"Look, miss, we have a mad house down here. Mr. Winrock was shot in his car."

"Where... When... Did..."

"I got to go, miss." There was a click.

Linda began shaking all over. Her teeth were chattering. She became aware she was repeating, "God, don't let him die," then thought that maybe he was already dead. The man said he had been killed. "Oh, God, no."

She made her way on rubbery legs to the private elevator and started down. Then she remembered that Daryl was waiting on the other line for news. The elevator was programmed to go directly to the second floor, which it did. As the doors opened, she could hear voices drifting up from the circular exit ramp, some shouts and commands. She knew the news was real. Something terrible had taken place.

Linda took the elevator, returned to her desk and picked up the phone. "You still there, Daryl?"

"Yes, I'm still here. Did you forget I was waiting?" he said with impatience.

"Yes, I did. Forgive me. Something terrible has happened." Her voice quivered. "Richard has been shot in the parking garage, in the head."

"*What* happened?"

"Someone shot Richard. That's all I know."

"My God. Who would want to shoot Richard? That's the craziest thing I've ever heard."

"I went down to the second floor. I could hear the commotion."

"God. What will I tell this group?" Daryl asked himself aloud.

"I don't know. Better verify before you issue any statement."

"I can't believe this," Daryl stammered.

"Neither can I," she said, holding back tears.

"Well, thanks, Linda. I had better call this function off. Won't set well."

"Screw those money changers. Richard may be dead." After Linda hung up the phone, she grabbed her purse and rushed back down to the parking garage.

Within minutes of the arrival of the police, the Houston Fire Department paramedics had arrived at the scene. They immediately called for an air ambulance. Despite the crowd, Linda was able to get close enough to see the two paramedics frantically working on Richard as he lay on a stretcher. He appeared to be unconscious, and she could see blood on the bandages on the right side of his head. Linda struggled to keep from fainting. Then, she saw Dan London, covered with blood, standing close to the stretcher. He kept looking at his hands but had no place to wipe them. As she pushed her way to him, she heard the blare of more sirens as additional police rushed to help.

CHAPTER
XII

Bewildered, Daryl slowly walked up to Bob McLean, who was surrounded by security analysts. "May I speak to you a moment, Bob?" Daryl whispered.

"Sure, Daryl." Bob followed Daryl to a vacant corner of the room.

"You are not going to believe this. Richard has been shot in the head; he may be dead."

"My God. When did this happen?"

"As he was leaving the parking garage."

"Are you sure? Who shot him? How did ..." Bob was almost speechless.

"I don't know any details, Bob. I called Linda to find out why he wasn't here. What are we going to do with this crowd? Do you want to give them the news?"

Bob thought for a moment then said, "No, it is more appropriate you tell them. I'm just a director. You are the host. I'll try to find out something while you give them the word. Did anyone say where they were taking

Richard?" Bob's first concern was the well-being of his friend, Richard Winrock.

"No. They didn't. Probably the Trauma Center at St. Matthews."

"I'll call over there and see what I can find out. I pray we have gotten bad information," Bob said, still hoping what he had heard was not true.

Daryl slowly walked over to a central table, leaned against it, cleared his throat and, raising his hands to signify silence, said, "Gentlemen, Mr. Winrock had an accident on his way here. I understand he has been seriously hurt. That's all I know. I'm sorry you have come out for nothing. Please feel free to enjoy our hospitality as long as you wish. We will reschedule this discussion as soon as we know more about Mr. Winrock."

The room had become increasingly quiet as he talked. When Daryl finished, there was complete silence as the crowd pondered what they had been told. Then the barrage of questions started. Daryl could disclose only what he had heard from Linda. He wanted to use the phone to learn more about the shooting incident but was unable to break away from the querying crowd.

Finally, he said, "Gentlemen, please excuse me. I must make some calls." With that, he looked frantically around the room for Bob McLean. Not seeing him, he turned toward the phone. There was now a line of people waiting to report this news to their companies. Daryl left the room and found another house phone. He called three direct Global numbers before he got an answer.

"Who is this? Oh, Layton. I got some bad news about Richard that I want to verify. What has happened over there?"

Steve Layton, a financial vice-president of Global, had been in the process of leaving the building right after the incident occurred. The ramp was blocked, so he got out of his car and walked down to investigate. What he saw he would never forget. There was Dan London sitting, frozen in the front seat of Richard's car, holding Richard's bleeding head. He had tried to get closer to the car, but people from the street had moved in around the car, making it impossible. Then two Houston police officers arrived and, waving their billysticks, herded people away from the car. Layton had rushed upstairs to his office to call Global's chairman, Rivers Kern. Now Layton described what he had seen to Daryl, who listened dumbfounded. Daryl headed back to the Travis Room to give his guests details of the shooting. Bob McLean caught up with him, saying, "I couldn't find out anything from the emergency room at St. Matthew's. What did you find out?"

Daryl addressed the group again. "Gentlemen, I have some bad news. Our president, Mr. Winrock, has been shot leaving our building. They are taking him to the Medical Center. I don't know his condition. Sorry."

He turned back to Bob. "Keep 'em happy. I'm headed for the building."

Bob went to the large picture windows of the Spindletop Club's forty-fifth story that gave him a view of the events taking place two blocks away in front of Global Tower. He contemplated the scene on the street and the group at the cancelled meeting and rushed out of the room. Thad Moore didn't need an invitation. He followed Bob into the express elevator, leaving the room filled with security analysts who had come to hear about the expected expansions at Global. The analysts were always looking for good stock. They were left in hushed silence.

Bounding out from the lobby into the street, Bob and Thad ran down Marshall toward the scene. Belaying his fifty-five years, Thad moved his large frame with long fluid strides; pumping his arms to keep the pace, Bob was close behind. Thad wasn't sure what he would do when he got to the Global Tower, but he had to know what had happened to his friend. If Winrock had been killed, he wanted to be there. If he was alive, there might be something he could do to help.

Thad and Bob slowed as they neared the crowds behind the police blockade in front of Global Tower. They pushed their way to one of the HPD officers at the roadblock and pulled out their company IDs; the officer let them through.

The two men could see the paramedics just inside the garage exit setting up an IV. They had started working in their direction when a helicopter's chop began to reverberate. The rotor noise was deafening as it bounced back and forth between the buildings. The chopper settled down gracefully, touching the helipad like a falling leaf. The two paramedics started wheeling Richard to the neighboring building to transfer him to the air ambulance

65

crew.

Thad moved closer through the crowd to get a better look. Usually the take-charge type, he felt lost. He wanted to help his friend but was certain he would be in the way. Thad watched Rich being rolled toward him. When the stretcher was right in front, Rich Winrock opened his left eye and looked right at Thad, and his right hand made a motion of recognition. Thad thought, Thank God he's still alive.

It did not take long for the air ambulance crew to get a quick report on Richard as they transferred him to their own stretcher. A few minutes later, the chopper rose straight up and then tilted forward and quickly disappeared over the tops of the buildings, headed for the Medical Center.

"I'm Thad Moore." He showed his ID. "Call upstairs. Ask transportation to have Clarence bring down the limo. I need to get to the hospital."

While Thad was shifting his two hundred twenty pounds from one size sixteen to the other, waiting for the company limo, he felt a tug on his sleeve. Thad turned to see Winrock's secretary in near hysterics. "Where have they taken him?" Linda sobbed.

"Now calm down," Thad said in a low voice as he held Linda to stop her from trembling. "He waved to me when he went by on the stretcher. He knew I was there. He waved. I saw it."

"Then he's alive," Linda whispered.

When the white Lincoln limo arrived at the building exit, the company driver, Clarence, recognized Thad. Clarence stopped close to Moore and motioned for him to get in.

"Come on, Linda." Thad put his arm around her and pushed her into the limo.

Clarence waited for the police to view his passengers and move a barricade. Then he worked through the crowd and the police cars to head south toward St. Matthews.

Sitting back on the soft leather, Linda Blake regained her composure.

"How could this happen?" Linda asked herself out loud. "Why would anyone do such a thing?" She looked out the window, watching the last of the flashing lights disappear.

Thad was still processing all that had happened. Gathering his thoughts, he answered, "Life's gotten cheap. I guess the gunmen got away."

"But why?"

"The police said it looked like a carjacking that went bad," Thad said.

"Did they say who did it?"

"No. Only that there were two of them."

"He won't die, will he?" Linda wiped her eyes on a silk scarf she was wearing, smearing her mascara. "How badly do you think he was injured?" Linda pursued, cautiously.

"It was hard to tell. There was a lot of blood."

Linda put her face in her hands and fell silent.

CHAPTER
XIII

Leo Solis cursed under his breath when cars failed to yield right-of-way to his blaring siren as he approached the scene in an unmarked patrol car. Finally, within one block of Global Tower, he swung onto the sidewalk and parked, getting some hard looks from people headed to see what the commotion was all about. Leo heard the helicopter getting close as he jogged up to the scene, weighted down by the extra twenty pounds he had put on and the .357 Magnum in a shoulder holster.

Looking at his watch, Leo said, "Not bad. The *Houston Courier* can't carp about that reaction time."

Before reaching the scene, Leo had been on his radio setting up the roadblocks and deploying six patrol cars to comb the downtown area in search of the two suspects who had shot the president of Global in an apparent carjacking. The sketchy description of the suspects would likely not turn up anything of value. But he'd been lucky before.

Arriving at the exit ramp, Leo pushed people aside, trying to reach the victim, telling them, "OK, let's give 'em some room. Get back. Get back." Leo bent over the two paramedics and said, "What's happening here?"

Normally the paramedics would have ignored this question, but the tone had authority. The older paramedic turned and looked at the ruddy-faced, dark-complexioned man with heavily scarred cheeks and asked, "Who are you?"

Leo was frequently not taken seriously by the public. His swarthy looks reflected a strong Mexican Indian heritage that still resulted in some prejudice in a city with a population that was over forty percent Mexican American. Leo had worked hard to become chief of his department, and the long, difficult process was present in his response.

Lowering the pitch of his voice but raising the volume, Leo answered, "I'm Leo Solis, chief of homicide. Now let's have it. What's happening here?"

The paramedic turned back to his task and answered in spurts between his actions. "We have a gunshot to the head."

"What's the condition?"

"He's still with us, pulse is weak, respiratory decline. We're preparing him for transport."

"How many times was he hit?" Leo couldn't tell from the amount of blood on the bandages.

"One shot. Small caliber. Passed through."

"Have they recovered the bullet?"

The paramedics turned and looked at Leo without answering. Dumb question, Leo thought. His job was to try and save this man, not worry about where the bullet was.

Leo looked hard at the victim. Based on his past experience, he didn't give him much chance to survive. He made sure the victim's car was secured and protected against further contamination before the laboratory was able to inspect it and obtain samples and prints. Then he barked out orders to his officers regarding the identification of the eyewitnesses and spoke briefly with one of them.

Continually scanning the scene, Leo noticed a man in the garage office surrounded by TV cameras and reporters. The man's clothes and hands were covered with dried blood. He looked at the officer, who nodded in response.

Leo walked in, quieted the reporters and said, "I'm Leo Solis, homicide. I'd like to talk to this man. Give us a break, will you?"

After the room cleared, Leo spoke up, repeating his introduction, as the man he addressed wasn't attending too much. "I'm Leo Solis, homicide. Who are you?"

"I'm Dan London, executive vice-president of Global. I was in the car with Rich—Mr. Winrock—when he was shot. It was awful."

"I'm sure it was. Let's go in this next room. Too

much noise," Leo said coldly.

It wasn't that Leo was inured to suffering and grief, but he had picked up so many bodies of buddies that had been shredded in war that he had learned to turn his feelings off during a crisis. But he could never purge his mind of the horrors he had witnessed. Years after the smoke and stench was gone, those images were still there—pieces of friends scattered about on the ground.

London saw the male strength in Leo's jaw set and followed him into a smaller security office.

Leo motioned to a security guard on the phone. "Give us some privacy, will you, son?"

The guard quickly finished his call, looked quizzically at Leo, then decided not to challenge the order he had been given.

"Suppose you take it from the top, Mr. … uh …"

"London. Dan London."

"Sure, Mr. London. Tell me everything you can remember."

Dan sat down, gripping his knees with his hands, now caked with blood, and looked at Leo pacing back and forth in front of him.

"Let's start from the beginning. Who was driving?"

"Rich—Mr. Winrock, our president, CEO."

"Where were you going?"

Dan looked up, wondering why that was pertinent. "To a meeting at the Spindletop Club."

"What time?"

"We were due there at five o'clock."

"Who knew about the meeting?" Dan did not respond. "OK, OK, what was the meeting about?" Leo said with some competence.

Dan didn't like this line of questions. He had already told the police that he thought the thugs who shot Winrock wanted his car. He hesitated then said, "About offshore drilling. What's that got to do—"

Leo ignored the remark. Shaking his head, he asked, "How did the suspects stop the car? Where was it parked?"

"On the second floor. We have reserved space. This is our building."

"I know," Leo responded and immediately questioned, "What did they say?"

"Get in."

"That's all?"

"That was enough."

"Then what happened?"

"They told us to drive out."

"What did they look like?"

"I don't know. They told us not to turn around."

"Did they have an accent?"

"Yes. I'm not sure what kind. It could have been Latin. Maybe Middle Eastern. I couldn't be sure. But it wasn't Texan."

"Did you see any of how they were dressed?"

"No. They were behind the seats."

"What were they trying to do?"

"I assumed they were trying to steal the car."

"Why didn't they just drive off with the car?"

"I don't know. I wondered about that."

"Did you have a car there? You're the vice-president, right?"

"Yes, I had one."

"What kind?"

Again, Dan thought this brash detective was overstepping his authority. "What's my car got to do with anything?"

"What kind, Mr. London?"

"I have a Lexus."

"It was parked in the same area, right?" Leo asked.

Then without waiting for an answer, he continued, "You had the keys, right?"

"Of course I had the keys."

"So they could have taken your Lexus if they wanted, right?"

"I suppose so."

"Why do you think they took both of you and the Mercedes?"

"I don't know, but I believe this questioning has gone far enough."

"Mr. London, I understand you told the security guard right after Mr.—"

"Winrock," Dan filled in.

"Yes, thanks, Mr. Winrock was shot and the gunmen ran off that this was a 'carjacking gone bad.' Is that right?"

"I guess I said something like that. I was in a state of shock. My president had been shot. His head was in my lap, bleeding."

"I'm sure you were. It doesn't really compute as a carjacking, does it?"

"I suppose not. I've not had time to think about it!"

"I don't like you tone. Sorry, but I don't like homicides. I'm investigating what could be a murder.

75

You are the best eyewitness we have. I don't want to miss anything. What you tell me now is uncontaminated by what you may hear or read, which could influence the impressions, the details, which may be useful, actually, vital."

Satisfied he had extracted everything of value from London for the time being, Leo stopped his questioning abruptly and said, "OK. Look, I'm going to the St. Matthew's Trauma Center. That's where they've taken the victim. Glad to take you." Believing strongly that the shooting would graduate to a homicide in the next few hours, Leo had decided to get firsthand information on the victim's condition from the hospital staff at St. Matthew's.

London answered, "Fine, I've had enough questions."

Changing his mood, Leo smiled and said, "Let's go. My car's up the street. You could never get out of here in your Lexus. I have the whole area blocked off."

"I'd appreciate a lift. I have to get there."

Leo started pushing his way through the crowd. "We may actually beat the air ambulance. It has to land on the roof of St. Matthew's parking garage. The Trauma Center is on the first floor. That transfer takes five minutes."

After they had left the downtown area and were proceeding south on Fannin Street, Leo said in a friendly tone, "Suppose you tell me a little about your offshore deal. I worked on a rig one summer when I was at U of H."

"I'm not the right person.   I'll give you an overview."

"Good."

Dan London stammered around trying to describe what he knew about the offshore drilling without revealing anything he knew that hadn't been made public. This was easy, as Winrock had kept most of the details to himself for security reasons.

CHAPTER
XIV

From the club, Daryl White watched St. Matthew's air ambulance as it took off, and he left a few minutes later, excusing himself from the analysts and their questions. He was able to make the trip to the Medical Center in twenty minutes—twice as long as usual but good time for rush-hour traffic. After parking in the emergency patients' area, he jogged to the entrance, stopped, straightened his tie with a jerk, smoothed his hair and stepped inside. He had to find Dan before the media got too much information out of him.

As White quickly moved through the ER, he saw Dan in the Media Room of the hospital, surrounded by reporters and TV cameramen, describing the shooting. Raising his arm, White got Dan London's attention and motioned for Dan to join him in the hallway. Dan cut the interview short and joined White at the end of the hall.

White looked over his shoulder, cleared his throat and said, "I hope you haven't given out anything on company plans. You've been doing a lot of talking."

Dan London would normally accept critical comments from White, but Dan was now in the driver's seat. He waited an unusually long time before answering White. "I know what I'm doing. What went on at the press conference at the Spindletop Club? How did *you* handle that?"

"Thad Moore got a call on his portable phone while I was stalling for time. He walked up, took the mic and canceled the meeting. Made me look like a fool. We have to get that clown off the board."

"Was any information given out?" Dan asked.

"Hell no. Rich was bringing the press kits with him. Where are they now?" White asked.

"They should still be in Winrock's car," Dan answered.

"We better get them before someone else does. We want to keep a lid on Richard's condition until after the offshore bidding." White lowered his voice.

"With Winrock out, the board will hang me if El Gato doesn't work." Dan winced.

"Frankly, I believe we've pissed off five million dollars on El Gato already. I can handle the board. I've built a good case for the file. Winrock was on his own in this deal." White smiled to himself.

"I'd better get back. They're going to operate on Rich," Dan said.

"He's still alive? I heard on the radio he was DOA."

"No, but he may not survive. They will need to operate to stop the bleeding in his brain. If he makes it, he'll probably be a vegetable," Dan said coldly. "We need someone at the helm, right away." White noticeably extended his chest.

Dan looked directly into White's eyes for five seconds without a word then walked back to the Media Room.

White pulled out his cell phone.

CHAPTER
XV

Following Sam Butler on his rounds was a special treat for the young residents because he described each patient in detail as a person, not a slab of mutton to be carved up. He described the logic of his diagnosis and the strategy of his operation and asked for comments from the other professionals. He also described the problems he had actually encountered in the operation and the prognosis. He did all this with a humility and little-boy quality that plunged each female resident into instant admiration. Sam enjoyed this enthusiastic company of residents on his morning rounds, but he knew it was taking its toll—his legs told him. He would need some fifteen minutes to rejuvenate afterward.

Sam had stopped in the doctors' lounge after his evening rounds. He sat down in the only chair that could accommodate his bulk and closed his eyes. His consciousness drifted through illogical images, driven by a combination of childhood and recent perceptions. It raced through dark, endless halls in an unfamiliar school as he searched for a class he couldn't find. Faceless forms leaning against the walls watched him and jeered his panic. A jab to his shoulder shocked him. He awoke, disoriented, barely recognizing the nurse who was shouting that he was being paged—*stat.* He rose slowly, as if in pain, and headed for the nurses' station, pacing himself so as not to consume the small amount of energy he had left. There he lifted the phone.

"Dr. Sam Butler here."

"Doctor, you're needed in Emergency, immediately," said a voice that reflected having paged Dr. Butler ten times before a response.

In a controlled, emotionless voice, Sam said, "I'm not on call in Emergency. Who wants me down there?"

"Dr. Levine asked me to find you. We have a VIP with a gunshot to the head. Dr. Levine thinks you should see him."

"Tell your Dr. Levine I wouldn't do this for anyone else. I'll be down."

As Sam Butler put down the receiver, he was aware that the two nurses at the station were staring at him. He was not handsome, but he was adored by many of the nurses on the floor, and they competed for the shifts that gave them the most contact with him. His large, lumbering frame misled the superficial observer; his six-foot three-inch body was loosely draped over a large, heavy frame, which had begun to sag the past few years. He was a gentle man. His open face framed large hazel eyes set wide apart below a bushy brow, a broad nose, full lips and a strong jaw supporting the beginning of a double chin. The years had added the creases in his face, adding dignity to his charm. When he smiled, which wasn't often lately, he charmed everyone around him. His usual friendly, low-key manner belied the awe with which the medical fraternity viewed his surgical skills. Sam turned to the two nurses, forced a smile and then walked briskly toward the elevators, the call having revived him.

He now needed to generate enough energy to activate his brain, his hands, his legs, his back and his perceptions that must be at their best, lest he make a blunder he couldn't rectify.

He was sure everyone knew how he felt about the emergency room. David Levine especially. He couldn't bring himself to say no if someone called for him, yet he wasn't sure it was wise to extend himself any further.

Sam's energy level had been subnormal since he got the final divorce papers in the mail. Of course, he knew they were coming, but seeing them in print with the judge's signature was still a jolt. He was almost grateful at first. But living in an apartment by himself, not seeing his children was not easy for him. It was especially hard when there was a big picture in the paper of Gladys and Clarence attending some social function. He knew he shouldn't have told the little prick off that night, as Gladys asked for a divorce the next day, but it was probably a question of time. He just brought things to a head. It had cost him the house, the Mercedes and over a million in cash. That was when Sam began to feel like his strength was flowing out of him through an open valve.

83

Sam had to take charge of his thoughts to avoid being enveloped by hostility. He realized he was breathing hard and grinding his teeth. As he reached the ground floor, he was in control again.

"Who is the patient?" he asked his accompanying nurse.

"A Mr. Winrock. President of an oil company."

Sam registered shock as he processed what he had heard about a man he had met socially. He had detested emergency surgery ever since his residency at Charity Hospital in New Orleans. That was when he made his first mistake. The mistake was still alive in an institution— unable to speak or walk—yet alive. He had made many since, but he had learned to rationalize them away more easily.

Sam lowered his shoulder to work his way through the crowd. Police, reporters, TV cameramen were everywhere, asking questions, trying to get medical information. A female Eyewitness News reporter recognized Sam Butler as the famous neurosurgeon who had operated on Crown Prince Mohammed bin Salman from Saudi Arabia last month.

She rushed up, followed by a TV cameraman, and shoved a microphone in his face, asking, "What can you tell us about Winrock? Is he still alive?"

The nurse was steering Sam through the crowded waiting room when Bob McLean grabbed him by the arm. "Sam, am I glad they found you. I was hoping you were still in the hospital. Richard Winrock has been shot in the head. I'm sure Richard's wife would want you to do any surgery necessary. Are you able to take the case?"

Sam responded slowly, "You're involved with Winrock's company, aren't you?"

"Yes, I'm a director."

"I'm on my way to have a look at him. What happened, Bob?"

"Richard was shot in the head in a kidnapping attempt about five o'clock this evening. Sam, please do what you can."

Sam nodded as Nurse Reese steered him around two more live TV cameras to Trauma #4.

Sam had developed a smoldering contempt for the media, particularly one of the dailies. They had elaborated on his statement about the procedure he had performed on Crown Prince Mohammed bin Salman to sensationalize a front-page story stating that the prince had died on the operating table, and Sam had brought him back with heroic medical skill. The prince's heart had actually stopped twice during surgery, but Sam reacted quickly and got it going both times. The article infuriated Mohammed's family and almost caused an international incident. Bill Miller, the hospital PR director, had used Sam several times on the hospital's VIP patients to publicize the hospital when the time came for the press conference routine.

Entering the examination room, Sam slowed to a

stop and said to himself, "Lord, let this not be too serious."

He assessed the situation and took in the activity. The emergency staff had cleaned the caked blood from Rich Winrock's face and head and shaved the area. Blood was still oozing through the gauze pads. A nurse brushed past him with vials of blood for typing and cross matching. Others were monitoring vital signs and moving equipment in place.

He walked up behind Dr. Levine, who was leaning over his patient and looking into his right eye with a small, high-intensity flashlight, and asked, "Who've we got, David?"

Dr. David Levine turned and answered, "Thank you for coming down, Sam. We need your help. Gunshot in the right hemisphere. Richard Winrock. Know him?"

"Only socially."

Dr. Levine stepped back to let Sam see the patient.

Winrock had been unconscious from the time he was placed in the helicopter. He had a peaceful expression on his face that Sam feared was close to permanent.

As he washed up and pulled on gloves, Sam asked a number of questions, requiring Levine to slow down his normally staccato speech to accommodate Sam's pace. When Sam was satisfied he had a grasp of what had transpired from the paramedics' arrival at the scene to the present, he said, "Nice job, David, let me have a look."

He put his large hands under Winrock's head, turned it then lifted the gauze to inspect the entry of the bullet and said, "Must have been a small caliber."

Sam pulled back each eyelid and looked carefully into Winrock's eyes with an ophthalmoscope and checked his reflexes. Turning, he reviewed the updated chart the nurse handed to him and said to Dr. Levine, "This man needs to go to surgery. Get X-rays and a CT scan immediately. There isn't much time to lose." He was imagining the bullet entering the patient's skull, ripping through brain tissue and neuron fibers, and finally exploding a piece of skull out of his cranium before exiting.

David Levine stood silently watching Sam then said, "Someone from the company has requested that you do whatever surgical procedures are necessary."

"David, I would feel very uneasy about all this if you weren't the one asking me. You know what's going on."

"I don't feel I'm ready to probe the brain of a man like Mr. Winrock. They tell me he's some kind of a genius."

"Well, it's just like they say: When you take off the cover, they all look alike."

"You haven't lost your sense of humor, Sam. Maybe you'll save this place."

"Look, David, you get consent from Mrs. Winrock, and I'll go in." Sam left Dr. Levine to arrange the transport to the operating room and went back up to the surgery floor to try and get his surgical team back together before they left the hospital. They would not be happy having to do another major procedure. Sam was not sure he was up to another surgery, but it would take too long to call another neurosurgeon. Winrock needed attention immediately. Sam had misgivings about operating on him, though. He was tentative when he knew his patient. A dear friend's wife died on Sam's operating table, and Sam knew in his heart he had made a fatal mistake. No one noticed but Nurse Carmichael, and she never acknowledged she knew.

While the operating room was being prepped, Sam returned to the lounge, poured himself a cup of black coffee and stretched out in his favorite chair. Sleep was beckoning in the shadows. Could he sustain three hours on his feet?

CHAPTER
XVI

Slightly less than thirty minutes later, Nurse Carmichael, who had stood watching Sam sleep for a full minute before prodding his shoulder, awakened Sam gently. He entered the operating room with new energy, stimulated by the challenge he would face. He scrubbed and held out his hands for Nurse Franklin to put on his gown and gloves. Sam walked quickly to the light board to study both the X-rays and CT scan film. Winrock, now in a coma, was having his head scrubbed in preparation for surgery, and the staff was monitoring his vital signs on a large console next to the operating table. Closed-circuit television cameras mounted overhead were recording the entire procedure. As Sam stepped up to his patient to mark the shape of the skull flap he would remove, energy was there waiting, borrowed from tomorrow or the next day.

Sam started slowly, then more rapidly he cut through the scalp, finding blood collected between the loose areolar tissue and the cranium. An electric pain passed through Sam's back as he cut on Richard. This happened only when he knew a patient or was a friend of the patient.

Sam called out, "Suction!"

The suction tube was placed firmly in his gloved hand. He drained the annulus then carefully folded back the large flap he had cut loose. "This is encouraging," Sam said, half to himself, observing that the parietal bone was not shattered, only punctured with a small round hole. The exit hole of the bullet had missed the coronal suture that joins the frontal and the parietal bones.

With an air-driven drill, Sam drilled three large holes in the skull section he would remove. He then used a large rotary saw to cut the oval section of skull that contained both bullet holes, removed the section and dropped it into a stainless steel pan with a clang, causing one of the neuro interns to jump.

As he closely surveyed the course the bullet had taken, Sam said, half to himself, "I don't think I've seen anything like this before. The bullet passed through without much damage." The two residents leaned closer to observe the brain area Sam was stroking with his gloved hand. "Now let's find those bleeders."

Sam gently moved the brain tissues in a circular motion to feel the small bone fragments that may have broken loose from the inside of the skull when the bullet entered, but there weren't any. He was confident the bullet had not splintered, as the exit wound was small and clean cut. After cauterizing the last small bleeders he found, he flushed the area until the solution was clear. Sam was concerned that if these vessels continued to pour blood into the brain cavity after the skull section was replaced and wired closed, this could cause pressure that would result in serious brain damage.

Where there was no more color, he suctioned out all the fluid and said to Sidney Long, the senior resident, "Let's take Rich Winrock home." Sam severed the suckers holding the segments of the tenacious white durra brain covering that he had tied off and began sewing them together with fine gut thread, using a small curved needle, the slender fingers of his large hands moving steadily and accurately. "I can stretch the durra to cover both the inlet and exit holes. Mr. Winrock is lucky the bullet was a small caliber."

The residents nodded their approval. It was considered to be a special privilege to observe Dr. Sam Butler in surgery. There was no hesitation in his actions. They were deliberate and continuous. Dr. Butler's particular trademark was his manner of communication with the team. He lacked the prima donna behavior of other recognized surgeons in the hospital who tended to abuse their assistants if they took too long to execute the surgeon's wishes. If asked, most of the staff at St. Matthews would characterize Sam as a "super nice guy."

Sam drew a long breath as he completed stitching the outside skin of Winrock's cranium and looked over at the clock—9:25 p.m. Sam was surprised that nearly two and one-half hours had passed so quickly. He said with a smile, "We've got to stop meeting like this, Carmichael."

Thanking his faithful surgical team, Sam cleaned up and went back to the lounge to prepare himself for Evelyn,

Winrock's wife, and two directors of Winrock's company, who were waiting in the visitors' lounge and were not speaking to each other, according to a messenger. As if telling Evelyn the news about Rich would not be bad enough, Sam dreaded having to meet the media that had been assembled by the hospital's Public Relations director in the Media Room after he finished talking with Evelyn.

Sam could only speculate on the effects to Winrock. His left side could be paralyzed; he could lose his sight, his reasoning power; and Rich might not regain consciousness. Walking slowly to the lounge, Sam felt a strange sense of foreboding—of being drawn into forces beyond his control or understanding.

CHAPTER
XVII

Global executives, having heard the original news through phone calls, social media feeds, on their radios en route home or on TV at home, had been filtering into the St. Matthew's emergency department in a steady stream. Seeing Dan's blood-stained suit, each approached him and asked him the same questions.

Dan liked being at the center of company activities. Although he was weary of explaining over and over what happened, he couldn't turn a question down from one of his associates. He suddenly became aware of a perceivable change in the manner in which he was being treated. He was now the big boss. He was not surprised at how quickly people switched their loyalties; he was surprised at how obvious they were. Even some of Richard's staunchest allies seemed to be patronizing him about his "terrible ordeal."

Tiring of talking to new arrivals, Dan decided to go to the OR waiting room. Despite their dislike for each other, Linda chose to follow. They headed upstairs and walked through the swinging doors to the hallway leading to the waiting area. Normally, only immediate family was allowed, but no one asked them to leave. Dan and Linda were both tired and grateful for a place to sit down. They began to watch the traffic area that led to the operating rooms farther down the hall, hoping the faces of the nurses and attendants leaving the area would give them some clue to the condition of Richard.

Linda was the first to recognize an anxious-looking woman and a gray-haired couple entering the hallway. When Dan saw the three, he jumped up to greet them. Mrs. Winrock was between Mr. and Mrs. Rivers Kern, holding onto their arms as they approached. She looked at Dan's blood-stained clothes, leaned forward and gave him a hug.

"You poor dear. Thank you for getting Richard here."

Dan then greeted his chairman with an exaggerated handshake. Linda stood silently, half-dazed, until Mrs. Winrock asked if she had seen what happened.

"No, Mrs. Winrock, I was upstairs."

"How is my Richard? Is he still alive?" Mrs. Winrock asked, with hope ebbing from her voice.

No one wanted to answer Mrs. Winrock, but Dan finally spoke up. "They are operating on him now. We have not heard anything since they started."

"My precious Richard. How could this happen to

him? He was feeling so good when he left for the office this morning." Turning to Rivers Kern, she said sadly, "How are we to get along without Richard? He must pull through this. He must," as if trying to convince herself.

Rivers agreed that Richard must survive and led her to a chair. Then they were all silent for a long period.

Rivers Kern had heard the news at the River Oaks Country Club as he finished a round of golf. He verified the news with a call to Global's offices then called his wife to ask her to call Mrs. Winrock, who lived only a few blocks away. Rivers rushed home, still in golf clothes, to pick up his wife and go to the Winrocks' residence. Getting no answer to their phone calls, they thought Mrs. Winrock might be outside in her rose garden. They found her with her cell phone in her hands, staring at a graft she had been doing. She had just hung up with the hospital. Mrs. Winrock walked slowly back to her spacious greenhouse, put down her tools, as if in a trance, and said, "Please take me to the hospital, Rivers. Tell me the truth. Is he still alive?"

"As far as I know, Evelyn. He is in the best hands. We can only pray at this point," Rivers said, hugging her.

Evelyn did not break down. She was a strong woman. Evelyn Winrock had lost both of her parents to cancer and one of her sons in war.

A short time later, Bob McLean found everyone he was looking for in the hospital, seated together. "I'm glad you're here, Evelyn," Bob said as he gave her a hug.

"The Kerns brought me here—didn't have time to change." Evelyn suddenly was aware she was in her gardening clothes.

After exchanging greetings and condolences, Rivers and Bob went off to talk privately down the hall.

"Things like this don't happen to us, Bob. I still can't believe Richard is in there."

"Yes. It is unreal. It is sad how two animals can destroy a beautiful man like Richard in the twinkling of an eye," Bob added.

"Well, he isn't destroyed yet. That's an excellent neurosurgeon working on Richard. I haven't given up."

"Nor have I," Bob said, feeling badly he had left the impression he had given up on Richard. "People have survived injuries like this," he continued.

"I hope they capture the thugs who did this. Why would they want to shoot Richard?" Rivers wondered.

"I understand from the radio they think the shooting was accidental. It was a carjacking gone wrong," Bob said.

"Yeah, I've heard all that crap, too, on the way over here. The media will have a field day with this one," Rivers said indignantly.

"We had a meeting scheduled with the security analysts today. Several came in from New York. I'm afraid they also will have field day with this," Bob confided.

"Damn. That is a pure case of adding insult to injury," Rivers said. "What did you tell them?"

"We told them to go home. We would call them when the meeting is rescheduled," Bob said.

"Oh well, the whole world will know about this by morning," Rivers consoled himself.

"This is a bad time for Richard to be out of service, Rivers, with all that is in the works."

"Couldn't be worse. I don't know what I am going to do. I will tell you what I'm *not* going to do: put Dan London in charge of Global."

"Who else have you got?"

"I have me, that's who. And I have you." Rivers looked directly into Bob's eyes, with his head forward.

"What do you mean?" Bob knew, but he wanted to be sure.

"I don't trust anyone in my shop but Richard. Since he is out—hopefully only for a short time—I'm going to move back in and assume the presidency. I decided on the way over here."

"I think you are wise. Hell, you built this company from a pup," Bob added.

"Well, I had a lot of help. But I do think I can run it for the time being. I do want to hear you say I can lean on you for the next few months. You understand a lot more about our business than I do, I'm afraid," Rivers said.

"Of course I'll help you. What are directors for?" Both men got a smile out of that statement. Feeling more relaxed, they returned to the waiting room.

As Sam walked into the room more than an hour later, Bob McLean stepped forward to greet him. "Thanks for working on Richard, Sam. I believe you know Evelyn Winrock and the Kerns?"

"Of course." Sam shook hands with everyone then returned to Mrs. Winrock and took her hand.

"How are you doing, Mrs. Winrock?"

"I'm all right. How is my husband?" she asked, searching Sam's face intently for a clue.

Sam said gently, "Please, sit back down. I have good news. Your husband is doing remarkably well under the circumstances."

Mrs. Winrock's face brightened. She whispered, "Thank you, Lord," as she sat down. "We've heard what the media is saying. What has happened to Richard?" Mrs. Winrock asked, almost hoping the doctor would not tell her.

Sam said, "He has sustained a bullet wound to the right hemisphere of his brain."

"Is it true the bullet went through his brain, then out?" Mrs. Winrock said, finding it difficult to say aloud.

"Yes, that is correct. The bullet was a small caliber, which does less damage."

"What does that mean, Doctor?" Mrs. Winrock asked, not liking what she was hearing.

"We cannot say to what extent this injury will affect Mr. Winrock. His vital signs are encouraging. He's breathing on his own. The most critical time will be the next twenty-four hours."

"You mean, if he will ... will live or not?"

"Yes, that is correct. I don't want to give you false hope, but I must tell you that he is responding very well, considering the injury."

"What did you do, Doctor?"

Sam knew he must choose his answer carefully. People who seemed so grateful for a surgeon's efforts during the time of crisis sometimes changed and became very bitter if the patient died, was incapacitated or sustained permanent deficits to his or her speech or mobility after surgery.

Sam looked carefully at Mrs. Winrock and said, "The X-rays and CT scan indicated the bullet passed into the interior of Mr. Winrock's right hemisphere before exiting. There was indication of bleeding in the cranial cavity. It was necessary to find the bleeding arteries and cauterize them. It was also important to remove skull fragments and any damaged brain tissue. That was done."

"Is my Richard going to live, Doctor?"

"There are a number of positive aspects to his condition. I feel encouraged, but I would be prepared, Mrs. Winrock."

With this, Mrs. Winrock finally broke into tears.

Sam held her hand tightly then said, "We are going to do our best for Mr. Winrock." He stood, nodded and excused himself, then plodded up the hall, a tired old man.

Linda seated herself in the chair Sam had vacated next to Mrs. Winrock and patted her arm. Everyone who heard Sam's words had the feeling that the doctor was expecting Richard to pass away during the night.

As Sam removed his scrubs in the changing room, he looked up at a large wall clock. Pushing ten o'clock. He was too tired to go home and come back for his first scheduled operation at seven. He would have the nurses on the ninth floor find him an empty bed.

Sam's days and nights had been blending into one continuous agony these past few months. His body was numb; his head was never completely clear; and between operations, his thoughts tumbled through one anxious fantasy after another. As he lay in the bed, he realized he was now almost beyond the point of sleep; his mind could not blot out what he had seen during his operation on Richard Winrock.

Rich should have had massive hemorrhaging and extensive brain damage. However, Sam had found what looked like the path of a surgeon's incision instead of a bullet's trail—something had separated the tissues of the brain with minimum damage. Winrock's vital signs had been remarkably strong considering the type and location of his bullet wound. Sam thought Rich had a good chance to recover physically, but he was unclear as to the effects of the wound on Winrock's brain function. A piece of bone that was carried ahead of the bullet must have acted like a scalpel, he thought. But why? God must have really wanted this man to live. There was no doubt in Sam's mind. This was the kind of miracle he had observed some years ago when he examined a man who had fallen from a tenth-story window onto asphalt and suffered only a concussion. There was no explaining either case medically. He must review the tapes of the operation as soon as he had time—and energy.

CHAPTER
XVIII

As Sam began to relax, his thoughts changed direction. They drifted to a few weeks prior.

Rounding a corner on the neuro floor, Nurse Carolyn Armas saw Sam approaching. She stopped to intercept him.

"Dr. Butler, I have been looking for you. I want you to have dinner with me this evening. I am planning something special I know you will like." Carolyn had rehearsed her speech for weeks.

"Thank you, Carolyn. I would like to, but I'm not good company just now." Sam didn't want to hurt Carolyn's feelings, but he was too tired to even think about going out.

"Nonsense. A home-cooked meal and a neck rub is what you need."

"I'm not sure what time I will get away. You know what they do to me around here."

"Yes, I do. It doesn't make any difference. Come over when you finish up, regardless."

"Do you really mean that? Midnight, perhaps?"

"You know I mean it. I will have everything on hold. Everything!" Nurse Armas smiled slyly, turned and left before Sam could decline.

Sam had watched Carolyn as she walked away, admiring the gentle sway her small body gave her green cotton operating gown.

Carolyn was twenty-eight years old and had served on one of Sam's operating teams for three years. Sam considered her the most competent scrub nurse he knew in the hospital. She seemed to anticipate his every move and had lightning dexterity, especially during critical operations. Nurse Armas's neck rubs after a long and tedious surgery were a delight Sam looked forward to as he neared the end of an operation.

Sam's wife had never given Sam a neck rub. Gladys Butler hadn't physically touched Sam for six months before their separation. Gladys's attention had been completely occupied with their two children, her bridge club and her garden club. Sam had left her alone a great deal of the time. As his practice began to expand, and Gladys filled her days with activity, she gradually lost interest in what Sam was doing and stopped talking to him about his work. Sam never volunteered any conversation regarding his practice of medicine and was obviously not interested in bridge or gardening; thus, their conversation eventually ceased almost completely.

Gladys was forty-seven years old but gave the impression of being in her late fifties, having let her hair stay the gray it had turned and having gained considerable weight the last three years of their marriage. Her clothes were those of an older woman, which helped create a matronly impression. Gladys had many convenient headaches or backaches over the years when Sam made an overture for sex. Hurt at being turned down so often, he gradually ceased trying, prompting Gladys to move to another bedroom. Sam thought this was the way Gladys wanted things and was stunned when she announced she was going to file for a divorce. Sam didn't ask her to change her mind as he had not been happy for years but tolerated their arrangement for the sake of the children.

Sam firmly believed that Gladys would be happier living alone with the kids. He began to wonder if his judgment was correct after they were separated. Gladys had gone on a diet, began to take dancing and skating lessons and dyed her hair. She began to look her age for the first time in years. There was a man in her life now, he was certain.

Sam had received a message from Gladys one day, which was left with his service, to call her after six o'clock at home. She had seldom called, so he surmised she had something on her mind.

"I'm glad you called, Sam. I'm going to Europe for a month." Gladys bubbled with delight.

"What about the kids?"

"They are going to stay with my mother. She's looking forward to it."

"Is she really. I can't imagine her babysitting **Rufus** and **Glenna**. I don't think she's done that twice in her life, much less for a month."

Gladys dismissed Sam's comments.

"I have everything arranged. You can have the children whenever you want. Just give **Big Gladys** some notice."

Soon after the divorce Sam had tried to arrange a weekend with the kids (for over a month) only to be told there was invariably some conflict—some activity the kids had to attend—that would make it inconvenient. Now that she was leaving the children for a month, she was making this generous offer. What a bitch! As Sam slowly walked down the hospital corridor after the call that day, he realized that every contact with Gladys upset him for hours and perhaps days afterward. She seemed to know just how to torment him. He wasn't sure she was tormenting him on purpose, but he was sure she was aware she was having a disturbing effect on him.

Oh, well, he now had someone who cared about him, who wanted him for himself.

CHAPTER
XIX

The tension in the operating room during Sam's third brain operation of the day was heightened by the nature of the surgery and the age of the patient. Dr. Edgar Shepherd, another neurologist, had referred a 14-year-old female patient to Sam for a medulloblastoma operation. Apparently, her family doctor had missed the obvious early signs of a brain tumor, and it had grown to an advanced stage.

He had tried to discourage Alicia's parents from proceeding with the operation and urged them to rely on radiation and chemotherapy until he realized that they could not live with themselves if they hadn't done everything possible for their only daughter.

When Sam first met her, he felt sad that the pretty girl's long golden hair would have to be shaved. Now she was under anesthesia, in Operating Room 9D with her head clamped stationary by a metal vise, two bars secured into her skull. Before he started, he turned and looked up into Carolyn's eyes for a moment, the only part of her that showed. As she stood on an elevated platform by Sam, her eyes glistened under the bright operating lights.

Sam opened Alicia's skull, observed the convolutions and arteries carefully for a full minute, and then walked to the X-ray display to verify his memory of the pictures. He stared at the X-rays and CT scans and began formulating exactly how he would enter this brain to remove the tumor. Returning, he worked his way through the soft white tissue of the brain to the densely crowded cells of the tumor and took a sample to send to the path lab for testing and classification.

Without waiting for the results, he began excising the massive tumor. Ten minutes later, Dr. Richard Wilkins spoke over a loudspeaker intercom system connecting the lab to the operating room and confirmed the medulloblastoma.

Sam continued to excise all the malignant tissue he could safely remove. Tiring, Sam put down his instruments, stretched his arms and shoulders, sighed aloud and said, "Let's wrap it up; we have done all we can." When he had completed restructuring the dura, he put down his instruments and said, "Gerald, close it up for me. I will be in the doctors' lounge if you need me."

Sam was not aware of how tired he was until he got a cup of coffee and spread out in the nearby doctors' lounge to relax. His arms, back, shoulders and neck ached from standing, bent over, for slightly more than two hours. As Sam stretched out on the sofa chair, he put his hands over his eyes to shield them from the overhead lights, but he had another reason. He didn't want anyone to see the wetness collecting in the corners of his eyes.

While Sam was operating, he would not let himself think of the effects of what he was doing would have on Alicia. But now that he was alone, he could not hold back the thoughts. Alicia's most serious deficit was her coordination problems. Sam hoped she would not have any complications from the surgery, such as bleeding, excessive brain swelling or infection, so that the radiology team could begin to treat that portion of the tumor he dare not remove for fear of destroying important functional parts of Alicia's brain. He thought that Alicia's age was on her side, but he knew she might not even live through the summer.

Sam prayed Alicia would reach her sixteenth birthday. Sam had a sixteen-year-old daughter whom he missed very much. Glenna was his favorite. He hated not seeing his children regularly and hoped he would not lose his relationship with them. They hadn't been enthusiastic about being at his apartment. There wasn't enough to do there, they had told him.

Sam's thoughts began to depress him. He realized what a treadmill he was on, performing one operation after another, having little interface with his patients before the operation and seeing so many discouraging results after surgery. He kept hoping someone would unlock the mystery of the cause of brain tumors.

Deep in his thoughts, Sam didn't respond to his

page. The senior resident on his team, who had followed him into the lounge, tapped him on the shoulder and said, "Dr. Butler, that's your call."

"I'm sorry you told me. I was going to ignore it," Sam said without opening his eyes.

Sam rolled his frame off the sofa chair and slowly walked to the phone on the wall.

"Butler here. Who's paging me?"

"Nurse Andrews in ICU, Dr. Butler. I'll connect you."

"Dr. Butler, we need you in ICU. Mr. Winrock has regained consciousness and is saying some strange things," Nurse Andrews said with an apologetic tone, knowing Butler's operating schedule.

"You're saying he's talking? He was in a deep coma when I left the hospital last night."

"Well, the first thing he said was, 'Call Sam Butler.' That's what we were able to make out of his whispering."

"Come on now, Andrews. There's no way he would know I operated on him last night. We nearly lost him three times," Sam said, his disbelief taking on the little-boy quality the nurses adored.

"Doctor, you really need to come down here. I'm not sure I believe what I'm seeing and hearing."

Sam turned to check the large clock on the wall in the lounge. "I don't have much time, but I'm on my way."

CHAPTER

XX

Sam lumbered down the polished hall—his running shoes making a loud squeaking noise—with Dr. Blanchard keeping pace. They took the elevator to the next floor and walked directly to the central nurses' station for neuro ICU. Sam walked behind the counter, picked up Winrock's aluminum chart, sat down and began flipping through the information that had been assembled since Richard Winrock was brought in the evening before. Sam was stunned at the strong vital signs Winrock was now showing. He became anxious to see the effects of the surgery for himself.

The head nurse came up behind Sam and watched him review the chart. When he finished his inspection, she said, "Dr. Butler, your patient has upset several of our nurses. He says things to them he couldn't possibly know. Who is this man?"

"He's head of the largest independent oil company in Houston. That's all the media has talked about since he was shot leaving Global Tower yesterday."

"That's not what I mean. I know all that stuff. He's got us all spooked with what he knows. I went in to check on him before you got here, and he said some things about "poor Alicia." Isn't that the little girl you operated on this morning? How could he—"

Sam turned to his head nurse. "Let's go see Mr. Winrock."

They both stopped abruptly in their tracks as they saw Winrock's penetrating grey eyes looking at them, eyes that were not of a man who had been near death just hours earlier. Winrock's head was heavily bandaged, with a large cotton cover over the bandages. Several probe wires emerged from under the bandages, and two IVs dripped into Winrock's arm, which was restrained to keep him from dislodging the IVs.

Sam frowned and moved forward, gripping the retainer bars on the side of Rich's bed with both hands. He uttered in an almost whisper, "Richard, I am Sam, Dr. Sam Butler. You are in St. Matthew's Hospital. You are doing fine."

Sam stopped, not sure Winrock was understanding him. Richard blinked both eyes several times, which Sam interpreted to indicate he did comprehend. As Sam talked to him, he continued getting the same response from Richard at appropriate times. Sam reached out and held Winrock's hand for a moment. He could see Rich's expression change ever so slightly. His eyes almost smiled. Sam turned to Dr. Blanchard to determine if he had noticed the response. He had.

Sam continued, "You're recovering very rapidly. Now, you go back to sleep. I'll see you later today."

Winrock blinked several times then began to move his mouth to make a sound. Sam turned off the sound of the heart monitor, leaned over and put his ear close to Richard's mouth to make out what he was trying to communicate.

Sam listened then turned to face Rich and said, "Again, Rich, try again." With his ear almost touching Winrock's lips, he could make out "Evelyn."

"Are you saying, 'Evelyn'?" Sam asked gently.

Winrock's expression changed again to a faint smile, and he blinked several times.

"I understand, Richard. I'll arrange for you to see your wife as soon as possible. She was here until four o'clock this morning and is probably still asleep."

Winrock moved his head ever so slightly up and down to signify he understood.

Sam decided this activity was too trying for Winrock, so he patted Rich on his upper arm and said, "Richard, go back to sleep. I'll take care of everything."

Sam closed the door behind them and motioned to the nurse to return. He asked Dr. Blanchard what he thought about Mr. Winrock.

"Sam, I have never heard of a patient regaining consciousness and being as well oriented so quickly after massive brain trauma. You did a masterful job on the old boy."

"Not so, Ted. All I did was clean up after a very masterful bullet."

"What do you make of him asking for you, Sam?"

"Are you sure that's what he said?" Sam asked skeptically.

"No, but the nurses think he did."

"Nonsense. I know him socially, but I doubt that he is aware of who I am."

"Don't be modest, Sam. Everyone in Houston has heard of you. I am puzzled how he knew you had operated on him. He was unconscious when he came in, and you were called off the floor to operate. Could he have regained consciousness earlier than we know and overheard some discussion in recovery?" Ted asked.

"That's possible … but highly unlikely," Sam said, shaking his head.

"I know. Well how do you explain it?"

"I don't," Sam stated flatly, wishing to end the discussion.

Dr. Blanchard continued, "Sam, don't you think we should get Mr. Winrock tested by one of our neuropsychologists as soon as possible?"

"Let's not rush him, Ted. Hold off a few days until

we are sure we don't have to go back in for any reason."

"OK. Fair enough." The two men nodded to each other and took off in opposite directions.

Returning to the doctors' lounge, Sam again fell into the comfortable sofa chair.

He was almost asleep when a warm hand cupped his chin and a voice said, "That was a beautiful piece of work, Sam."

He opened his eyes to find Carolyn standing there smiling, with her green surgical cap still covering her rich brown hair.

"You are the only beautiful piece of work I know, young lady."

"Flattery will get you a return engagement, sen□ or."

"That's what I was hoping you would say."

"Well, I've said it, and I'm glad. What time will you finish today?"

"I have two appointments at my office before it closes but have to come back here to make sure everything is in order."

"What time do you think?"

"I can be at your place by nine—I hope."

"Wonderful. I will have dinner prepared and

waiting. By the way, quite a few people noticed you came back to the hospital in the same clothes you left in the last time. It wouldn't be a bad idea to bring some changes over if you are going to be my roommate."

"That's a good idea. I will stop by the apartment before I come over."

Carolyn was gone, leaving Sam alone again. How had he so quickly become close to this precious young girl? They hadn't discussed the future. They hadn't even seriously kissed until recently. Now he was considering moving in with Carolyn. He was sure everyone on the hospital staff who knew him was aware of the latest events. Somehow, he didn't give a damn. He was a big boy and could do whatever he pleased. What would Gladys say when she heard? And she would hear. Oh well, he would worry about that some other time. Right now, he needed to relax, to relieve his shoulder muscles that were now so tense they were ready to spasm. He had only ten minutes before his meeting with Leo Solis about Richard Winrock.

CHAPTER
XXI

Thursday morning, Global's office began to fill with four thousand anxious people. The previous evening's late news had been dominated by reports of the shooting of their president. His condition was still listed by the morning reports as critical. Almost every conversation in the building related in some way to the dramatic events of the previous evening.

Rivers Kern had arrived at his desk at 7:10, an unusual event. In recent years, he was more interested in his bank, golf and his thousand-acre ranch in Brenham, Texas, than in Global. He spent only thirty percent of his time at Global's offices and almost never came in early. A champion golfer, Rivers was thin and muscular for his seventy-eight years, a surprise to those who knew his age. With his full head of slightly curled snow-white hair and tanned skin, he looked more like he was in his early fifties. Kern had started Global Oil and Refinery eighteen years before and had guided it to the two-billion-dollar level, maintaining a stunning forty-three percent of the common stock.

He often spoke of the times when he knew all the employees by name. Now he felt like a stranger in the elevator—thus, his decision to build a private elevator to the executive floor. The majority of Rivers's present employees who knew him did not understand him well. He was usually quiet and appeared shy to new acquaintances. Yet his powerful strength of will came through to those who worked with him. People moved when he issued an order. His square Welsh face, jutting jaw and penetrating eyes caused considerable uneasiness to the executives who had been hired since he became less active in the company.

At eleven o'clock, Rivers convened a meeting of the top executives and department heads in the formal board room to announce his intent to run the company until Richard's future was known. The words he used to his glum, nervous staff revealed his pessimism at Richard's return or, even, his recovery. Rivers scheduled an emergency board meeting for ten days later to ratify his actions, a legal formality, as he held the control interest in Global.

Recently, Dan London and Richard Winrock had been locked in a bitter controversy regarding the company's future plans. Richard wanted to plunge into a vigorous offshore exploratory drilling program in California, Louisiana and Texas at the time that most of the operating and drilling companies were stacking rigs. Richard's rationale was that it was *the* time to drill. London would counter with how demand was down and inventories were up and the excessive cost for exploration and drilling. This dispute had caused considerable division in the company.

Rivers Kern was aware of the diverse opinions of his top two executives; however, he felt more confident of the company's direction when there was healthy debate present. Actually, the chairman encouraged such controversy if it did not develop normally. Kern expected Dan London to make his move as soon as the company had recovered from the shock of Richard's injury.

Rivers commented on his distaste for an article in the business section of the *Houston Courier* regarding Global's future. He reflected on the good communications Global had enjoyed with the security analysts who had attended Global's aborted meeting the night before and stated that the tone of this article was damaging to the future of Global, which already might be threatened by the injury of their president and which was in considerably poor taste due to its timing.

As Rivers stood addressing his staff, his secretary handed him a note. Before opening the folded paper, Rivers was sure it was word that Rich had passed away. He took a deep breath, opened the note and then gasped before breaking into a broad smile and announcing the news. There was spontaneous joy from the staff when they heard Richard had regained consciousness and spoken. Winrock was a popular president, sensitive to people's feelings and showing little pomposity or ego. He was also greatly respected for his keen analytical mind, which devoured numbers and financial statements. Kern then rephrased some of his earlier statements in a more optimistic tone, using the expression *when* rather than *if,* and adjourned the staff meeting.

Upon hearing the news, Dan London had mixed emotions, which he disguised successfully. He had longed to reach the president's job but had resigned himself to failure, as he was two years older than Winrock and did not seem to fit the profile Rivers Kern had structured for his chief executive. Suddenly, when Richard's life—or at least the recovery of his full mental competency—was in jeopardy, Dan had thought that maybe now he would get his chance, although he wasn't glad for what had happened. In spite of his personal dislike for Richard, he was genuinely sorry for his misfortune, yet he could not ignore the benefits that might accrue to him as a result of Richard's condition.

CHAPTER
XXII

It was difficult to anger Rivers Kern. When someone or something finally did offend him, he went to great lengths to even the score. The morning newspaper's editorial cast a shadow over Global's future. The article stated that Global was curtailing their exploration and drilling program due to reduced earnings. The most damaging statement implied that Global may be the target of a takeover attempt due to the uncertainty of the medical condition of its president, "who was gunned down in the parking area of his own building." It was obvious that portions of the article had been prepared before the scheduled meeting and before the shooting to preempt the comments that the various financial journals would publish following Global's presentation to the investment security analysts. Someone had merely injected the comment on the shooting at the last minute. Since no information on the company plans was released at the aborted meeting, the *Courier* had done its own research.

Rivers Kern had some dark thoughts concerning the motivation of this article. He thought some motivation might come from the differing political views he and the

Courier's board chairman, Klegg Allen, held. Allen wasn't above doing something to hurt Kern's company for political reasons. Kern's even darker thought was his suspicion that one of the business editors may have written the negative article to manipulate the stock price. Rivers met with his security director after the article appeared and authorized a clandestine investigation of the stock trading done by the *Courier's* editorial staff. Global's security department was one of the best small private organizations in the United States. If one of the editor's second cousins sold Global stock, the security department would find out. This time, Rivers had prepared the press release with considerable background information on the financial condition of the company to counteract the negative statements by the *Courier.*

Entering the boardroom, River's confident smile changed momentarily to an expression of disgust when he saw Vernon Billings, business editor of the *Courier.* Rivers glared at him. In contrast to Rivers's trim, blue surge suit and regiment tie, Vernon Billings had on a rumpled tweed sport coat and black knit tie. Vernon smiled weakly through his cigarette-stained teeth, adjusted his glasses to use the upper portion of his bifocals and sat back to hear what Rivers had to say. Rivers, the professional administrator, did not let his disgust for this man distract him from his task at hand. He greeted the group, thanked them for making the press conference then announced he had good news to report.

"Mr. Richard Winrock has regained consciousness

and has spoken to his doctor. He is doing remarkably well for the injury he has sustained. Barring any setbacks, Mr. Winrock should be returning to his position as president of Global."

Rivers went on to say that the company was having a good year despite the downturn of the economy and had had sustained satisfactory earnings for the first two quarters of their fiscal year. Rivers's statement was made with an air of confidence. He was a polished public speaker who chose his words well. When Rivers finished, he motioned to Dan London who handed each member of the press corps one copy of the prepared press release. Everyone in the room made some effort to review the information in the bulletin except Vernon Billings. He stared coldly at Rivers, waiting for the opportunity to ask questions.

He was the first to speak up. "Mr. Kern, who will replace Mr. Winrock during his absence?"

Rivers Kern could feel the anger building inside of him. Being chairman of the board did not allow him the luxury of telling Billings to go to hell. He looked down at his papers then slowly turned to his tormentor.

"Mr. Billings, I have assumed the role of president until Mr. Winrock's return."

After several questions from the representative of the *Wall Street Journal,* Billings again spoke. "Mr. Kern, Global is well into the fourth quarter, yet you haven't commented on the third-quarter earnings."

"I don't have the final figures on this period yet, Mr. Billings." Kern turned to the other side of the table, hoping to move on to another question. No questions were forthcoming. In fact, the faces he saw suddenly looked unfriendly to him. He must have indicated in his voice or his manner that he was avoiding saying what everyone suspected.

"What is the indication, Mr. Kern?" Billings said slowly and deliberately.

Kern decided to face the issue head on as he had done all his life. He imagined Billings as a linebacker he would run over as he charged through the line of scrimmage.

"The third quarter will probably be down slightly, with a recovery in the fourth quarter, giving us a typical successful year."

Billings made notes on the back of the handout and moved around in his chair, signifying his anxiety to leave.

Rivers Kern closed the meeting with a comment on the kidnapping attempt: The police were investigating it as such rather than a carjacking, which he was happy to say was a failure, particularly with the remarkable recovery of Mr. Winrock. Kern stated that he hoped the "massive" efforts to bring the kidnappers to justice would be successful. The group responded in the affirmative and left, hurriedly.

As the media were leaving the meeting, Hunter, Rivers's son, was entering the office. Rivers saw Hunter stop twice to engage in conversation with the media representatives. The exchange was animated and substantial, as if the parties had a mutual concern in the topic. Rivers had a strong premonition that Hunter was the source of the leaks to the media. Rivers was appalled. He would find out the truth, and the consequence to Hunter would be serious.

CHAPTER

XXIII

Complying with Richard's one-word request earlier that morning, Sam called Evelyn Helm Winrock to advise her that her husband had regained consciousness and was asking for her. Evelyn was so astonished at this news she was almost speechless.

"Thank God," she kept repeating after she caught her breath.

Evelyn agreed to meet Sam outside the ICU at two o'clock, the earliest Sam could arrange a gap in his scheduled activities. She came to the hospital early, but after arriving, realized she had made a mistake, as the nurses would not allow her to see Rich without authorization. Sitting in the waiting room, Evelyn studied the faces of the people there. She was surprised at the number of nationalities represented and was still guessing where people had come from when Dr. Butler arrived.

When they walked into Richard's room, Evelyn noticed that Rich's eyes were on the entrance, and he was definitely smiling. Evelyn hurried to his side and attempted to lean over to kiss him, but the steel bars on the side of the bed made this impossible.

Sam spoke up, "Here, sit here by the bed."

Winrock turned his head, and his eyes looked into Evelyn's. She did not speak for a full minute, as she was saying the prayer she had repeated over and over the previous night. Rich's eyes were both bright and intent. Evelyn was thrilled. She slipped her hand under his and held it gently, so as not to disturb the tubes in the back of his hand.

As she sat there, Evelyn became aware of the sound and picture of his heartbeat on the miniature monitor on the other side of the bed. She watched it as Rich attempted to shift his body toward her. The repetitive oscilloscope picture of his heartbeat suddenly went crazy and made wide swings up and down. Evelyn's heart almost stopped as she gasped for air and motioned for Sam to look. Calmly, Sam patted her on the shoulder and advised her that Richard's movement, not his heart, had caused the changes in his oscilloscope heart pattern.

"He is quite stable."

Evelyn sighed with relief and started to cry, letting all her pent-up emotions pour out.

Sam stepped in and asked Rich how he was feeling and if there was any pain, not expecting an answer. Rich took a deep breath and exhaled, making several sounds. With this, Sam turned off the monitor's sound and asked Rich to repeat his answer.

Rich said, unmistakably, "OK."

Evelyn was thrilled. Her tears turned to those of joy.

"Say that again, Rich?"

"O ... K ... OK."

"Wonderful! You are doing better than I expected."

Richard responded by taking another deep breath, waiting for Sam, Evelyn and the nurse, who remained in the room, to be listening then said in a faint whisper, "Lenny's ... arm."

Evelyn was the only one who understood. She stared, putting her hand to her mouth to stifle the exclamation she nearly made.

"But how could you know? I don't understand. Doctor, what's going on?"

"What is it, Mrs. Winrock? What did Mr. Winrock say? I couldn't make it out."

"He asked about Lenny's arm. Our grandson. He broke it this morning. But how could Richard know about that? Lisa called after you called. I'm confused. I thought you said that no one but you has seen Richard."

"That's correct. Well, almost correct. Dr.

Blanchard, his neurologist, was with me this morning."

"Then how?" Evelyn stood and looked down at Rich. "I'm thrilled with your recovery, my darling. I wasn't going to tell you about Lenny for fear of worrying you. He's doing fine. Lisa called back, and it's in a cast. She will be coming as soon as she can get away." Evelyn looked around the room.

"Did my daughter call here?" she asked the nurse, who was standing with her mouth open in surprise.

"No, ma'am. There are no phones in these intensive care rooms. We have received no messages," the nurse answered.

"Has anyone been in to see my husband?" Evelyn asked, ignoring Sam's previous answer.

"Just the duty nurse and one of the residents who checked his IVs."

"Then how—"

Observing the frightened look on Richard's face, Sam terminated the visit, taking Evelyn back to the waiting area.

"Dr. Butler, suppose you tell me what's going on?"

"What do you mean, Mrs. Winrock?"

"You know very well what I mean. Someone has been talking to my husband. Who could it be?"

"I don't know what to tell you. I know of no one

128

except **Dr. Blanchard** and the floor nurses who have seen him. I understand he has been asleep since I saw him this morning with **Dr. Blanchard**. I have no idea how he knows about his grandson. Are you sure that he asked about Lenny's arm?"

"Of course I am sure. Oh dear. I hope I didn't upset him asking all those questions. The important thing is he is recovering. I had all but given up last night. I just won't worry about how he knew."

"I think that is the right approach," Sam said as he left her to return to the operating area.

CHAPTER

XXIV

The shooting of Rich Winrock was now dominating the news throughout the country. There was wild speculation as to the identity and nationality of kidnappers. Fearing international involvement, Chief Winslow of the Houston Police Department wisely invited the local **FBI and CIA** representatives to assist in the case.

Leo was six minutes late to the three o'clock meeting to review the case and establish a cooperative program for the various agencies. He had waited impatiently in his office for the fact sheets he had prepared to be copied for distribution at the meeting. While the group was waiting in the chief's conference room, Chief Winslow used the time to present Leo's credentials. He was saying, "Leo Solis is the sharpest and most successful detective in Houston," when Leo walked in with the information booklets under his arm. The remarks embarrassed Leo, and he frowned as he looked down at his scuffed shoes.

Chief Winslow said with a grin, "I've gotten their attention, Leo; it's up to you to hold it."

Leo set the stack on the conference table and said, "I plan to give each of you a copy of all the information we have accumulated on this case at the end of the meeting."

He began reporting in detail the events just preceding the attempted kidnapping, the actual kidnapping attempt and the escape of the two kidnappers. Next, he presented the known information on the description and behavior of the two suspects and followed this with background information on Global's international activities, their current financial status and their president. Leo summarized his formal presentation with his conclusion that the kidnappers appeared to be international terrorists who had selected Global Oil and Refinery as their target for a kidnapping to embarrass the United States and raise dollars for their terrorist activities. Global presently had operations in four Middle Eastern countries and was particularly vulnerable to retaliation by any of these governments, should the kidnappers be apprehended.

During the question and answer period that followed, Leo impressed the group with the precision and depth of his answers to probing questions. There were few avenues of investigation that Leo and his local team of officers had not considered over the short period.

The meeting closed with a comment by a CIA representative that expressed the general feelings of the assembly. "Gentlemen, we should give this case our most serious attention. We in the United States may be experiencing the violent terrorist activity that is commonplace in much of the world and has recently intensified. How we handle this case can have a most serious consequence to our national security in the future. You will get our full cooperation."

The room remained silent for a full thirty seconds. Then the police chief stood, walked to the end of the table, and began outlining the general plan that he and Leo had formulated, setting up manhunt task forces that included the Houston Police Department, the Harris County Sheriff's Department, the Texas Highway Department, the Texas Rangers, the CIA and the FBI, and establishing administrative and communication lines. After the discussion, Leo distributed the information booklets and the meeting adjourned.

CHAPTER

XXV

After her phone call with Bob McLean Wednesday morning, Lenora was excited by the prospect of selling a twenty-million-dollar piece of property to the Italian investors. She sensed that her efforts would be successful. Lenora had closed several large commercial transactions in the last several years; however, there had been other brokers involved, which reduced her commission substantially. On this deal, she was the sole agent and would have to share it with no one. The two Italian investors were holding the money in a Houston bank. They were anxious to start the project as soon as possible to take advantage of a favorable construction proposal they had received.

Shortly after her phone discussion with Bob McLean, Lenora was able to reach the investors in Dallas. She learned they would be returning to Houston at six thirty in the evening of the next day. Lenora advised Rodrigo Carranza, the principal, that she would be willing to meet him and his brother at the airport and have the purchase agreements drawn and ready for their approval and signature. Rodrigo accepted her offer immediately.

Rodrigo had heard about Lenora through real estate channels. They first described her as a stunning young lady with the "mind of a computer." Further investigation revealed that she was five-foot-seven with the body of a fashion model and a face that always prompted a second look by both men and women. He found Lenora had an interesting combination of features that haunted his memory, from her wide-set eyes that changed from light green to light blue depending on the colors she wore, her small nose that could have been made of flawless porcelain, to her small, full mouth. When she smiled, her eyes, not her lips, gave away her emotions. He could tell from the set of her jaw that she had a mind of her own, yet her overall appearance showed warmth—the kind people wanted to relate to. During Lenora's first meeting with Rodrigo, she had been surprised at several of his statements. This surprise seemed to dilate her pupils as she looked squarely in his eyes. That was when Rodrigo decided to pursue the hotel venture with Lenora as his agent.

After a busy day at her office, Lenora went home early to relax and prepare herself for what might be a long evening. She anticipated Rodrigo and his brother asking her to have dinner with them and would be dressed for the occasion. She had her white Lincoln Continental Town Car washed on the way home.

Lenora had found Rodrigo attractive, but she suspected he had a wife and children in Italy. He had never spoken of his family, but she detected signs that told her he was a family man. During their business meetings, if alone, Rodrigo had dropped hints that he was seeking a relationship with her. She handled this by acting as though she did not understand his subtle propositions.

When she arrived at the parking garage of her upscale townhouse on Woodway, her head was pounding again, as it did daily now. She took two Advil and decided to rest before dressing for her trip to the airport.

Lenora's family doctor had checked her over two weeks previously and found no cause for her persistent headaches. He advised her to take at least a week off and relax, attributing her problems to business stress. Lenora did not believe this was the cause because she had lived with business stress for several years while building her real estate business. She had forty-seven agents in her firm and was earning over a half a million a year for herself. Her office in the nearby Post Oak Towers was considered to be one of the most elegant in Houston.

As she lay on her king-size bed, staring at the ceiling, she had to admit to herself that she did not have the usual drive and stamina lately. At times, she dreaded getting out of bed in the morning. Her thoughts drifted back to the early years in business following the loss of her husband. In her view, she and Randall had been happy for ten years, and then he had died of a heart attack in his secretary's bed. Only a few people knew the circumstances surrounding his death. Lenora remembered what mixed emotions she had had at the funeral. She doubted that she could ever trust another man.

Lenora had sold their large house herself and bought the townhouse with enough money left over to launch her real estate business. Lenora had never liked the snobbish crowd Randall French had called his friends. She gave her business most of her time and energy, leaving little opportunity for social activities. She did attend the River Oaks tennis tournaments, an occasional polo match and most of the prominent annual charity balls. A small group of older, successful, divorced men usually competed to take Lenora to the Museum Ball or the Junior League Charity Ball. However, since she had met him, Rodrigo Carranza seemed to occupy her mind and time. She did not understand why.

As she followed the delicate molding on her ceiling with her eyes, she realized her life was lacking meaning and purpose. Her financial success and recognition didn't seem important. There were few she could really call her friends, although now that she was successful, many people referred to her as their "close personal friend." She had no man with whom she could discuss her feelings— she could discuss only her activities. She enjoyed the excitement of putting a real estate deal together, but even that was not as stimulating as it had once been. When she closed this land deal with Rodrigo, she would go to Europe for a much-needed vacation. She made this promise to herself.

CHAPTER
XXVI

Sam did not care for the kind of activity his ex-wife, Gladys, and her mother thrived on, yet he had felt left out when he heard about it and was not involved. He realized as he hurried through his evening rounds that he needed someone to love and hold. He was excited about holding Carolyn this evening, regardless of her social standing. Having seen all his patients and issued instructions for their overnight care, he headed for Richard Winrock's room to have one more visit before departing the hospital.

Richard Plimpton, the hospital administrator, had personally advised Sam that a Detective Solis was placing a twenty-four-hour armed guard at Mr. Winrock's room. Sam was actually pleased. He wanted to insulate Rich from the outside world until he found out more about Rich's strange statements. The guard would probably please Mrs. Winrock since she was beside herself with worry about her husband.

The ICU for neurosurgery was relatively quiet as Sam approached Winrock's room. The uniformed policeman standing guard stopped talking to a pretty Latin-American nurse as Sam thrust out his special ID

137

card and entered the room. Rich's eyes were open and turned toward the door. The nurse on duty had fallen asleep while reading a magazine. When she heard the door close, she awoke with a jerk and dropped her magazine.

"Nurse, how long has Mr. Winrock been awake?"

"Oh—Mr. Winrock has been asleep, Doctor."

"I see; it's Mr. Winrock who has been asleep! Well, he's awake now. Why don't you go get some coffee while I examine Mr. Winrock?" Sam placed Rich's chart on the bed then sat down close to Rich's head.

"How are we feeling, Mr. Winrock?"

Rich's lips moved, and he exhaled air through his mouth. There were no discernable sounds this time, but the reaction Sam was observing was meaningful. Rich was aware of the question and was attempting to answer.

"Are you in pain?"

Rich shook his head slightly. Then he was able to whisper, "No."

"Excellent. Mr. Winrock, you are doing very well."

Rich's expression changed slightly, indicating a smile.

"Mr. Winrock, do you remember the events that put you in the hospital?"

Rich moved his head slightly up and down and

138

again tried to speak.

"Blink once for yes, twice for no."

Rich quickly blinked once.

"Excellent. Now, Mr. Winrock, do you know your first name?"

There was one blink as Rich's face clouded up at this question.

"Your middle name?"

One blink.

"Do you know what hospital you are in?" Sam had mentioned to Rich earlier that he was in St. Matthews and wanted to test his short-term memory.

One blink.

"Have you been here before?"

Two blinks. Sam was delighted. Rich Winrock was attending to his questions and answering them quickly and decisively. Each time before he blinked, Rich's lips moved and he exhaled.

"Mr. Winrock, would you move the fingers on your left hand, please."

There was a hint of a smile on Rich's face before he moved all his fingers together up and down about one inch without moving his hand. There were two tubes and several monitor probes attached to his left arm, confining its movement.

"Excellent, Mr. Winrock."

Sam now knew that there was likely no massive damage to Rich's right hemisphere, which controlled the movement of the left side of the body.

"Mr. Winrock, do you know my name?"

This time Rich exhaled loudly enough for Sam to hear. He was saying yes.

"Say it again."

Sam put his ear next to Rich's mouth. Sam could clearly make out a yes—at least an attempt at yes.

Do you know what day this is?"

Again, a yes.

"What day is it, Mr. Winrock?"

Sam could make out "Thursday."

He uncovered Rich's feet then asked him to wiggle his right toes then his left toes. Rich responded correctly.

"That is good news, Mr. Winrock. You are doing extremely well." Sam held Rich's right hand as he continued, "Your vital signs are all stabilized. You are recovering rapidly. You might just make medical history."

Rich blinked once, and a faint smile emerged, his eyes still fixed intently on Sam, as if he wanted to tell him something.

"I want you to rest. I will visit you tomorrow. The nurse will be able to get in touch with me if you need me."

Sam leaned over to hear what Rich was whispering. He drew back, stunned by what he heard. Rich had whispered something that sounded like "Go ... Carolyn."

CHAPTER
XXVII

Lenora French felt beautiful as she waited for Flight 520 from Dallas. She was eager to tell Rodrigo and Pepe about her phone call with Bob McLean and of his reaction to their offer and get them to approve the earnest money contract.

When she first met them, the apparent fun these two men had investing their money and their families' money in various business ventures in Texas intrigued her. From what little she could find out from both men, they had selected Texas for their target and Houston for their American base quite by accident. Now, after only eighteen months, they were well-known and respected in Houston's business community.

Pepe saw Lenora first, and he punched Rodrigo in the back, directing his attention toward her. Rodrigo gave her a large grin and a flamboyant wave of his arm. He walked up, leaned over the rail and gently kissed Lenora on the cheek.

"Hello, darling. You look wonderful!" he said, as

though they had known each other for years.

Lenora was not expecting his greeting and was unable to answer. She blushed and began to walk parallel along the ramp.

"You are a dear to meet us. Pepe will take our car back.

That devil, Lenora thought. He had his car at the airport all the time. Oh well, at least I'll get the earnest money contract signed by coming out to the airport.

They were in the car headed back into Houston with Rodrigo looking quite pleased with himself when she asked, "Where can we go to review the documents I have prepared for you?"

"Aha, let's see. What about Tony's? We can have an early dinner there after we finish."

"It's kind of noisy, Rodrigo. Also, the light isn't good."

"You are right. Let's see—how about Sullivan's? The lounge shouldn't be crowded at this hour."

"That's a good idea. Very well. Sullivan's."

Rodrigo watched her and tried to keep the conversation on a personal basis during the entire forty-minute drive, making it clear he was more interested in Lenora than in their business deal.

Sullivan's was just starting to get busy. The maître d' smiled at Rodrigo with a knowing twinkle when he noticed that Lenora was carrying a briefcase. Lenora caught the look he gave Rodrigo, and she began to become angry. Realizing what she had at stake calmed her down. As she walked past the maître d', she acted as though he did not exist. She must take some time off. Lately, each slight put down that she experienced for being a woman was setting her off like a rocket. She knew she was reaching a dangerous level of tension.

A Sazerac cocktail relaxed Lenora and prepared her to discuss business with Rodrigo. He tried to delay this discussion until after dinner, but Lenora said she would be able to enjoy their having dinner together only if they had first completed their business.

After he had carefully read the documents Lenora had prepared, Rodrigo took off his reading glasses, leaned closer to her and said, "Darling, I don't question your judgment, but why did you offer him fifty dollars per square foot right off when you knew this is our top offer? I can't go any higher and make the project fly."

"Mr. Carranza—"

He put his large hand over hers and said, "Please, Lenora, my name is Rodrigo. No more Mr. Carranza."

She would avoid saying either one. "The reason I gave him our best offer is he is really not interested in selling the project at any price. I checked on him before I called. Bob McLean is a successful and respected chemical engineer. Real estate is a hobby with him. He started investing in real estate to tax shelter his income. McLean started Dixie Petrochemicals, United Texas

Industries and Elemental Gas Technologies plus some smaller publishing companies I can't remember. He is on the board of Global Oil & Refining, two banks and a dozen companies. I estimate Bob to be worth between forty and fifty million dollars. He's not playing games. He's just not interested. My only chance was to overkill."

"What do you mean *overkill?*" Rodrigo said briskly. He glanced away from Lenora as if trying to contain his anger.

"Offered him fifty dollars per square foot. He was a bit surprised by that."

"I'll bet he was," Rodrigo retorted. His fingers were making a staccato pattern on the table.

"I hope he will accept it." Lenora's eyes belied the calmness of her voice.

"Yes, well, I have mixed feelings about what you have done. I understand what you have told me about Mr. McLean. I know about him. At the same time, I have always done some trading before a deal is closed. Now we have no room to trade. None whatsoever."

"Bob McLean doesn't trade from what I understand. He usually makes one offer when he buys and that is it."

"He's selling this time."

"The same would hold."

"I thought you suggested the fifty-dollar figure."

"I did. What I mean is, the only way I got his attention was to give him our best shot. I understood you would be willing to pay fifty dollars for this tract."

"I am—or at least I was. I may still."

Lenora turned white. "What do you mean?"

"You see, Pepe has been looking at a tract on Westheimer and the West Loop. Not as large as this one but large enough if we redesign around it."

"You didn't tell me this." Lenora's voice had an angry edge.

"I know. Pepe had a serious discussion with the present owners just two days ago," Rodrigo replied with a gesture of his hand.

"What do they want for that tract?" Leonora asked without hesitation.

"I'd rather not say, but it is less than your fifty dollars."

"I know the tract you are talking about; a German owns it now. The man who operated the shopping center and service station sold it last year. He also owned about six houses on Alabama."

"You keep up, don't you?" Rodrigo smiled. His eyes showed admiration for this bright and charming woman.

"Mr. Ca—Rodrigo—that tract is only about 5.1 acres as I remember."

"I think you are right."

Lenora tried to hide her bitter disappointment at this development. She had understood that McLean's site was the only one that satisfied all the criteria for the project and that the Carranzas would be willing to pay fifty dollars per square foot if she could provide a purchase/sale agreement.

"I have a meeting with Bob McLean tomorrow morning at ten. I told you on the phone. I am to bring an executed earnest money contract to Mr. McLean, or we can forget that tract."

"Relax, Lenora. You are getting yourself all worked up. You are too lovely to be upset."

Lenora resented Rodrigo bringing the conversation back to a personal basis. They were talking serious business. What she looked like had nothing to do with this business.

"Rodrigo," she found it easier to call him Rodrigo when she was angry with him, "I explained all this on the phone. I had the impression it was satisfactory."

"I must admit, I was surprised at your discussing fifty dollars over the phone with McLean, knowing you could not improve it. Wouldn't forty-five have impressed him? That would have left some room."

"McLean is a one-shot man. If you miss, you lose."

"So you have told me."

"I am sure of this. I guess you don't believe me."

"OK, OK. Where do we go from here?"

"You sign the agreement and give me a check for two million one hundred thousand dollars."

"I can't do that."

"What do you mean?" Again, Lenora felt a weakness come over her.

"I can't give you a check. But I will have arranged a letter of credit for the amount you need. Much better."

Relieved, Lenora said, "I hope that will be satisfactory with McLean. What bank will you use?"

"First Consolidated. Tell you what—I'll meet you there tomorrow morning at nine at the main office. Ask for Ron Girard."

Lenora was so pleased at this news that she thought she might faint. She tried not to show her excitement, but Rodrigo could see it in her eyes. Had he been teasing her all this time? The bastard. He must have already talked to the bank. He had made her suffer. But no matter, she would make this deal. She knew it.

Rodrigo patted her on the arm. "Lenora, my dear, is this man going to take our offer? You know this letter of credit will cost me twenty thousand dollars, more or less."

"I can't guarantee he'll take it, but he would be a fool not to."

"I agree with that statement."

Rodrigo signed the earnest money contract with flourish, rubbed his hands and said, "Now, enough business for one evening. Let's enjoy ourselves."

Lenora retrieved her papers, placed them into her briefcase then settled back into her chair and finished the ice that had melted in her cocktail glass.

"My dear, you can't drink those awful things all night. Let's start on a nice wine and finish it with our dinner. Wait, I have a better idea. Let's have champagne. That will give us an appetite."

Lenora nodded her approval.

Rodrigo ordered a bottle of expensive champagne then leaned back and looked at Lenora as though she was a delicious pastry he hungered for.

Lenora excused herself and went to the ladies' room to repair her makeup and regain her composure. She could feel Rodrigo's eyes on her backside as she walked away from the table.

CHAPTER
XXVIII

Later, although he already knew the answer, Rodrigo asked, "Are you enjoying yourself, Lenora?" Lenora's eyes were sparkling. Her speech was more animated than normal. Lenora had become completely relaxed with Rodrigo. She put her hand on Rodrigo's arm several times to emphasize a point she was making—quite a change from her previous cool behavior. Rodrigo was impressed with the quickness of Lenora's mind and the absence of the silly or inane remarks so many of the Houston women he had met used. He considered how she thought like a man but was all woman.

Rodrigo was also impressed with the number of people in a restaurant like Sullivan's who knew Lenora. He watched the men carefully as they stopped and greeted Lenora, and he sensed their respect for her. Rodrigo was sure he would be able to discern the subtle familiarity in a man's behavior if he had been really close to Lenora. He observed nothing that upset him. We shall see how strong-willed this woman is, he thought. Lenora seemed to charm information out of him. She was shocked to learn that Rodrigo owned a 727 airplane. It was presently receiving routine service at Hobby Airport. Lenora also learned that Rodrigo and his brother were large investors in the Four Star Towers condominiums located near The Galleria. When it was first developed, she had been amazed at the size and timing of the two elaborate thirty-five-story towers that the two Italian investors had built, but the Carranza brothers were never mentioned publicly as participants. Initially the towers had not been successful, with only ten percent sold after one year. However, the word circulating through the real estate channels was that the owners built the towers with their own money and could easily sustain the slow sales performance.

Lenora confirmed that Rodrigo had interests in her other than real estate when he asked her to dance. Sullivan's had a small room in the lounge area with a tiny dance floor. Lenora accepted coyly and followed Rodrigo onto the floor. Rodrigo looked her squarely in the eyes as he slowly slipped his arm around her. His hand came to rest at the small of her back, where it gently guided her through their first steps.

Then he stopped, leaned back, looked at her squarely again and said, "Relax, my dear. Just follow me."

His remark made her laugh, and then she relaxed in his arms. She glided around the floor, gracefully following his smooth, strong lead. For a large man, he was light on his feet. The affluent couples, mostly in their forties and fifties, who were seated at tables in the lounge, began to watch them as Rodrigo got more dramatic.

Rodrigo perceived Lenora was tiring after two dances, and he guided her back to their candlelit table in the dining room. He ordered a flaming dessert that was prepared at the table.

"I am not used to so much food, Rodrigo. I would be enormous if I ate like this all the time."

"You could use a few more pounds, my dear."

"I understand Italian men like their women full figured."

"*Se son rase fior iranno.* Actually, this Italian likes his women just like you."

Lenora wasn't sure what Rodrigo had said but asked, "Why are you trying to fatten me up, then?"

"I am only trying to relax a very tense woman whom I find to be intelligent, beautiful and charming."

"What a nice compliment."

"You know, Lenora, the more I am around you, the more I think of you. It is usually the reverse with me."

"Do you have many lady friends in Houston?"

"On the contrary. I have very few."

"Have you ever been married, Rodrigo?"

"Yes, I have been married." Rodrigo's face clouded, and he reached for his glass as though he would crush it in his strong hand.

Lenora changed the subject. At this point she would rather not know more about Rodrigo's past. Suddenly she felt compassion for him. It was as though this large, handsome, strong man was only an overgrown boy who needed to be hugged, needed to be loved.

When the conversation stopped, Lenora became aware of the throbbing in her head in the same place it always was. Now it gave her flashes of pain that made her close her eyes and clench her jaws.

"What is it, Lenora?" Rodrigo asked gently as he took her hands in his.

"I have a bad headache."

"I'm so sorry. Have you had it all evening?" His attitude changed to one of concern.

"No. It has been building. I noticed it was getting worse after we stopped dancing."

"Is it a migraine?"

"I don't know. I have been having them a lot lately. The doctor says it is tension."

"He is probably right. You are an intense lady."

Rodrigo used the word *tense* differently than Lenora had intended. She thought that they had communicated quite well, and his accent, which appeared to be natural, not an affection, charmed her. His chuckles seemed to come from deep within, and his warmth toward her made her feel serene. There was no doubt in Lenora's mind that

Rodrigo loved women. He might try to dominate or possess them, but he loved them in the Old World tradition.

Lenora fascinated Rodrigo. He had first thought Lenora used her femininity to enhance her business success, but after spending an evening with her, he was convinced her business success was the result of her brains, judgment and stamina. Actually, she went to extremes not to use her feminine wiles on her clients. It was only after several hours together that Lenora began to relax and reveal her femininity.

When they arrived at the west tower of the Four Star Towers complex, Rodrigo insisted she come up for a cup of hot tea. Lenora was concerned about leaving her car at the entrance, but the doorman's enthusiastic reaction to Rodrigo's request to look after the car reassured her.

They walked through the elegant marble lobby to the elevators and were whisked up to the thirty-fifth floor. They stepped out into a paneled hallway that had only two doors, one on either end. Rodrigo guided her to the door on the right. He stopped in front of a camera monitor. Speaking in Italian, he issued several abrupt commands. An electric lock clicked, and the door slowly opened. A dark-skinned, Latin-looking butler in a black uniform held the door. He bowed as Rodrigo and Lenora entered. What she saw took her breath away: an enormous, dark living room lined with curved walnut paneling; the black marble floor outlined with a small gold stripe some two feet from the walls; and groups of ornate French provincial furniture arranged atop oriental rugs. Lenora's practiced real estate eye estimated the room to be over one hundred feet long. Her focus rested on the magnificent carved Italian marble fireplace at the end of the room, large enough to roast a full-grown steer. A series of heavy crystal chandeliers hung from a twenty-foot ceiling.

"Let me take your coat, my dear. Let's go sit by the fire." And suddenly, where there had been darkness, there was a beautiful fire licking around real logs.

"I don't understand how that happened, Rodrigo," she said as she nestled down in a large wing chair facing the fire.

"*Delto, fatto.* ... Modern technology makes it easy: an electric starter and gas jets."

Rodrigo issued more instructions in Italian to his servant, using a harsh tone that puzzled Lenora. He positioned a second wing chair at a slight angle next to Lenora's so they could see each other while resting back in their chairs. Shortly, a beautiful young girl in a black maid's uniform appeared with hot tea on a silver tray. Rodrigo inquired how Lenora wished her tea then conveyed the message in Italian. His large hands seemed out of place handling the delicate china, but he did so with consummate skill.

As they sipped their tea, Lenora focused on an enormous oil painting of a woman seated in a heavy gilded chair. The strikingly beautiful woman wore a Victorian-style green velvet evening gown with a high neck. Lenora could see Rodrigo in her eyes.

"Who is this, Rodrigo?" She motioned with her head, already knowing the answer.

"That is a portrait of my mother."

"I thought so. Does she live in Italy?" Lenora did not want to appear intrusive, but she wanted to learn more.

"She died a few years ago."

"I'm so sorry. And your father?"

"He is fine. He lives in Milano." The sadness in Rodrigo's voice signified enough on this subject. Lenora struggled to change the conversation.

"You have a beautiful apartment. Did you decorate it yourself?"

Rodrigo's laugh conveyed the answer as he shook his head and ignored the question. Instead, he responded, "We have a nice view of The Galleria from here."

Lenora turned toward the windows that lined the room. The display of lights through the expanse of tinted glass left her speechless.

"Towers Three and Four will not affect my views."

"Yes. ... I noticed there were only two doors from the elevator lobby to this floor," Lenora mentioned casually.

"My brother and I share this floor."

Lenora walked to the window and stood there for a

long time watching the dynamic city. She could see at least ten major buildings under construction from this one location. Lenora felt Rodrigo's arms cradle her as he stood behind her looking at the view over her shoulder.

"I like having you share my view with me."

Rodrigo said this as though he owned the view and was letting her borrow it. Maybe he would literally own a lot of the view if his acquisitions continued at their present level. Rodrigo put his chin into her hair.

"You are a very special woman."

"You are a very special man."

Rodrigo chuckled at this remark, and she could feel his stomach shake with his laughter. He turned her toward him and said, almost in a whisper, "Young lady, I am not going to let you drive home by yourself. I will have my driver take you home then deliver your car in the morning."

Lenora was not sure whether she was relieved or disappointed by his remark. She did not wish to be pampered, but she also did not feel well. Her headache was back, more painful than ever. A call from the doorman signaled that the car was waiting at the front door. Rodrigo escorted her downstairs and into a limousine, kissing her hand before he closed the door.

What an incredible man, she thought as she sped away in a nine-passenger Mercedes limousine. The driver dutifully stood by her side until she had gained entrance to her townhouse, and then he bowed and departed. As

Lenora walked through her living room, she was stunned by the difference between Rodrigo's world and hers. Until tonight, she considered herself one of the affluent Houstonians, possessing much of what was available to the wealthy. Now she realized there was another level of wealth she had never known before.

CHAPTER
XXIX

Leo Solis was still at his office at nine forty-five Thursday night. His body was spent. His back ached as he hunched over the files he had assembled. He kept leafing through them, hoping to notice something he had missed previously. But he knew that would not happen. The case needed something to break his way.

Once he had learned more about Global, Leo had instinctively known the kidnappers had not intended to shoot Rich Winrock but were likely trying to abduct him and hold him for a large ransom. Global, the largest company in the Houston area that was not owned through a widely distributed public stock, was a good target for this type of threat, and Rich was the correct person to abduct. Rivers Kern was a major stockholder, and Kern cared about Richard Winrock—his protégé. The kidnappers could likely have extorted several million dollars if they had played their cards more skillfully.

Leo now had compiled verbal descriptions of the two kidnappers and planned to bring a group of eyewitnesses together in the morning to guide the police artist in completing composite sketches of the suspects. He would then circulate these sketches and descriptions to various security organizations in the U.S. and Europe. The CIA had information regarding the movement of various terrorist groups they had infiltrated. They would supply information on the prime candidates for the kidnapping attempt in Houston from people they had placed in international terrorist communities.

Leo had no doubt they were Middle Easterners, or else someone had gone to a lot of trouble to make them look and act like Middle Easterners. They had spoken an Arabic dialect, as yet unidentified. The police did not have any meaningful information on the third man who drove the car. Both kidnappers had beards and fairly long dark hair. They would likely have shaved their beards and cut their hair short by now to thwart their identification.

The airports and bus terminals were under twenty-four-hour surveillance for men fitting the description, but Leo believed the kidnappers would stay in Houston. He was certain they would make another attempt to kidnap Rich Winrock or another prime target. If only the lab would turn up some prints on the getaway car. Leo had hoped there would be prints on the gun but was disappointed to learn the gunman had worn gloves. This might explain the accidental shooting and their losing their gun during the struggle that followed. Leo had instructed the lab to recover as much as they could from Rich's car—to make a match—should he be fortunate enough to apprehend the kidnappers. If only ... The phone rang, the first time in over an hour, startling Leo.

"Leo Solis here," he barked out.

Leo listened then gave instructions. After he hung up, he balled his hand in a fist and banged it on the desk.

"Beautiful!" he said out loud.

A car fitting the description of the one the kidnappers used to leave the scene had been found on Delgado Street only thirty minutes from the Global building. The owner had reported it stolen the previous day. The car was a 1984 Ford, in poor condition, a classic nondescript car. Leo had received over ten descriptions of the car, none of which were exact, but they were close enough to find it. Leo had given instructions to have the car brought to the lab for a complete inspection, not only for prints but for analysis of the smallest sample that might help to identify where the car had been and who the recent occupants were. Hopefully, something would turn up.

Leo decided to cruise the neighborhood where they found the car to get a concept of why the car was dropped there and where the occupants could have gone. He would put five plainclothes detectives on the street the next day questioning everyone in the vicinity.

The streets were virtually deserted around Delgado. He wasn't surprised since this neighborhood consisted of commercial one-story buildings and warehouses, most of which closed between five and six. Some of the businesses hired private security firms that employed patrol cars similar in looks to police cars. Hopefully, Leo would find a private security officer who saw something the night before.

Arriving at the location where the kidnappers' car was found, he parked his unmarked car, locked it and walked slowly in the area, trying to get a feeling for what had happened when the car was abandoned. Leo used his instinct as a weapon—sharp and deadly. Several times in his police career he had felt the presence of someone threatening his life and found there was someone there. His instinct had saved him from certain death. Leo employed his instinct when questioning people. He seemed to know if they were lying or telling the truth or hiding something important. Prosecuting attorneys had learned to value Leo's judgment about important testimony and statements, as well as his recall of details. Approaching the corner, Leo stopped and, without moving his head, rotated his eyes over everything that could be of value to him.

Leo returned to his car and circled around the neighborhood for thirty minutes before heading home, having formulated the plan he would institute the next morning for questioning the various business and security personnel in the vicinity. Leo knew in his gut that he would catch the kidnappers and ultimately learn what their objectives were.

CHAPTER
XXX

As he stood at her front door, Sam thought about how wet his palms had been the first time he met Carolyn at her apartment. There he was, after all these years, going on a date and feeling an excitement he could only vaguely remember. As he waited for Carolyn to open the door that night, he wondered why she was taking so long or if she had forgotten he was coming. Tonight, the door opened slowly, and Carolyn stood there as though waiting for Sam's approval. He looked over her silky, flowing hostess gown and noticed how she had put her hair up. She looked radiant.

Sam said warmly, "Well, hello. Don't you look beautiful?"

He wanted to sweep this precious little woman up and hug her but only walked in and smiled. He loved how Carolyn moved around gracefully and followed her into the living room, where he sat on an overstuffed sofa. Carolyn's tastes were modern, in complete contrast with the antiques Sam and Gladys had collected over the years, yet the room was bright and friendly.

Carolyn fixed drinks then came and sat close enough to him that he could actually feel the warmth radiating from her body as they listened to some soft music. Sam discussed the events of the day at the hospital, trying to decide if he should mention what he had heard Richard Winrock say, until Carolyn put her hand to his lips and said, "No more shop talk. You have practiced all the medicine you are going to do today." Her hand smelled of perfume.

Until he started dating Carolyn, Sam had forgotten what a delight it was to be close to a woman—a feminine woman.

Gladys had lost her femininity, at least for him, years ago. She was playing the role of a River Oaks matron, not a wife or lover. Carolyn was definitely playing the role of a lover this evening, and Sam was enchanted.

Carolyn served Sam a delicious, elaborate dinner. She glided back and forth to and from the kitchen with her gown flowing gently around her. Sam's gaze followed her everywhere she went, delighting at her grace of movement.

After dinner, Carolyn asked if Sam would care to watch television. He said it sounded like a great idea and followed Carolyn back to her bedroom where she had her only TV. From the closet, Carolyn took out two large pillows that she propped against the headboard for each of them and motioned for him to make himself comfortable. She gently took off his shoes, quickly walked around the bed, and crawled up next to him against the pillows. They found a program that looked interesting and settled down to drink the coffee she had prepared.

After a time, the movie they were watching turned to an explicit bedroom scene. Carolyn said, "Oh dear," under her breath and gave Sam a quick glance to see how he was reacting. She saw he was watching intently. She could see he was getting excited, perhaps because they were watching together. When the television scene had changed, Carolyn put her hand gently on Sam's thigh. Sam began to breathe hard and could hardly believe he was getting so aroused. He turned and slipped his arm around Carolyn and pulled her to him. They kissed long and hard. He delighted in the feeling of her warm, firm body in his arms. He explored her with his hands until they both were trembling. Carolyn slowly undressed him, then herself, and they snuggled under the silky sheets for an evening that left Sam sound asleep in Carolyn's arms.

Sam awakened early to a gentle kiss and the smell of fresh coffee.

"Good morning, darling," Carolyn whispered into his ear, folding his hair back out of his sleepy eyes.

Sam looked up with a start, momentarily forgetting where he was. He sipped the coffee, dressed and found Carolyn in the kitchen completing a large breakfast.

"We need to get to the hospital."

"We have time. It's better you have some breakfast. You can't make love and do surgery on just coffee, young man."

Sam looked at Carolyn curiously and then gave in,

finishing the breakfast with an appetite he had not known for a long time.

Driving to the hospital, Sam's head was clearer than it had been in recent months. He felt good all over. Sam anticipated with excitement, not the near dread he had felt lately, the procedure he would perform that morning. What a difference being loved makes to our entire psyche, he thought. Sam felt like a young surgeon once again, anxious to use his skills, not worrying about the risks or the aftereffects.

CHAPTER
XXXI

Friday morning couldn't arrive soon enough for Leo Solis. He decided to meet it halfway. He rose and dressed at four, ate what was left of a cold pizza, and was at his desk at four thirty to clear out some accumulated paper work before heading to a meeting with the eyewitnesses to Richard's shooting and the police artist. It was set for seven to minimize the time that would be lost from the participants' work.

The Houston police used a software of layers of individual facial features, overlaid one on another, to gradually build up a complete face. The variety of eyes, noses and mouths available were sufficient to cover all but the most extreme features.

The police artist had already constructed the face of one of the kidnappers from the descriptions. The witnesses all agreed that the initial composite was not accurate. The artist quickly made substitutions, and there was a spontaneous affirmative reaction from the group of two security men, two pedestrians and Dan London. The procedure continued until the artist assembled a composite that achieved unanimous approval. Next, they began to frame the second kidnapper, which was more difficult. Only one person had noticed him to the same degree as they had the first suspect. Nonetheless, everyone present confirmed the final composite.

The only information that had been gathered on the third suspect, the driver of the getaway car, was that he was white with a lot of dark hair and a beard. Leo sat silently at the side of the room and observed the procedures. When it was complete, and the composites were projected on a large screen, he walked to the center of the room, leaned forward, put his weight on the back of a chair and said, "Thank you for coming here this morning. Before you leave, I would like to ask each of you if you believe the composites here," he pointed to them, "are what you remember. Are they really 'right' or just 'close'? The smallest detail can be important. Mr. London, how do you feel about suspect No. 1?"

Dan London stood up, pleased with the attention focused on him and said, "It is very good. My only comment is that his face looks just a little wider in the composite than I remember. Also, his skin was bad. He had acne. That would be hard to show on the composite, I guess."

"Not at all, Mr. London. This suspect can't shave off his acne. That's valuable information."

Leo elicited final comments from those present then

shook each person's hand as he or she left the room, looking longer than normal into their eyes as if searching for something that they were hiding.

"Nice job, Bruce. Run fifty copies of your composites and have them on my desk in one hour," Leo instructed the police artist, leaving no doubt about his order. Leo waited until he received an acknowledging nod from Bruce before striding out of the room and up the hall to wait for Chief Winslow.

Leo wished to advise the chief of his immediate plans for combing the neighborhood where the car was found and of his instructions to the lab regarding the car and the crushed burner phone they found. Both operations would be time-consuming and expensive and would take manpower away from other important police activities. Leo was counting on the lab finding prints that could be sent for possible identification to the division of the CIA that was concerned with international terrorists' operations. Maybe they would get lucky with the burner phone, though it had been rather crushed.

As Leo sat waiting for the Houston police chief, he wondered if he would be pleasing his dad if he were still alive. "Buck" Solis had been the sheriff of Fredericksburg, in the Texas Hill Country, for twenty-six years when he was killed while chasing a sixteen-year-old drunk driver. Leo had worked with his dad in the department for eight years, but left for Houston after his father was killed. He realized that, like his father, Leo's work was his life.

On his next birthday, Leo would be forty, with not

much to show for it. He lived in a small apartment in a tough part of town, had a car half paid for, a few suits of inexpensive cloth and a modest gun collection. Leo sent enough money to Fredericksburg each month to take care of his mother and divorced sister. Leo seldom saw them and heard from them only when they needed additional money. He had the feeling his mother was still trying to punish him for leaving Fredericksburg. She probably appreciated the money, but she seldom expressed any thanks. He would have this thankless financial obligation until his mother died. Then, he would tell his sister to get her ass out and get a job. He would tolerate her staying at home as long as she was taking care of their mother.

Leo was grinding his teeth when the chief breezed up saying, "Come on in, Leo. I heard you were waiting. What have you got?"

Leo described his basic plans briefly and immediately got the chief's approval. He strode out of the office with a private smile knowing he had again handled his business successfully.

CHAPTER

XXXII

The downtown business community began to come alive at seven Friday morning. By the time Lenora arrived at the Global parking garage at 8:42, the morning traffic rush hour was over. Standing outside the bank entrance in the main elevator lobby of the Global Tower, Lenora watched the parade of people passing by. Male executives with their briefcases streamed into the jaws of the elevators that seemed to chew them up and simultaneously emit young, well-dressed secretaries headed for the coffee shop. Lenora marveled at how stunning many of the girls looked wearing the latest fashions, with appropriate shoes and jewelry. How could they afford the cost of clothes today on a secretary's salary, she wondered as she stood by the large glass doors, waiting for her appointment.

Lenora hoped Rodrigo would not be late so there would be time to arrange the letter of credit and make her ten o'clock meeting with Bob McLean. She hated tight schedules. They put her under pressure, which lately seemed to start her persistent headaches. Maybe she wasn't getting enough sleep. Last night she kept thinking over being with Rodrigo in his apartment. Rodrigo had been a perfect gentleman, although he did drop some hints that indicated he was not used to platonic relationships. She would face that problem after she had closed the land deal. Rodrigo was a charming man in control of himself and his environment at all times, and she felt his strength when she was around him. She liked the way he looked at her even though it often embarrassed her. Rodrigo made her feel like a woman—a desirable woman.

At nine o'clock sharp, Lenora entered the bank, immediately seeking Mr. Ron Girard's office. She was shocked to find Rodrigo calmly seated there. Rising, Rodrigo warmly introduced Lenora as the most beautiful realtor in Houston. Not the best realtor—the most beautiful. The chauvinist, Lenora thought, sitting down next to Rodrigo without a side glance.

"Mr. Girard will have your LOC shortly, Lenora. We have worked out all the details."

"I didn't see you come in," Lenora said, confused by the events.

"I've been here since six forty-five, Lenora. Mr. Girard was nice enough to come in early."

This puzzled Lenora momentarily, but she surmised that Rodrigo had called Girard at home and requested the early meeting. Rodrigo's business must be important to the bank. He could probably arrange anything he desired.

A tall, stately secretary brought in some papers for Mr. Girard to review. As she left, she smiled at Rodrigo then looked Lenora over very carefully.

"I think you will find this in order, Mr. Carranza," Mr. Girard said in his banker's voice.

Rodrigo handed the document to Lenora without looking at it.

"Let's hope Mrs. French finds it in order."

Lenora reviewed it hurriedly and, nodding her head, said, "Yes, this is exactly what we need."

"Lenora, I have some further business with Mr. Girard. Please call me at my office after your meeting. By the way, McLean is on the board of First Consolidated. You were pretty accurate about him."

As Lenora headed to her car, she wondered whether Rodrigo already had background on McLean when they discussed him last evening. He apparently loved to bait her, and she never knew what he was thinking or what he knew—almost never.

CHAPTER
XXXIII

Downtown Houston was growing at a rate that left many of the streets partially blocked with construction. Lenora had just over twenty-five minutes to make her appointment with Bob McLean, and she wanted to be prompt. Until this point, she had been occupied with getting her offer to buy in the proper order. Now she began to be concerned about McLean's acceptance. He had agreed only to "meet" her if she brought with her the nonrefundable LOC and the earnest money contract. What if he really wasn't interested in selling, only playing a game with her?

Lenora steered her Continental from one lane to another as she traveled south. The heavy traffic made her wish she had chosen a different route. However, it was too late to backtrack. Her tension was building as she waited through another red light. When she arrived in front of Mr. McLean's house on Lazy Bend, her head was pounding. Normally, she had the severe headaches only in the late afternoon, but today started with one. She had drunk more than usual last night. That must be the difference, she thought.

She gazed at the magnificent antebellum-style main house, with its large columns on three sides, set in the middle of at least five acres. This must be one of the true show places in Houston, she thought as she started up the driveway looking for the two-story building Bob McLean had described. She felt awkward meeting him in his garage, but that was the way McLean wanted it. It was his apartment project, and she must convince him to sell it.

The handsome white two-story building in back surprised her as she rang a bell and heard an electric buzzer unlocking the door. Climbing carpeted steps, she found Bob McLean in flannel slacks and a golf shirt, waiting to greet her in a large paneled room. Books and binders filled bookshelves lining all four walls. With his reddish hair, ruddy complexion, rosy cheeks and young eyes, she guessed the tall, thin man to be about fifty years old.

Bob extended his hand in a friendly yet business-like manner and said, "Good morning, Mrs. French. You are here right on the stroke of ten."

"Lenora could hear a clock chiming with ship's bells as she walked into Mr. McLean's office. In the corner, Mr. McLean's desk was piled high with stacks of papers. She took notice of several computer consoles and a fax machine next to his desk. It was difficult to determine his business from what she saw. She glanced at the long glass-topped Queen Anne conference table in the center of the room, surrounded by antique chairs upholstered with red leather.

"Where would you like me to sit, Mr. McLean?"

"Anywhere that suits you, Mrs. French."

Lenora picked a chair in the middle of the conference table. Bob McLean helped her be seated then settled next to her on the same side of the table. Lenora nervously unsnapped her briefcase and extracted the papers she was carrying while he watched.

"Mr. McLean, I have here an earnest money contract for the property signed by my clients and a letter of credit for two million, one hundred thousand."

"A letter of credit, Mrs. French? I thought we discussed a check?"

"We did. We did. This letter of credit should accomplish the same thing," she said with a slightly persuasive tone.

Lenora handed Bob the contract and **LOC**.

He said, "I'm sure that my partner, Sam Butler, will be satisfied with this. He was too busy operating to join us." Suddenly, Bob said, "I'm sorry, Mrs. French." He stopped as her pupils dilated. "I didn't offer you anything. Would you care for coffee or tea?"

"No thank you," she said with relief, aware of the adrenalin that had entered her system, making her head pound, "but some water would be nice." She put her hands against her temples and leaned back in the chair. "I'll be all right in a minute."

Bob looked at her quizzically, wondering if there was something really wrong. After they quickly finished the meeting, she was up and out of the house, leaving him wondering about her health.

CHAPTER
XXXIV

Leo Solis was excited about the developments in his case. The lab had just verified that there was a positive match on the palm print from the getaway car, and a moment later, he received a trace on a car that had been stolen two blocks away the day of the Winrock shooting. He could hardly contain his joy. Leo called his task force together within an hour and outlined the next steps.

"Let's get on this trail before it gets cold," he admonished his crew. "We have a good description of one of our quarry and a general description of the second man. I am confident they are roughly hiding out within minutes of the car switch, which circumscribes a circle roughly two miles in diameter. I have analyzed what is within the circle and think the best hunting is south-southeast. We are mobilizing twenty men in civilian clothes to look like bill collectors."

Leo walked to the large map on the display board marked with the key locations and the target circle.

"Each of you can pick up your assignments after this meeting. It will describe your territory, how fast you should cover it, and the general language you should use when you talk to people. Let's stick close to the script. We are doing our operation simultaneously, concentrating on the prime target area first, to catch them before they can relocate. I have reason to believe these three, or more, are well trained and well financed—probably international terrorists. It's not the same as dealing with local punks. Be prepared. We don't want anyone getting hurt. Remember, this crew thinks nothing of their lives, much less yours."

After a series of questions, Leo adjourned the meeting and returned to his office, closing the door behind him. He put his feet on the desk, leaned back in his chair and concentrated on his prey. Leo tried to place himself in the same situation as the kidnappers. How would they use their skill and cunning to evade a massive police search? What would they do? Leo thought through all the measures he would take to protect the secrecy of a hideout. This type of exercise had worked for him successfully several times.

The telephone's ring broke Leo's concentration. "Solis here."

The caller was from the CIA. Leo gave the caller the proper code name and received a report on the first results of the prints. There was a partial match on a known terrorist in Saudi Arabia. The composite search was extending to the CIA's operations in Europe and in the Middle East. Leo instinctively felt that someone in the service would recognize at least one of the men, which would help identify the terrorist group and motive.

With this latest news, Leo headed back to the chief's office. He requested that four patrol cars be placed on alert as backup should any of his men confront the suspects directly. Everyone would be wearing Kevlar. The entire area had been combed with modest results, but the house-to-house search scheduled might in turn provide valuable information.

Leo had a different feeling about pursuing the terrorists rather than hunting down what Leo called "scum" who robbed and killed for money to buy dope. This case had international consequences. This was a professional challenge—a battle of international wits—the kind of challenge he thrived on. However, when a case started well, it usually ended in disaster. Leo hoped his good fortune would continue. Just a few breaks, and he might have the group within his grasp. A quick solution to this type of activity in the U.S. would discourage other terrorists from trying, at least for the time being. This was the most important police work Leo had done in some time, and he wanted his program to be carried out just as he planned it. He would not tolerate any variations. The chief would be pleased with how the investigation was coming together.

CHAPTER
XXXV

Her immediate staff greeted Lenora French as she walked into the office after her meeting with Bob McLean and phone call with Rodrigo. The deal was a success. McLean was sure that his partner would be on board. He would let her know as soon as he met with Sam Butler. Lenora had called in the news on her drive over, to the excitement of her office. The staff hung on Lenora's every detail of the deal.

"Just relax, you guys. I haven't closed on the property yet," she admonished as she flopped into her huge judge's chair and sighed with relief. "Mr. McLean isn't as bad as I thought. Actually, he seems to be a very fine gentleman."

One of the older female agents in the office, Melinda, chuckled as she said, "That means he didn't try to put one over on you."

"No, he really is a nice man."

"Is he going to take your offer, Lenora?" Jeff Wilson asked.

"I don't see how he can turn it down. He is a very mathematical man. He will find we have offered an excellent deal, and his partner will too."

"Is there any competition?" Jeff asked.

"I suspect we are the only ones trying to buy it. He will either sell it to us or keep it."

"We have all decided you need to take the rest of the day off," Jeff said.

"Oh, you have, have you?" Lenora acted surprised.

"Yes, and the vote was unanimous. Melinda and I want to take you to lunch first," Jeff said in a tone that would not be denied.

"OK, OK. Sounds great. I'm ready."

The three quickly left the office and headed for Polo's. On the way to the elegant restaurant on the ground floor of a building near the Uptown area, Lenora admitted she was very tense and already had her daily headache.

"It's always in the same place." She pointed to the right side of her head just behind her temple.

"You have been working too hard—classic tension symptom," Jeff said.

"I guess you're right. I do need some time off. When this deal closes, I really will take a break."

They both looked hard at Lenora and laughed.

"No, I really will take some time off; I promise," Lenora said with a chuckle.

"Seeing is believing," Jeff said, smiling.

The three had a delightful lunch in the dimly lit dining room filled with antiques, crystal chandeliers and attentive servers.

Eleven years younger, Jeff was a new agent in the firm and was fascinated with Lenora. He talked Lenora into a game of tennis at the University Club after lunch for both the exercise and relaxation, and they agreed to meet at three in the lounge area between the indoor courts high above The Galleria.

When Lenora arrived home to change clothes and pick up her tennis gear, she was sorely tempted to cancel their engagement. She was tired and in pain. Stretching out on her large bed was more appealing than a game of tennis. However, she knew the game would be good for her.

Jeff arrived at the University Club early and busied himself watching a hotly contested doubles game with a foursome all easily over sixty years old who missed few shots that were in their reach. Seeing Lenora entering the tennis lounge area, Jeff jumped to his feet and greeted her with a big smile.

As they walked to their court, Lenora noticed how athletic Jeff appeared. She had not styled him as an athlete, but the signs were unmistakable. She began to be concerned that she would embarrass herself by not being able to offer him much of a game, since hers had deteriorated recently between her schedule and her headaches.

Jeff seemed to sense her thoughts because he said, "Let's just hit the ball around for a while. I haven't played lately."

Lenora's game started out very poorly but improved as she began to get the rhythm of her swing. Jeff was very patient and returned most all of Lenora's shots directly to her. Only occasionally would he hit the ball with any pace that made its return difficult. Lenora began to reach for more difficult shots, began to distribute the shots from side to side. Lenora was enjoying herself as she stretched out for a forehand shot when she suddenly fell. She put out her left arm to break her fall and landed on her wrist. Jeff was around the net and kneeling at her side in seconds.

"Oh, Lenora, I'm so sorry. I hope you didn't hurt yourself," Jeff said.

Lenora rolled onto her side and held her left wrist in her right hand with her eyes closed. Jeff could see she was in real pain.

"Let me see." He gently took her wrist and slowly moved it. "I don't think it is broken," he said.

"I don't know what happened. I didn't slip or anything."

"You haven't played in a while. I guess you didn't warm up enough."

"That's not it. I really don't know what happened," she said as she tried to stand up.

"Don't get up. Just sit there."

"OK."

"Just relax, and maybe it will stop hurting."

After a time, Lenora said, "I think I can stand now, Jeff."

Jeff helped her to her feet and walked beside her, holding her right arm and offering her reassurance.

Lenora leaned on him slightly and said, "You are a dear, Jeff. I am sorry this ended our game."

"Nonsense. I am sorry you got hurt."

Jeff took charge of getting her bag and escorting her to her car. He offered to drive her home, but she insisted she could drive herself. He did follow her and helped her into her townhouse and onto the sofa in her living room.

"I am going to get some ice for your wrist and something for your pain and stay with you until you are OK, so don't say a word."

She had intended to dispatch Jeff as soon as possible but agreed to his offer and told him where to find the Advil. He found an ice bag, filled it and placed it on her wrist, and then he brought her a glass of water and Advil.

Lenora curled up on her sofa. He removed her

tennis shoes and spread an afghan from the back of the couch over her. In five minutes, she was sound asleep. Jeff found several magazines to read and quietly kept a vigil nearby.

CHAPTER
XXXVI

Leo Solis needed a witness to help move the case along. Just as Leo finished reviewing the complete work-up from the lab, he got a call from the lead member of his investigation crew who was questioning people in the neighborhood. Bingo, again. They had found a member of an office cleaning crew who saw three men leave a car, walk down the block, and get into another large car with some difficulty the night of the shooting. He remembered the men had beards and one was limping. The El Salvadoran was a little suspicious, but it was the way of the neighborhood to look the other way. He had asked the driver of his van to slow down as they drove past, and he got a good look at the men at approximately six fifteen, the time they normally reported to their office cleaning assignment.

It was sheer luck that Officer Eduardo Martinez had found this man. The witness had been returning to one of the office buildings to retrieve an extension cord he had left the previous evening. It was good fortune that Martinez was the officer involved, not only because the witness spoke little English and Martinez spoke Spanish, but because the man was in the country illegally and would have hesitated to say anything to a non-Latino. Eduardo assured him he would not be arrested and sent him to police headquarters with two officers. Leo Solis was pleased: two breaks within one hour.

However, by the time the witness had reached Leo Solis's office, he was terrified. His eyes were those of a caged animal looking for a way to escape his captors. Leo had seen this frightened look many times. Leo excused the two officers and waited for the man to be seated before focusing his attention on him.

Then he walked around his desk and held out his hand, saying in gentle Spanish, *"Muchas gracias, amigo. Nos puede ayudar mucho."*

The witness hesitated then took Leo's hand, shaking it cautiously.

"Yo soy Leo. Como se llama usted?"

"Yo soy Ruperto Alverez," the man said, barely audible.

"Quere café?" Leo asked reassuringly.

"No, gracias."

Leo tried to persuade Ruperto to please have some coffee with him, adding that it was actually pretty good for gringo coffee.

This remark, along with the twinkle in Leo's eyes,

melted Ruperto's anxiety. He smiled then laughed and agreed to join Leo. Leo talked to Ruperto about his family, his job and his living accommodations in Houston for twenty minutes before approaching the subject of the car incident. By then, Ruperto had regained his composure and was able to give a description of the second car. What he saw had made an impression on him. Finally, Leo returned to his desk, took out the composites of the two suspects, and returned to his seat next to Ruperto.

Laying the two pictures on the desk, Leo asked Ruperto if the pictures looked like the men he had seen.

"*Habían tres hombres*." Ruperto was now anxious to assist Leo.

Leo explained in Spanish that they didn't have a picture of the third one and then said slowly, in precise English, "Tell me what you think, Ruperto."

"*Sí, sí.* Them the men." Ruperto excitedly moved his hand downward over his chin to demonstrate that they had beards.

"I understand you got a good look at them in the car," Leo said.

"*Sí.* Car. Van go. I see real good—*creía que eran*—friends—El Salvador."

"Excellent. You have done real good, Ruperto. By the way, I hope you haven't missed any work time coming here." Ruperto looked puzzled. Leo asked again, "Are you missing work?"

"No, señor. *La compania* say go get electric line—my time."

Leo switched back to Spanish and said, "Glad to hear that. Now, Ruperto, I am going to have one of my men in plain clothes and a plain car drop you off at the place you live. He speaks Spanish and can follow your directions. Thank you for your help. We may call you again—just to repeat what you told us today—no more. Understand?"

"*Como no. Gracias for el café.*"

Leo studied Ruperto's eyes as he shook his hand, getting a good feeling about his important witness. Ruperto left, walking with confidence, knowing he had a new friend in Houston. Leo was convinced Ruperto had no idea he was identifying two of the suspects in the Winrock shootings. If Ruperto figured out the puzzle, Leo might lose his witness. Then again, Ruperto might be a brave young man after all, if Ruperto trusted him.

CHAPTER
XXXVII

Hillard Tinhauser, president of Tinhauser Manufacturing, was the first at Elliott Slizer's mansion. He came early to have a private talk with Slizer before the arrival of the other Global directors who were invited to the meeting. Slizer had called three of the twelve directors of Global Oil and Exploration Company the day before without disclosing the purpose. He had cautioned each not to disclose to the others that there was to be a private meeting at his house.

Hillard drove his two-door Lexus to the back of the house so that the ten-foot brick wall around the property would hide his car. Hillard was often in Slizer's home, but not at seven fifteen on a Saturday morning. Hillard stepped out of his car with his briefcase, set it down, smoothed his hair and straightened his tie to his image in the driver's side window, and walked toward the back door with the bounce he had developed since he became a serious runner.

Hillard's gentle knock set off a high-pitched barking and scratching on the back door. Usually when

Hillard entered the Slizer house, he was afraid he would lose part of his pants or perhaps a finger before Ping and Pong, the Slizers' feisty toy poodles, recognized him as friendly. A familiar voice scolding Ping and Pong quickly followed the barking. Rosie, Elliott's wife, opened the door with a dog in each arm and let out a waft of perfume that overpowered any smells of food from the kitchen.

Rosie was a perfect wife for Elliott Slizer—upbeat, personable, politically correct and wise enough never to contradict Elliott in public, no matter how far from the facts he got. Behind the scenes, Rosie was the dominant personality. It was her money that had originally financed Elliott's trucking business. She had forgotten that fact long ago, but Elliott never did.

Rosie leaned forward to greet Hillard with a kiss on the cheek, which allowed Ping and Pong to plant their wet noses on Hillard's shiny silk suit, leaving two round spots. When Hillard saw this, he had some dark thoughts about the future of Rosie's dogs. Recovering quickly, he greeted her with a big smile.

She led Hillard across the kitchen to the breakfast room where she had prepared an elaborate breakfast. Rosie was not much on formality. She had on a pink warm-up suit, size ten, that was attempting to stretch itself around a size fourteen body, high heels and a bouffant hairdo that was two days old.

"That looks great, Rosie, but I've already eaten," Hillard said, carefully.

Rosie clouded up. "I told Elliott to let everyone

know I would have breakfast for them. I guess he forgot. He's got so much on his mind."

Hillard always covered for Elliott. "Oh no, he told me, but I have only coffee and toast in the morning."

"I hope I didn't fix all this stuff for nothing. I'm on a diet, and so is El. He's waiting for you in the den."

Hillard walked through the house and found Elliott sitting in his large red leather wing chair, reading the *Wall Street Journal.*

"Good morning," Hillard said respectfully.

Elliott looked up over the top of his reading glasses, nodded and said, "There's breakfast in the dining room. Go help yourself."

"Thanks, I've already eaten."

Elliott looked at his watch, noting Hillard was fifteen minutes late for their meeting and asked, "Did you run this morning?"

"No, I've been finishing the plan you asked me to prepare for this morning. I brought four copies," Hillard said.

"Let's take a look," Slizer said as he carefully folded his *Journal* and placed it on the massive coffee table in front of him.

Hillard selected a chair to the right of Slizer, put his briefcase on his lap, and began spinning the wheels of the combination locks on it. His hands shook, knowing Slizer was watching him. One lock didn't snap open on the first attempt, so he slowed the process, mumbling to himself. His second attempt was successful. Hillard carefully handed three typed pages to Slizer and waited for his reaction.

Elliott Slizer pushed his glasses back on his nose, sat back in his chair and slowly read the document. Hillard took out a copy and simulated reading it, turning the pages in unison with Slizer's progress.

When Slizer had finished reading, he nodded to Hillard and said, "You've covered everything. Be sure to get all the copies back after the meeting."

Hillard waited until Slizer had straightened the papers then asked, "Have you gotten any response from the others?"

"I haven't told them anything. I just asked them to be here at eight," Slizer said.

"Do you think they will go along?" Hillard pressed.

"They will, or they won't be in the control group," Slizer said, his face hardening.

"You think you can swing this without them?" Hillard continued.

Slizer looked over at Hillard, shook his head and said, "Let's don't waste time speculating. We'll know soon enough."

"Yes, sir," Hillard responded with enough of an

edge in his voice to indicate his displeasure at Slizer's remark, but not enough to constitute disrespect.

"What did you find out about Winrock?" Slizer asked.

"There's nothing new on his medical condition, but I picked up something about his mental condition," Hillard said.

"Let's hear it." Slizer motioned with his hand to speed up the process.

"The head nurse on the ICU floor told me one of the private nurses Global hired had quit. She told the staff that Winrock had terrified her," Hillard reported.

"What does that mean?" Slizer was growing impatient.

"I'm not sure. He apparently said things that frightened her," Hillard said.

"At least you found out he was talking." Slizer's eyes narrowed.

"He's talking all right. This nurse said he was making strange statements." Hillard chose his words carefully.

"I still don't know what the hell's going on in that hospital," Slizer said. "Let's get to the essential point. Is Winrock going to survive? Will he have his mental facilities? Is he impaired physically? That's what I sent you to find out." Slizer's voice deepened in irritation.

Preparing himself for an answer, Hillard swallowed several times, pursed his lips, folded his hands on his knees and said, "Global has put a tight lid on information about Winrock. They even have a police guard outside his room."

"What's that for?" Slizer asked.

"I couldn't find out. I get more information listening to the news than I do at St. Matthew's. They still don't know who shot him."

"I take it you haven't talked to Winrock's doctor, Sam Butler?" Slizer asked.

"No. It's impossible to reach him. He's operating all day and half the night."

"What about Evelyn Winrock? She should know what's going on," Slizer said.

"That's a good idea. I'll go over and try to see her at the hospital," Hillard said.

"Let's get some facts, not hearsay or media bullshit. If we're going to remove him from his position at Global, we need concrete reasons." Slizer began pacing in a circle in his den. The exertion calmed him down. He returned to his chair, leaned forward and said in a near whisper, "Have you got everything wired in Global?"

"I think so. I met with—" Slizer's large hand in his face interrupted Hillard.

"I don't want to know any details. I'm not involved,

understand?" Slizer made the point with his index finger aimed between Hillard's eyes.

"I understand," Hillard whispered back.

"Remember, get all these copies back after the meeting, destroy them and erase the computer file, understand?" Slizer's eyebrows came together.

Hillard nodded acceptance of his assignment. His throat had tightened up, so no words came out. When the bell rang, he jumped up and walked in a near jog to open the front door.

CHAPTER
XXXVIII

Three hours of restless sleep wasn't sufficient to rejuvenate Leo Solis's tired body. The events of the previous evening had insulted his entire emotional system. One of his men had been badly shot up carrying out an assignment he ordered and was now on the critical list. Leo felt completely drained of energy, yet he was too agitated to stay in bed. Finally, he got up, fixed himself some instant coffee, and still wearing the previous day's skivvies, he sat in Buck's worn chair, the only piece of furniture he had brought from Fredericksburg and one he loved. He sipped the hot brew. His mind was blank.

When seven o'clock arrived, he got up and called headquarters. The detective told him that when he left the hospital, Charles Howard was still holding on. A meeting Leo had called for the entire task force was scheduled for eight. Searching through his jacket's pockets, he found the note that had the name and direct line to a phone in the doctors' lounge in the emergency room. He called to inquire about his officer. The phone rang twenty-three times before someone picked it up and gruffly said, "Hello."

"Could you get Dr. Amery on the phone, please? It's important."

"I'll try," came back the tired, indifferent voice.

Leo waited for ten minutes before he heard Dr. Amery on the other end. Solis inquired about Charles and got an encouraging report. Charles had a stronger heartbeat and didn't show signs of internal bleeding. His vital signs were stronger. The doctor said infection was the next hurdle to overcome. The report got Leo's adrenaline flowing, and he hurriedly dressed and headed for his office. Listening to the police channel gave him a feel for the current activities. He had a full head of steam by the time he arrived at his assigned parking place.

Striding in with his usual half-run, half-walk gait, arms swinging, he was accosted by a young man in a too-large suit who was waiting in the hall.

"Mr. Solis, may I speak to you for a moment?"

"Who are you?" Leo asked, looking at the man's mouth rather than his eyes.

"I am Gus Angler, with the *Courier*."

"Sorry, I don't have time."

Leo continued down the hall, ignoring Gus Angler's repeated plea for some answers. Leo was trying to tune out the questions, but he heard this young reporter ask if Charles Howard had been shot by terrorists. Anything that was said in the papers at this point was damaging to their campaign of finding the terrorists. If it was them, they would find out the police knew. If it wasn't them, they would know the police were chasing the wrong trail. News that the getaway car had been found had made the front page of yesterday's paper. The newspaper account strongly suggested that the kidnapping attempt was for a big ransom. Leo Solis had been livid when he saw the article. He had taken every precaution to keep what little information they had confidential. Now Leo snapped. He wheeled around and stuck his finger in Gus's face.

"You better get your facts straight if you print anything, buster, or I'll have your ass."

"Can I quote you, Mr. Solis?"

"Be my guest." He mumbled, "Little prick," as he continued down the hall.

The majority of Leo's task force was waiting for him when he entered the special conference room on the second floor. A group of tired faces looked at him. A lined face looked back.

"I hate to mess up another weekend, but we need to talk," he said as he sat on the edge of the table facing his men. "Charles Howard was hurt badly, as you know. He's hanging in there right now, and the doc thinks he will make it if he doesn't get any bad infections."

The news really pleased Leo's men, and several slapped each other as though someone had made a touchdown. Charles was a popular officer.

"I don't think Charles was involved with the terrorists. He just stumbled onto some pushers who decided it was easier to take him out than hassle with him about what they were doing there. It was a bad deal."

His men nodded in acknowledgement.

"I don't need to remind you that I am asking you to nose around in some bad areas. I don't want anyone else getting hit. I want you to travel in pairs. I am going to ask for some more men when I can corner the chief. Now don't take any—"

"Pardon me, Mr. Solis. You have a call from Washington in the chief's office. He wants you there right now," a young officer stuck his head through the door and interrupted.

Leo told the crew to grab some coffee, and he'd return shortly. He jogged down the stairs to the chief's office well ahead of the messenger who had been sent to get him.

"What's up?" he asked, out of breath, as he entered the chief's cluttered office.

"We have a break. Here, they want you," the chief said with a little hurt in his voice.

"Leo Solis here." Leo listened intently. First, a smile covered his face, then, just as quickly, his face clouded. He punctuated the conversation with "Sure ... Yes, sir ... I got you ... I understand ... Sounds good ..." and, finally, "I'm sure he will. Here, let me put him on." He handed the phone back to Chief Winslow.

The chief listened then agreed with the suggestion

to allow twenty special FBI agents to assist in the case. Leo had learned from the director for the FBI unit that dealt with terrorist activities in the U.S. that the other print had matched with prints obtained from France belonging to a Libyan who was reputed to be in league with al-Qaeda. This man was known to INTERPOL as Ijaz Moka.

The FBI had decided the incident in Houston had grave, long-range consequences for the United States and were going all out to apprehend the culprits. Chief Winslow heartily agreed with what he was hearing, and when he hung up, he had a pleased expression on his face, like he was sucking on a butterscotch candy, his favorite. Leo had been wise in forcing the FBI director to speak directly with the chief.

The men stared at each other, stunned by the information they had heard. This was no ordinary kidnapping incident. They were indeed dealing with international terrorists who had likely been trained and should be well financed. Adding twenty well-trained agents to the already large task force would allow much work to be done that was not possible within the Houston Police Department's budget or manpower availability. The director had also mentioned that the CIA would be contacting them to arrange for providing additional advisors.

Leo broke the silence. "What do you make of it, Chief?"

"Looks like we have a wing-tailed bitch on our

hands," he answered, shaking his head. "It is going to be hard keeping this out of the press like they want."

"I better get back to my crew upstairs. I would like to go over all this with you as soon as I get them straightened out."

"Sure. Come on back down. I will wait for you."

The magnitude of the operation they would be conducting and the attention it was receiving from Washington excited both men.

Leo returned to find his crew now seated in the conference room with coffee in their hands.

"Any good news?" one of his men asked.

"Yes and no." Leo struggled for a way to inform his men without disclosing information the FBI had asked he keep confidential for now. He paced back and forth then said, "We are going to get some help on this case, lots of help. The people we are looking for are not amateurs. The FBI has asked that we not disclose any facts about them. I can think of lots of reasons for this."

"Do they know who they are?" the same officer asked.

"One of them. I can tell you this much. The people we are looking for wouldn't hesitate to take out a whole block to cover their tracks or achieve their objective— whatever that is. We have got to be real careful. I don't want anyone else getting hurt. Understand?"

No one nodded. No one had to. They all understood only too well. Leo went on to outline what he had planned for them that weekend if they found something. He wanted them to know he was working, also.

"Any questions?" he asked, knowing that all present knew that was Leo's way of saying meeting adjourned. Leo hurried back to the chief's office to discuss what they would do with another twenty men and several advisors entering the picture.

CHAPTER
XXXIX

The telephone rang and woke Lenora from a deep sleep. The voice on the other end of the telephone said, "Good morning, Lenora, how are you this morning?"

"I am fine, Rodrigo, but I didn't get much sleep—lots on my mind."

"What I have planned for us will make you happy," Rodrigo announced with excitement. Lenora winced at his making plans without her input, but said nothing, and Rodrigo continued. "Now, Lenora, listen carefully. I am sending my car for you at eleven o'clock. We will go directly to the restaurant and then to a soccer game."

"What time is it now?"

Rodrigo chuckled and said, "It is nine thirty."

"Oh dear. I'll try, but it may take me longer to get ready with my wrist sore. I can hardly use it."

"Very well. My driver will ring your bell then wait outside until you are ready."

This is against my better judgment, Lenora said to herself. Rodrigo had caught her when her resistance was low. "Yes, I'll go."

"Splendid, Lenora. By the way, we are having lunch with some friends from Europe."

"Glad you told me," Lenora said half under her breath. "Fine, I'll try to be ready." Lenora sat straight up in bed, shocked at the thought of having to get dressed for a luncheon and a game. "What in the world can I wear?" she said out loud as she hung up the receiver.

Promptly at eleven o'clock the bell rang, but Lenora had yet to put on her shoes. She did so and then rushed around her bedroom, hoping the day would not be an ordeal. She emerged from her townhouse looking dazzlingly beautiful in a rust-colored silk suit, and Rodrigo's driver bowed as he opened the door to the limousine. The driver pulled up in front of Rodrigo's high-rise building to find him waiting out front holding two pairs of binoculars. He entered the car, kissed her hand and told his driver to proceed to the Houston Country Club. She doubted that he belonged and thought he must have gotten a guest pass from one of his wealthy friends.

"Well, now, my darling, you look beautiful," he said with his delightful Italian accent. He took her left wrist and gently held it, inspecting the bandage she had wrapped around it.

"I am so sorry you fell. What happened?"

"I don't know. My leg just seemed to give way."

"You should be careful, my Lenora. We can't have you hurting yourself."

His tone was quiet but authoritative; with it he was in command of everyone around him. He frightened her in a way. She was usually in control of her environment, but with Rodrigo she felt like a young girl on her first date. He did not intimidate her exactly, but his strong personality and charm completely overwhelmed her.

At the club, Rodrigo seated Lenora in a large upholstered chair in a salon by the dining area and then disappeared to speak to the head waiter. She sat quietly, trying to take in the luxury and influence to which she was being exposed. Seeing the way she was being treated, she mused to herself that Rodrigo must be a true multimillionaire. But where did the money come from? Then she realized that perhaps she would rather not know.

Rodrigo came back to the table, and they sat in pleasant silence enjoying the atmosphere as they waited. A few moments later, the server appeared carrying an elaborate tray of hors d'oeuvres.

The server approached Lenora and asked, "Madam, may I fix you something to drink?"

"It's a little early for me, thank you, but I'll have some water."

"You sure you won't have something? I am having a milk punch. You can have one also. We can ask that they include only a little bit of cream."

Lenora declined the drink, and the server left.

Soon, three men, decidedly Italian, approached the table. They broke into grins when they saw Rodrigo and gave him a hug, each speaking endearingly in Italian. All three were older than Rodrigo, the oldest of the three being quite short and dark complexioned.

They sat down after the introductions only to stand again as two stunningly dressed ladies approached their table. The two younger men introduced them as Lila and Constance—no last names. Seated again, Rodrigo continued his greeting of his dear friends while the ladies inspected each other, trying to look casual. Lenora noticed their jewelry and clothes were exquisite. Both women were in their early thirties, she judged, and were probably the mistresses of the two younger men.

After an awkward period, Lila said in as heavy an accent as her friend had, "I understand you are an important lady in Houston. I have never been to Texas before."

"Yes, I am a native Houstonian, rather rare to find one, today."

"How lucky to be from this sparkling modern city. We have been to the excellent museums and even managed to visit the tunnels under downtown," said Lila.

"I have not done that myself. But those who work downtown enjoy its restaurants and boutiques every day. I hear that there are ninety-five blocks of tunnels," Lenora responded.

"We have just come from The Galleria—not too far

from here."

"My, you can find every elegant European and American store there, almost four hundred stores," Constance interjected. "We've been to Neiman's, Saks, Cartier, Tiffany and others with clothes by Channel, Armani, Estrada. What choices you have!"

"My, you really have been busy. I guess you have been to Uptown also?" Lenora said with a smile and waved her hands as if in surprise. "Where are you from?"

"We live in Milano. My husband works for Rodrigo's family in Italy," said Lila.

"I see. What does your husband do?" Lenora asked, not really wanting to know.

"He is the president of Ferroital, a steel company."

This was not the answer Lenora expected. Taking another look at Lila's husband, Lenora decided she was misjudging Rodrigo's friends. She relaxed and began engaging more in the conversations with greater interest.

The club had servers hover over them the entire meal. Lenora had difficulty opening the shelled shrimp with her wrist problem without splashing hot sauce on her clothes, but with Rodrigo's help, as he devoured a huge plateful, she was able to get enough to eat. These people obviously enjoyed each other and apparently had not been together for a time.

As the men allowed the attentive servers to fill their wine glasses repeatedly, Lenora learned the other younger man was married to the older man's daughter, and the older man was the director general of the Carranza family's construction company. No one gave Lenora the name of the company, but she learned that they operated on a worldwide basis, particularly in Eastern Europe, the Middle East and Africa.

They spoke about Italy, about American and Italian clothes, and their excitement in planning for social events they will attend. Apparently, thought Lenora, the girlfriends had fun while the wives stayed home to take care of the children.

The game would not start for nearly one hour, so the group sat in a circle and visited. Lenora apparently fascinated the Italian men, particularly because she had her own highly successful business. Women did not engage in that kind of business in Europe, certainly not in Italy. Rodrigo's friends treated Lenora as though she were to marry Rodrigo shortly, and they wanted to know all about his bride—to the point of embarrassing her. She was feeling closed in but wasn't sure what she could do or wanted to do about it.

They arrived at the VIP club of the BBVA Compass Stadium a few minutes before the game. When the game started, they followed it with the binoculars, Rodrigo explaining every aspect to her.

"Did you play soccer, Rodrigo?"

"Not professionally. I did play for the academy."

"No wonder you know so much about the game."

"Everyone in the world knows about this game except the Americans, and they are learning fast."

The game became increasingly more interesting as Lenora began seeing it through Rodrigo's eyes to the point that Lenora jumped up and cheered when the Italian team scored a goal. The Italian team lost to a stronger German team; however, the game was one of the most enjoyable sporting events Lenora had seen since she was in college. Everyone was emotionally drained as the group headed for the downtown Four Seasons to drop off the Italian visitors. Rodrigo hugged all the men and bid them warm good-byes.

Halfway home Lenora realized her head was throbbing again. Her contentment was so complete she decided to try to ignore the pain. She began to relive the events of the day, amazed at how smoothly everything had worked. There was no frantic arranging. Rodrigo made no phone calls, gave only a few instructions in Italian, yet everything happened like clockwork. It was as though the lane he traveled in had no other travelers. They were quiet on the return to her home, having said everything there was to say.

Rodrigo took her hand gently in his and kissed it as Lenora prepared to walk up the steps to her townhouse.

"My darling, Lenora, you were fantastic. My friends loved you. I hope I didn't tire you with all the activity."

Suddenly Lenora fell forward. Rodrigo quickly reached out and caught her before she completely lost her balance. In the process of reaching for Rodrigo's arm,

Lenora struck her already hurt wrist on the rail of the steps, causing her excruciating pain. She became dizzy and had to sit on the steps for fear of fainting.

Rodrigo knelt down beside her and said tenderly, "Thank God I caught you," not knowing she had hit her wrist. Seeing the pain in her face, he asked if she was OK. She told him haltingly that she had hurt her wrist again.

"My poor little chicken. I am so sorry. Here, let me get you inside. If you will give me your key."

Lenora pointed to her purse, which she had dropped. Rodrigo found her key, opened her door, then scooped her up in his arms and carried her inside, and then set her gently on her living room sofa.

"What happened, my dear? Did you trip?"

"I don't know, Rodrigo, my leg just seemed to give way. This is the second time in two days."

"We will have to get you checked over by a doctor. I am worried about you."

Lenora was visibly shaken by the near fall and the pain in her wrist. She began to tremble and was unable to control her teeth chattering. Rodrigo became frantic with concern for her. He rushed into her bedroom and brought back a quilt Lenora kept at the foot of her bed. He wrapped it and his arms around her and talked softly to her until her trembling stopped and she regained her composure.

Lenora kept apologizing for her clumsy behavior, but

Rodrigo would not hear of it. He fixed her a brandy and held it up to her lips.

The effect of the brandy began to work. Lenora looked up at Rodrigo, who had been hovering over her, and thanked him for being so dear.

"Nonsense. I cannot stand to see you suffering."

This was a complex man in her house. In control of everything around him with a forcefulness that frightened her, yet tender as a lamb with her simple problem.

Rodrigo stayed until Lenora had regained her balance and could put herself to bed without any risk. Rodrigo insisted that Lenora call him when she was prepared to go to sleep to assure him everything was OK. She agreed, and Rodrigo kissed her hand again and left.

As Lenora lay in her bed, she realized she had acquired a protector in the last two days. For someone who had prided herself in being self-sufficient and independent, she had trouble accepting the fact that her vulnerability had brought out these strong protective instincts in a strong man. She admitted to herself that she enjoyed being taken care of.

CHAPTER
XL

Sam was thirty minutes late meeting Bob McLean in the main dining room of the country club. Bob had enjoyed the wait, visiting with a number of his friends as they filed in for Saturday lunch.

When Sam arrived in his turtleneck sweater and handsome tweed sport coat rather than his usual tired brown corduroy jacket with suede elbow patches, Bob could tell before he reached the table that there had been some changes in Sam's life. Bob noticed his complexion was ruddier, and he looked rested and walked with a more confident air.

"Good to see you, old friend," Sam said with sincerity as he shook Bob's hand.

"Good to see you, Sam. I can see you are taking better care of yourself these days," Bob responded.

"Actually, I am getting better taken care of, Bob."

"Whatever you are up to, it agrees with you."

"Thanks. I needed that," Sam said.

"Care for a cocktail?" Bob asked.

"No thanks."

"Fine. Let's order lunch then get into our discussion," Bob said. "But first, how is Richard getting along? I haven't talked to you about him in a couple of days."

"Not only have no complications developed thus far, but he is making a remarkable recovery. In fact, *remarkable* is not strong enough. We plan to have a neuropsychologist test him on Monday."

"Already?"

"I told you, *remarkable* is not strong enough to describe his recovery. By the way, I wish I could have Helen examine Richard, but it would probably be better to use our staff. How is Helen these days? I ran into her but didn't have time to talk."

"She's fine. How is Richard's attitude, Sam?"

"He is doing as well as can be expected. It is not uncommon for brain trauma patients to be depressed during their immediate recovery."

"Is he depressed?"

Sam hesitated to discuss Richard with anyone, even his oldest friend. "Well ... let's say he is having some difficulties accepting his confined convalescence. We have not allowed him much movement yet."

"Is there any paralysis?"

"Not that we have detected. We will know more next week."

"Thank God for that," Bob sighed.

"Yes. He is an incredibly lucky man to have come out of this with no apparent deficits," Sam added.

Wanting to change the subject, Sam started ordering lunch, and then Bob led into the discussion about the offer from Lenora French.

"Since I called you, I have analyzed a land venture that has been in the back of my mind for several years. I am satisfied that my numbers are realistic and reflective of the kinds of long-range benefits we can derive from this approach. So we have three choices: hold what we have and let the market continue to grow up around us, sell at an excellent price to this Italian group, or the third choice, the one I have been studying, promote a hotel on our property."

"God, Bob, I have a hard enough time deciding what tie to wear in the morning. How do you expect me to help you in this matter? You are over my head."

"You must have been completely indecisive this morning."

"Why do you say that?" Sam asked.

"No tie, my feather-headed friend."

"Oh yeah. Well, Carolyn wanted to see me in a turtleneck."

"Carolyn, is it? Splendid. Who is Carolyn?"

"A divine nurse at the hospital."

"She must be good for you. Now, back to our project. Sam, we can sell the project now and take a long-term capital gain of just over sixteen million. Your share would be four million."

"You have an offer?"

"I have an earnest money contract with a two million dollar walk-away penalty. Not much chance of collecting two million from the Carranza brothers."

"Who are they, Sam?"

"Two real-polished Italians who have a tanker load of Euro dollars to spend over here."

"Ah so."

"How do you feel about selling?" Bob asked.

"Four million would feel good, Bob. I don't know what I would do with it, though. I'm billing more fees now than ever. I was planning on asking you what I could with my cash."

"Doesn't sound like a sale would be particularly timely for you, unless you wanted to go back into the real estate market with your four million plus my twelve."

"What do you recommend we buy?" Sam asked.

"I don't have anything specific in mind, Sam. It will take some searching to find a larger revenue-producing property that is for sale in this down payment price range and is worth having."

"How large a project could we buy?"

"Oh, we could perhaps buy something between seventy-five million and one hundred twenty-five million."

"That's getting into the big leagues, isn't it?"

"I suppose you could say that."

"What would you be looking for—what kind of property?"

"Again, I don't have anything specific in mind. Possibly an office building, a shopping mall, a hotel. I would look at all three."

"How large an office building could we buy for that kind of money?"

"We could say grace over more than one million square feet if we catch one that is in the process of being built. We also need to secure good financing."

"You mean we buy someone's building and lease it back to them?"

"Precisely."

"These big numbers scare the hell out of me, Bob. We would be taking a big risk if we did something like this, wouldn't we?"

"Everything we do has risk. Every time you operate, you are taking a risk of malpractice."

"What a nice thing to say. Is that what you think of my surgery?"

"You know what I mean. Frankly, if we don't leverage too highly, our risk will be minimal, provided we select a sound project, buy it right, get a really good financial package, either from the owner or from the outside, and manage it properly."

"You know, Bob, the only investment I have made that has turned out to be really profitable has been this one. I don't have the time or the inclination to pursue it, but I don't mind. I will depend on your judgment. After all, all I did on the Antebellum Apartments deal was send you a check. You did everything else."

"You know, Sam, you are the best real estate partner anyone could have."

"Well, partner, what about the other alternative you mentioned: the hotel?"

"Yes, the hotel. Sam, I have used all my own numbers, but I think the projections I have made tell us what the potential can be to this approach. Basically, we would establish a joint venture with a hotel chain to build a high-rise hotel on the ten acres. We might have to use only part of our ten acres, or we might retain fifty percent ownership in the hotel."

"What size hotel are you thinking about?"

"The size of the two hotels in California."

"That would be exciting, Bob."

"Actually, it would."

"You know, Bob, who would have thought thirty-five years ago when you were carrying me through algebra that we would be building hotels together?" Sam said, looking out over the golf course with a far-away expression.

"We have been friends for a long time haven't we, Sam?"

"I am afraid I can't help you much on these decisions. I will go along with anything you want to do. I don't need money now, so I am willing to let it ride if you are. I think, Bob, we could also start a search for another larger investment while getting into the nitty gritty with some hotel chain, all the time keeping the offer to buy alive."

"Your craft has improved your basic logic, Sam. That is an excellent way to go if our Italian buyers will give us enough time to run out the bunt."

"There you go. You might make a real estate tycoon out of me yet."

Having dispensed with the business considerations, Bob returned to the subject of Richard Winrock.

"When do you expect Richard to be on his feet again, Sam?"

"I wouldn't be able to comment on that. It would not be expected for several weeks, then only on a limited basis."

"Is he the same old Rich I know?"

Sam stared at Bob for a long time, searching for a clue to this question. Then he said, "Why do you ask?"

"I understand from Helen that brain trauma sometimes changes people's personalities, particularly when the frontal lobes are involved."

"That's true; however, Richard had no damage to that portion of his brain," Sam said in his professional voice.

"The world is going to be knowledgeable about brain trauma with the coverage Richard is getting in the press. Even the *Wall Street Journal* had a full-length story about Richard's injury. Where do they get all that information? The article only mentioned you as his neurosurgeon."

"Reporters have been around the hospital like flies since he was brought in."

"Is there anything else you have to do to him?"

"No, not unless complications develop," Sam answered, again in his professional voice.

Bob noticed that Sam grew increasingly more

nervous as they continued to discuss Richard.

"Sam, Evelyn Winrock is distressed—not with Richard's condition but with what he is saying. Now, level with your friend. I know you too well. What is going on?"

"Nothing is going on, Bob. I'm not sure what you mean."

"You know what I mean. It is all over the hospital. Richard is acting or talking strangely."

"He is talking remarkably well for the recovery time he has had," Sam answered, distressed.

"You are still not answering me. Perhaps you won't or can't. But there is something going on with Richard in the hospital that you have not been telling me. I want to help. God knows I want to help. I am your oldest friend, and I consider Richard and Rivers dear friends. How can I help?"

The weight of the burden on Sam became oppressive. He wanted to—needed to—confide what he knew despite his responsibility to his patient. Since Bob was a board member of Global and the kind of friend who would never hurt anyone, Sam impulsively began to tell Bob his story starting with, "I know you are not going to believe this and will question my sanity ..." Sam then recounted the events from the beginning, describing them in detail to his fascinated listener. Bob leaned forward, taking in every word without uttering a sound.

When Sam had finished, Bob put his hand to his mouth, gave a long sigh and said, "Fascinating!"

"I don't have a word to describe how I feel about this, Bob."

"You are certain there is no communication you may not know about?"

"Bob, you must not have been listening. Richard knows things no one at the hospital would know. There is no question he is getting information—so far, accurate information—on any subject, on any person he focuses on. I have begun to think that I must be suffering from a mutual illness when I try to accept as factual what I can't deny."

"Fascinating."

"Is that all you can say about it?"

"Helen is the expert in this field, not me. What do you think is causing it?"

"I have no medical explanation. Everything within me, my entire training, tells me the whole affair is a fantasy, yet I know what I have observed and experienced is real." Sam laughed, "Bob, I had hoped you would help me reject the whole business."

"From what you and Rivers tell me, Richard needs help. I am not sure either of us can give it to him, but if we can just begin to understand what might be at the bottom of his behavior, we may begin to understand."

"I know," Sam answered, resigned.

"Tell me more about Carolyn." Bob decided it was

wise to change the subject although his mind was racing about Richard.

Sam thought for a moment then said, "Carolyn has taken my mind off of myself. I guess I have been feeling sorry for myself, guilty, so I punished myself by working all the   time."

"You have nothing to feel guilty about. Gladys left you, didn't she?"

"Yes, she did. I guess I would have put up with our lousy marriage for the rest of my life. It was easier to ignore what was wrong with it than to try to change it."

Bob waited a moment and then said, "Oh, by the way, the offer for our property came through a rather charming young lady by the name of Lenora French. I rather think you two would get along famously."

"Lenora French. I have heard that name before."

"More likely you have seen it. She has real estate signs all over town. Smart young woman."

"How young?"

"I can't really tell, Sam. Maybe mid-thirties."

"I'll keep her in mind if Carolyn throws me out."

"You are staying at Carolyn's. How interesting."

"You are a nosey old bastard, aren't you?"

"You know the ancient Eastern custom: Once you save someone's life, you become responsible for him the rest of his life, having interfered with destiny."

"So that's it. Why didn't you tell me this years ago when I was struggling to pay Gladys's bills at Neiman Marcus?"

"I think my timing has been perfect."

"Bob, I could be in a heap of trouble for telling you as much detail as I have about Richard. Please keep everything to yourself. Why don't you forget the whole thing? That is what I want to do."

"So you said. What about Richard?"

"I am trying not to get personally involved with Richard. He is my patient."

"Well, I am involved with Richard—have been for years. Don't worry. I won't say anything that would hurt him any more than he has already been hurt."

"OK, OK. I won't worry."

The two men walked through the elegant club to the exit, where Bob McLean excused himself and went down to the men's locker room to wait for a threesome he would join for tennis doubles at three o'clock. He was certain he would have a bad match as he could not take his mind off the information Sam had told him about Richard. Helen would be even more fascinated than he was but would likely reject the whole story.

CHAPTER
XLI

Bob's prediction was correct. His game had been less than brilliant. He had been distracted and was not anticipating the direction or velocity of the balls coming into his territory. He made heroic efforts to get many of them, but his skillful opponents put away many shots down his lane. Bob was actually glad that the two sets were over, as he could hardly wait to discuss with Helen what Sam had told him. She will probably think both Sam and I are crazy, he thought.

Helen had specialized in the brain localization of behavior. For a number of years now, she had worked with brain trauma patients and stroke patients regularly. As head of the psychology department at Memorial Hermann Hospital and professor of psychology at the affiliated medical school, Dr. Helen Parker-McLean had recently developed a test called the PALI—Parker Assessment of Language Impairment—which was gaining worldwide recognition. Bob thought she would certainly have something to offer for the strange behavior Rich Winrock

226

had been exhibiting since his shooting.

He didn't bother to shower and change clothes after the tennis game; he walked into the locker room with his partner then bundled up his stuff and headed home in his 1936 Mercedes convertible. Entering the house from the back entrance, he called to Helen. She answered from the library where she was busily engaged in reviewing some recent letters she had received pertaining to the genealogy of the McLean family. Bob came into the room, set all his gear on the table, walked over and gave Helen a tender kiss on the lips

"My dearest, I have something I want to tell you that will take some time. Can I interrupt what you are doing?" he asked.

"When have you needed my permission, Bob McLean?" she laughed, bundling up her numerous papers into files.

"I'm not sure where to start."

She eyed him out of one eye, waiting impatiently.

"I had lunch with Sam, as you know. Well, he told me a story I don't know how to handle. It seems that our friend Rich Winrock has had a dramatic change take place since his injury."

Helen smiled at Bob. "I have heard through the staff. He has upset some of the nurses."

"It's much more complicated than that. Sam tells me—Helen, forgive me—but Sam says that Rich is now clairvoyant."

Facetiously, Helen asked, "Would Sam recognize clairvoyance if it thumped him on his cranium?"

"I know what you mean, but let me tell you all the facts."

"Facts?" Helen queried with a trace of amusement in her voice.

"Yes, facts. At least 'hearsay' facts. First of all, Rich recounted everything that happened to him from the time he was shot until he regained consciousness."

Helen's eyes narrowed as she began to listen more closely.

"He has told Sam things that happened in the hospital, things he could not possibly know."

"For example?" Helen asked, wondering why Sam would discuss details of a patient's condition with someone outside the patient's family.

"Oh, let's see. Oh yes, one I remember: Sam walked directly up to Rich's room from an operation, and Rich knew what he had done, the name of the patient and the prognosis."

"Couldn't someone have told him?"

"Not possibly. Rich has guards at his door. The nurse on duty had been with Rich for four hours without leaving his room. She knew nothing of the activity in neurosurgery. Rich knew the details of the operation as though he was in the amphitheater watching the whole thing. Sam is convinced Rich has ESP powers."

Helen stared at her husband, trying to understand what she was hearing. "Does Sam attribute his ESP to the injury?"

"He doesn't attribute it. He did not know Rich before the accident, so he doesn't realize how out of character Rich's behavior is now."

Helen closed her eyes momentarily, trying to put the facts she was hearing in perspective.

"What is Rich's present condition? I read about him in the papers, but what does Sam say?"

"He says Rich has made an extraordinary recovery. I would classify it as a miracle, although Sam would not use that term."

"How is Rich's speech, his motor functioning?"

"Apparently his speech is fine. He has had quite a lot to say at any rate."

Helen sat with her hands in her lap, waiting for Bob to continue.

"Sam at first thought Rich had had an out-of-body experience. Sam has encountered this phenomenon several times over the years while his patients were under anesthetic. Now, he is sure that it's more than that. Rich seems to recall anything he wishes to know about, past or present"

"For example?" Helen asked, beginning to focus on a series of questions she would ask a typical patient.

Bob went into more detail. "My dear, Sam says that Rich has described everything that has happened to him since the injury. The number of the helicopter, the names of the paramedics, the resident's name who first worked on him, remarks that were said in the operating room. That's bizarre enough. But even more incredible, Rich knew about his grandson's broken arm that Evelyn had barely heard about. He blurted out the name of a nurse who had never been in his room before. He knew Sam's lady friend's name. He knew the name of a detective who was requesting a visit. Sam gets strange feelings he must go see Rich during the day, and when he arrives, Rich is expecting him at that precise time. Sam is worried that Rich may be controlling Sam's actions in some strange way. Each of these items can be suspect, but taken collectively, Sam is convinced Rich is an incredible clairvoyant."

Helen could only shake her head. She sat back in the Barjelo wing chair and held her hands together as though she were going to pray.

"Has a neuropsychologist examined Rich?"

"Sam mentioned that would take place Monday."

"Who is doing the examination?"

"I don't know. Sam said he wanted you to do it but felt obliged to use the hospital staff. I feel a special obligation to Rich, sweetheart. He has been a friend for years. He seems to be in a strange state now. His physical recovery is remarkable, and his mental recovery has no reference point. I don't know what is going to happen to him."

"I wish I could get an opportunity to evaluate him. It is difficult to understand everything you are telling me."

"I will talk to Sam and see if he can arrange it. You know, a second opinion or something."

"I don't want to interfere. Sam will have to call me in."

"Sure, I understand. I'll call him tomorrow."

Bob picked up his tennis gear and left Helen to wrestle with her thoughts. She sat still for a long time trying to make sense of the information Bob had given her, with little success.

CHAPTER
XLII

Mrs. Henry Brennand, Rich's daughter, walked with her mother down the long corridor leading to Rich's room, recognizing it by the uniformed officer who was standing guard. Lisa Brennand had been devastated by the news that was splashed all over the media, even in the paper in Columbus, Georgia. She had arranged to come to Houston as soon as possible. Lisa held her mother's arm tightly for both moral and physical support. When they arrived at Rich's room, the officer courteously asked who they were, checked his instructions, and then informed them that Rich's daughter was not authorized to see Mr. Winrock.

"That is ridiculous. This is my daughter—Mr. Winrock's daughter. Please check with whomever you have to check with. Who does Dr. Butler think he is?"

"Ma'am, I am just carrying out orders. I will do my best. Excuse me."

He picked up his radio mic and called someone. Shortly, another officer came up, and they discussed the problem. The first one left to use a phone at the nurses' bay, which took fifteen minutes.

When he returned, he started in an apologetic tone, "I'm sorry ma'am. I can't do anything about your daughter. You can see Mr. Winrock if you wish."

"I have never heard of such a thing. Darling, you go wait in the lounge for me. I'll visit with Rich then we'll both see if we can reach Dr. Butler. The very idea."

Mrs. Winrock entered Rich's room, and the attending nurse stepped out. His eyes were much brighter than they had been the last time she had visited yesterday. She noticed his arms and head had fewer tubes attached and his bed was elevated at the head so he could see her as she sat down beside him.

"Don't be upset. Lisa will get to see me later." Rich nodded toward the door.

"How did you ... Rich ... I don't understand." A frightened look crept into Evelyn's eyes.

"Don't try, my dear. Sit down and tell me how you are," Rich said slowly.

"I'm fine. It's how *you* are that concerns me."

She was thinking how normal his speech had become yet how abnormal what he was saying was.

"I'm making medical history, actually, my dear."

"Oh, Rich." Evelyn burst out crying as she put her head on his hand. "I have been so worried about you.

Thank God you are **OK**. I don't know what I would do without you."

"You won't have to. I'll be out of here in no time."

"Oh, God, I hope so. It has been so difficult not being able to stay with you. I don't understand all this security business."

"It is necessary, my love," Rich said gravely.

"I guess so, but I hate it."

Rich had noticed the huge Sunday paper Evelyn had brought. His eyes caught the front page, and he laughed out loud.

"What is it, Rich?" Evelyn sat up, startled.

"Nothing, dear. I was just looking at the paper you brought in."

"What about it?"

"Nothing."

"Yes, there is. What were you laughing at?" she gently probed.

"That article on the front page about the Soviet SS20 missiles—it quotes the current German chancellor. Actually, the current chancellor made no such statement; it was made by the former chancellor. There will be a big flap about it tomorrow."

"But how would you ... Rich, have you been

watching television?"

"No, I haven't. There is none. Sam will have a fit when he hears I saw the morning paper."

"That's ridiculous. Why can't you see the paper if you are recovering so remarkably?"

"He doesn't want me to develop any anxiety over the bad news I guess."

"Well, I don't agree. I don't like the way they are isolating you. We don't want any gunman coming here, but your daughter—and the paper—I never heard—"

"Dear, Sam knows what he is doing."

"I certainly hope so."

"You know, I have always marveled at the misinformation that is printed," Rich continued. "Take that story on the sixth page about silver prices becoming stable. Silver prices are going to drop thirty percent in the next three months."

Evelyn reached over and picked up the front section of the paper and opened it to page six. There was an article stating that silver prices were expected to stabilize.

"Rich, are you playing tricks on me? How did you know about this article? Has your nurse been reading to you?"

"Actually, yes." Rich could think of no other explanation that Evelyn would understand.

Rich prolonged her visit by inquiring about things at their house, their daughter and grandchildren.

Finally, Rich said, "Tell Lisa I like her hair short."

Evelyn's mouth fell open. She stared at Rich for a long time. How could he know? She was certain she hadn't said anything about Lisa's hair. Rich began to worry her terribly. She was completely confused. He seemed to know all about his children, his grandchildren, international events in the paper, even mistakes in the reported news. She was badly shaken. Rich, of course, realized that he had upset his wife and tried to placate her, with little results. She quickly kissed him and hurried out of the room to call Dr. Sam Butler. The attending nurse agreed to try to reach him through his service then returned to Rich's room. When questioned, the nurse assured Mrs. Winrock that she had not discussed any news items with Mr. Winrock per Dr. Butler's instructions.

CHAPTER
XLIII

Dr. Butler was sound asleep in Carolyn's bed when his cell phone rang. Carolyn was embarrassed at having to tell the operator of the hospital service, "Just a moment," then have Sam's half-asleep "Hello" follow.

Mrs. Winrock had relentlessly pursued reaching Dr. Butler with the hospital staff until they agreed to call him at an unlisted number, his cell phone, to be used only in emergencies.

"Dr. Butler, this is Evelyn Winrock. I have just seen my husband, and I must talk to you right away. How soon will you be coming to the hospital?"

Sam had not intended to go the hospital at all, except in an emergency. "Is there a problem?"

"Yes, there is. I am worried about Rich. He has upset me, Doctor. Could you possibly come over now? I will wait for you in the ICU waiting area."

"Yes, I guess so. It may take me forty-five minutes to get there. Can't we discuss this over the phone?"

"No, this is too urgent. I will wait."

"Very well," Sam answered and hung up with a long sigh as he looked at Carolyn.

"I know. You have to go to the hospital," Carolyn said sadly.

"I won't be long, dear. I'll come back as soon as I see Mrs. Winrock. What time is it?"

"It is exactly 10:22."

"Mrs. Winrock sounds really upset after seeing Rich," Sam said as he got up and grabbed his shirt.

"He upsets a lot of people, I understand."

"This hospital has a hell of a grapevine."

Sam hurriedly shaved, dressed and headed for the hospital with a good idea of what had happened to upset Evelyn Winrock. Meanwhile, Evelyn was sitting with her daughter and was trying to explain the strange feeling she had about her visit with her husband.

Striding down the hall toward Rich's room, Sam's legs felt heavy, without spring. Carolyn was relaxing him almost too much, he thought. He didn't see Mrs. Winrock but assumed she was in the waiting room.

Nurse Crenshaw said, "Good morning, Dr. Butler," with a mischievous smile as he passed the nurses' station.

Evelyn and Lisa both stood up as Sam rounded the corner and entered the waiting area.

"Good morning, Mrs. Winrock." Sam shook her hand with his best professional manner.

"Dr. Butler, this is my daughter, Lisa Brennand. She was not allowed to see her father. She has come all the way over here from Columbus, Georgia, and they would not let her in. Apparently, your instructions—"

"I am sorry, Mrs. Winrock. I didn't know your daughter was in town. Of course, she can see her father. Since she is direct family, I can give the guard the authorization she needs. We will have to get her a special card, however."

"Can she see him now?"

"Yes, of course. I will arrange it. Excuse me."

Sam identified himself and produced his card before discussing the problem with the guard on duty. Then he returned to the Winrocks. Mrs. Winrock suggested Lisa visit her father alone while she talked to Dr. Butler.

"I am pleased to see how bright my husband is looking, Doctor."

"Yes, he is responding better than we could have hoped."

"I am concerned, however, with all the security that doesn't seem to be working."

"What do you mean?"

"Well, first of all, Rich tells me he isn't allowed to watch television or read the papers."

"That is correct. I don't want him placing himself under any stress these first few days."

"But he is doing both."

Sam looked puzzled. He had explicit instructions against either TV or any news material. "Are you sure?"

"It's the only explanation I can give. He told me about an article in the paper. And as you know, he had also gotten the word that his grandson had broken his arm. I don't know how. I certainly didn't tell him."

"I see."

"The guard told me that you and I were the only people authorized to see him. Who else is seeing him, Doctor?"

"Leo Solis had a brief visit Friday, and several of the residents have checked him over. No one else."

"Well something funny is going on around here, Dr. Butler. I don't like it. I don't like it one bit."

Sam knew he had better give Mrs. Winrock a plausible explanation, or they would all be in trouble. "Mrs. Winrock, some of the nurses do talk a lot. I guess they have been keeping Rich informed."

"I asked the nurse on duty, and she said she hasn't said anything to Rich like that."

"Well, Mrs. Winrock, she may not even be aware she has said some things. She may be afraid of getting in trouble."

240

"I guess so. I don't know why she didn't tell me the truth. I don't care, though. You are the one who is all fussed up about keeping Rich isolated."

"He's doing so well. We will relax the restrictions as soon as possible."

"I hope so. It has been very difficult not to really visit with my husband."

"I'm sure it has. Let's go see how ..."

"Lisa," Mrs. Winrock prompted.

"Yes, how Lisa is doing with her father."

Sam and Evelyn entered Rich's room to find Lisa laughing, almost in hysterics.

"What is it, Lisa?" Mrs. Winrock asked anxiously.

Continuing to laugh, she recounted the story Rich had told her about the time she had broken her arm sliding down the bannister of their inside stairway onto a pile of her mother's best pillows on the floor. The visit continued until Sam could see Rich's eyes tiring.

"I think Mr. Winrock has had enough excitement for one day. Why don't you both visit him tomorrow?"

Evelyn and Lisa both kissed Rich on the cheek and, looking back over their shoulders, left his room.

"Rich, you really upset your wife with the newspaper business. I wish you would try not to say things you aren't supposed to know."

"Sam, I am trying. It's just that I lose track of where the information comes from. What really upset Evelyn was my mentioning Lisa's hair."

Sam sat down and began using his professional voice. "You are saying it is difficult for you to distinguish what information you have obtained through ... normal channels and what information through ... through ... other channels."

"Go ahead. Say abnormal channels."

"Is that true?"

"Yes. I saw the paper in Evelyn's arms. Evelyn didn't realize I couldn't see it from where I was. I knew the *Courier* had made a serious mistake."

"What kind of mistake?"

"Oh, there was a front-page story that stated that the chancellor of Germany had taken a position on the Soviet-era SS-20 missiles. Actually, it was the former chancellor. Someone must have botched up the story."

"You mentioned this to Evelyn?"

"Yes."

"Oh, boy. What is going to happen next?"

Rich said, "Tomorrow the chancellor is going to raise hell about the story, which was apparently sent around the world."

Sam looked exasperated. "When Evelyn sees that,

we will all be in trouble."

"I am afraid so, Sam. She will really wonder."

"What else did you tell her?"

"Nothing much." Rich looked sheepish. "I did comment on a story about silver prices."

"What about silver prices?"

Rich chuckled, "If I tell you, you will become an insider; you know that."

"What about silver prices?"

"This article said silver would become stabilized for an extended period."

"And ..."

"Well, actually, silver is going to take a dive down to its level of two years ago."

"Why is it going to do that?"

"Because the U.S. government is going to dump some of its surplus, and Russia will follow suit before prices fall any more, with the net result being quite a nose dive."

Sam looked long and hard at his patient. This bit of information could be worth millions of dollars. Sam would not react to it. He didn't need more money with the prospect of making four million on his real estate with Bob McLean and his current income well above four hundred thousand. Sam was so sure Rich was right, he did feel like an insider who should not take advantage of in-house information.

"Rich, I suggest you stay away from any discussions with Evelyn—with anyone—involving information you are not sure of."

"I'll try, Sam. It just seems to slip out."

"Rich, I don't think you realize how serious this whole … How can I say this? I understand … No that's not right either. I accept what has happened to you, Rich, although I do not understand. I am not sure anyone else is going to accept your situation. I don't want you to end up in a psychiatric ward, Rich."

The sound of Sam's words reverberated through Rich's mind. Rich closed his eyes as if trying to close out the hyperconsciousness he experienced constantly.

"Rich, I have restricted your visitors to your wife and now your daughter. Please be careful. Hopefully, this awareness you have now will subside as your brain adjusts to the insult it has received. Until then, please be careful."

"Of course. I understand. I'll do my best. You don't know how hard it is being here while things are happening all around me—things I can help!"

"I can imagine."

"No, you can't. For example, your Mr. Leo Solis has his policemen combing the wrong area. He has already gotten one of his men shot over on Live Oak."

"You know about this?"

Rich looked at Sam with impatience. "After all I've told you, you ask a question like that."

"Sorry. Continue."

"I wish you could get word to Leo Solis that the terrorists are in an old building on Lenehan Street."

"Where is that?" Sam was fascinated with this news.

"It is a short street off of Velasco Road, yes, Velasco—North Velasco—close to railroad tracks and Buffalo Bayou."

"Have you known this all along?"

"No. I became aware of Leo's efforts this morning. It seems he had a meeting with a group of officers and gave them areas to search. The location I mentioned is within this area but won't be recognized as a place anyone would be living. Do you think you can get word to Leo Solis?"

"Rich, I am getting to feel more unprofessional every time I talk to you. Now you want me to be a tipster."

"No. I just want you to somehow get word to Solis where to look. They are there right now. Don't you understand? They are the people who shot me."

"That isn't going to be easy. What pretext can I use, Rich?"

"I don't know. You will think of something."

"I'll do my best. What about an anonymous tip?"

"That would work. Be sure and tell Leo, no one else."

"OK. I understand. I'll do my best. Now stay calm and please monitor your comments, Rich."

Rich shook his head ever so slightly up and down then closed his eyes. Sam patted him tenderly on the arm and left his room, motioning for his nurse to return. Sam was getting more deeply involved in this strange turn of events. He did want to help Rich but knew that his entire professional career would be jeopardized if this whole ESP business were to come out. Sam should have put all the information on Rich's ESP experience into his record without interpreting it. Knowing what effect this might have on Rich's future, he withheld this information. He was now liable for malpractice and censor by the hospital, but it was too late to turn back. He would continue to protect Rich as long as he could and hope this phase he was experiencing would pass.

Deciding to make a few Sunday rounds, Sam called Carolyn and then proceeded to see the rest of his patients. Sam dreaded making his rounds on Sundays because he would see many of his patients' families who would want some encouragement from him. He seldom felt sincere with what he said. There was always hope, but not very much, with his typical brain tumor patients. He would need Carolyn's warm embrace when he finished his rounds and returned to her apartment.

Sam realized he had forgotten about Rivers Kern's request for a visit with Rich when his pager snared him, and he heard the voice of the angry chairman of the board of Global. Sam told Mr. Kern he would attempt to reach Leo Solis by telephone to obtain his authorization, believing success was unlikely on Sunday. But Sam didn't know Leo. Sunday was just like every other day to Leo. The officer who answered advised Sam that Leo was headed for the hospital. Sam was not sure which one or why. He would be at this hospital for another hour, which would give Leo time to arrive.

CHAPTER
XLIV

When Leo arrived at Ben Taub, he went directly to the Intensive Care Unit to check on Charles and then to the waiting area and found Charles Howard's wife. She was sitting by herself with a dazed expression on her face. Sitting beside her, Leo took her hand and asked, "How is our Charles doing this morning?"

"Oh, hello, Mr. Solis."

"Have you heard anything this morning?"

"Yes, a doctor came by about an hour ago and said his condition was more stable."

Leo had already gotten a report, but he didn't want to let Mrs. Howard know what he had heard until she had received the news directly from the hospital staff. They visited for thirty minutes. Leo stayed until he felt Mrs. Howard no longer needed to vent her feelings then headed for St. Matthews to inquire about Rich Winrock.

While circulating around the doctors' parking area looking for a place to leave his unmarked patrol car, he saw **Dr. Sam Butler** walking across the lot. He pulled up alongside, put the window down and said, "Dr. Butler, got a minute?"

Sam did not recognized Leo immediately, nor did he decode Leo's remark. He looked strangely at Leo and continued to walk.

"Dr. Butler, may I talk to you? I'm Detective Leo Solis," Leo said in clear English.

Sam stopped, apologized, opened the door to Leo's car, sat down and said, "I have been trying to get you. They said you were headed for the hospital. I was not sure which one."

"What did you want?" Leo asked flatly.

"I wanted to let you know that **Rivers Kern**, the chairman of Global Oil and Refining, wants to see Richard Winrock. I thought it would be all right from the security point of view but have been delaying this type of activity to give Winrock a chance to recover."

"Do you think this type of visit is wise? He took a pretty hard hit."

"I think Kern just wants to verify that his president has, in fact, survived his injury and is talking."

"It's OK with me if it's OK with you. I'll advise the security detail. When does he want to do this?"

"I set it up for Tuesday morning," Sam answered.

"Now, how is our patient doing today, Doctor?"

249

Leo asked.

"You won't believe how well Mr. Winrock is doing."

"I am pleased to hear this. I didn't know whether to believe what I have been reading about him. Where does all the garbage come from?"

Sam nodded. "I know what you mean. I feel the same way. The fact that we haven't given out much officially on Richard Winrock seems to intensify the media's interest in his condition."

"When is he going to be up and around? It will be more difficult to protect him then. I need some notice to set things up."

"I can't tell you that. He has had a thorough examination of his gross and fine motor skills, and we plan a neuropsychological exam on Monday. He has improved markedly since you saw him."

"What do the tests show so far?"

"There is apparently no damage to his motor system. We will begin getting him on his feet soon."

"Is he out of danger from any complications, Doc?"

"Except for infection, I would say yes."

"Can I visit with him soon?"

"Is that necessary?" Sam did not want to expose Rich to any further chance of his disclosing his clairvoyance, particularly to this detective.

"I would like to question him further about his company's activities in the Middle East. It is critical, Doctor."

Sam sensed Leo knew something he wasn't telling him. "I thought you discussed that with Rich on Friday."

"I did, Doc. You were there. I now have more specific questions."

"I see. Well, I guess a short visit won't be harmful. When do you want to see him?"

"Whenever I can, Doctor."

"Let's make it Wednesday morning."

"What time?" Leo asked.

"How does ten o'clock sound?" Sam replied.

"Perfect." Leo shook his head with finality.

"How is your investigation going?" Sam had been keeping up with the media accounts.

"We are making progress," Leo said.

"Sorry about the officer who was shot Friday night."

"Yeah, tough break. He is really a good man. Got careless."

Sam struggled with his conscience. Could he withhold what he had learned from Rich? He knew in his

251

heart this was what Leo needed to catch the monsters who shot Rich.

He impulsively said, "Leo, you get all kinds of scuttlebutt around a hospital. For what it is worth, check a Lenehan Street off Valesco. Someone around the hospital must know of an old building by some railroad tracks near Buffalo Bayou that could make a good hideout."

Leo searched Sam's face for a clue to his strange tip. "Who gave you this?"

"I don't remember. I didn't think it was important at first."

Sam sensed he had stepped in over his head. "One of the employees must have picked it up, but it might be worthless," Sam stammered.

"Yeah, I know. Thanks. We'll check it out. What was the street again?"

"Lenehan Street—old building—off Velasco."

"Got you. When did you get this tip?"

"Yesterday, I believe."

Sam said goodbye to Leo and hurried to his car, angry at himself for having gotten involved. He could hardly believe he had told Leo about the hideout. His pattern throughout his medical career was to be a loner, to perform his specialty and not get to know his patients or their families too well, certainly not to get involved to the extent he had with Rich—or Leo Solis.

As he headed for Carolyn's apartment, he wondered whether Rich actually had the power to influence other people's actions. He had tried to humor Rich about passing on the hideout information without actually planning to tell the police, yet he had done just that. He had placed himself in the middle of a raging series of events that was making spectacular news throughout the country. He shuddered as he thought of himself splashed on headlines: "Dr. Butler locates terrorists" or "Dr. Butler linked to terrorists." He said, "Damn, what the hell have I done?"

This was almost an irrational action. He was beginning to lose touch with reality—certainly his reality. Then, being easier on himself, he thought of how painful it must be for Rich to know where the gunmen are and not be able to communicate that information to anyone. He was Rich's only confidant. He knew Rich desperately needed him if Rich was to keep his sanity.

CHAPTER

XLV

Sam was glad they had chosen Ruggle's when he saw Carolyn's short, gold-sequined dress with a large satin bow on one hip. The numerous gold necklaces and bracelets she had chosen did not complement either the dress or each other. Between her teased hair in a large bouffant style that made her small head look even smaller and her heavy makeup, she did not look much like herself. Sam paid a weak compliment when she asked him how she looked. His navy blue blazer with gold buttons and charcoal grey flannel slacks were the most formal clothes he had brought to Carolyn's apartment.

Arriving at Ruggle's, the hostess led them to a table close to the entrance. Sam wisely suggested they be given a more private table. The hostess smiled shyly at Sam and said, "Surely," and led them to a dimly lit corner in the back of the restaurant. When she returned to the entrance, she mused to herself, "The old goat doesn't want his wife to find out he's with a young chick."

Several cocktails later, Sam's outlook was less apprehensive and less cautious. He was enjoying his young lady friend, and he was enjoying the reaction he was getting from the outside world at being with an attractive young woman. Carolyn's clothes, jewelry, hair and makeup had cheapened her natural beauty, but she still came across as a stunning young woman. They enjoyed their roast beef and left arm in arm.

Returning to Carolyn's apartment, they went to the bedroom and began to undress as though they had been married for years. As Carolyn stepped out of the last of her clothes, Sam placed his hands on her shoulders, turned her around and kissed her hard. Then he picked her up in his arms and carried her to the bed, maintaining a kiss as he moved.

In the morning, Sam awoke with the realization that he couldn't continue using Carolyn this way. He was glad that he hadn't run into anyone he had known at the restaurant, ashamed at how Carolyn had dressed. It was her youth and inexperience. She was nearly twenty years his junior—much too young for him.

He carefully unwound himself from around her and touched her cheek. Sam grabbed his clothes and put them on then came back in, finding Carolyn still asleep. He bent down and kissed her gently on her forehead, waking her up.

"Good morning," Carolyn said sleepily and with a smile. It broke Sam's heart to have to say what he had to say next.

"Carolyn, sweetheart, you have been so good to me. Exactly what I have needed for a long time. Thank you."

She smiled at his admission, and he took her hand. The look on his face melted her smile, and she sat up concerned. Sam continued, "I can't do this anymore. It can't work."

"What are you talking about, Sam? We are good. This is good. What more could you want?"

"I feel like I am using you, and I can't do that anymore. You are much younger than me and deserve to find a man you can have a family with. I've already had mine. I'm done."

"I don't understand! Please don't go," Carolyn pleaded as tears dripped down her face. Sam squeezed her hand and began to leave, pausing at the door.

"You will understand one day, Carolyn. You need to be with someone who can match you in every way. Eventually you would come to resent me if we continued this. Take care, Carolyn." And with that, Sam left her apartment, not waiting to hear her protests.

CHAPTER
XLVI

Monday morning, Lenora had no sparkle at all. Despite the wonderful weekend, she felt depressed, tired and, somehow, lonely. Her headache greeted her like an old friend as she opened her eyes and turned her head to see the time—8:05. Lenora was usually dressed and on her way to her office by now, particularly on a Monday. Lenora stretched out under the covers and enjoyed the feel of satin textured sheets against her body. She pulled an extra pillow on her large bed down under the covers and wrapped her arms and legs around it, snuggling into just the right position to go back to sleep.

But her thoughts would not let her sleep. She wanted to relive the previous day. So often Lenora resented being a woman, one who was not always taken seriously by businessmen. They didn't expect her to be knowledgeable or informed about commercial real estate and would infuriate her with their obvious lack of attention to what she was saying, attending only to the "package" that was doing the saying. Lenora could draft real estate contracts with the best of the agents in Houston and had a keen knowledge of Houston demographics, economics and judgments of appraised values. Being what several men called beautiful was often a drawback in closing a commercial property. Lenora often threatened men in her field. They could not accept her as an equal and tried to make a secretary or messenger out of her.

But right now, Lenora was hyperaware of her gender. She let her thoughts drift into fantasies with Rodrigo holding her and caressing her while she struggled to decide if she would give herself to him. He made her feel like a sensuous woman, a feeling, she realized, that had been suppressed for some time. Lenora had loved Byron French, and theirs was a strong physical relationship. The last few years of their marriage he was often "too tired," but she attributed this to his frequent late working hours. After his death, she had been devastated to learn he had been living with his secretary for almost six months. No wonder she had avoided any involvements. Now, she was on a path that might well lead to involvement. Rodrigo was charming, handsome, incredibly rich, tender, dangerous, mysterious and probably married. Lenora's thoughts swirled around in her head as she attempted to unravel the puzzle of who and what Rodrigo Carranza was.

The phone's ring seemed to be connected directly to her nerve endings as it interrupted her thoughts. She wanted to put her head under the pillow and ignore it but finally answered it. As if summoned by her thoughts, the voice on the other end of the phone was Rodrigo telling her he had not slept for worrying about her, and he had called a neurologist he knew and arranged for Lenora to see him at ten. Lenora thought Rodrigo must be drinking. She could hardly believe he was telling her what she "must" do, immediately.

"Who is this doctor?" she asked, not really caring.

"His name is Jim Nidert. He is the best neurologist in this part of the world."

"How do you know him?"

"He treated my mother."

Rodrigo had not talked about his mother except a comment about her beauty. Lenora was not aware that his family had ever been to Houston, and the information surprised her.

"When were you and your family in Houston?"

"A little over four years ago."

"I didn't know."

"My mother came to Houston to see Dr. Jim Nidert."

Lenora's wheels were turning. This doctor must be good for someone to come halfway around the world to see him.

Rodrigo continued, "Jim has arranged to see you this morning as a special favor to me."

"Why must I see him this morning? I am fine," Lenora said, knowing she was anything but fine. She began to shake all over, unable to stop her teeth from chattering. "What time is this appointment?"

"Ten. I will pick you up at nine thirty. I don't want you to worry about where to go and where to park. I know you will like Jim Nidert. He's the best."

"What is he again?"

"A neurologist."

"Why would you want me to see a neurologist? Aren't they for nerves, vertebra problems, like that?"

"They treat the nervous system, yes. Dr. Nidert specializes in diagnostic work."

"What would he be trying to diagnose?"

"Lenora, you have had headaches for some time now. You have fallen twice. I just want him to check you over, for your own sake, really."

"Not for my sake, Rodrigo, maybe for yours. Certainly not for mine."

"Lenora, please let me pick you up. You don't like your headaches, do you?"

Lenora paused and then, resigning to a situation she knew was inevitable, said, "No, I don't. Very well, but why this morning?"

"Dr. Nidert is going to a meeting in Chicago this week, and I wanted you to see the best."

"All right, Rodrigo. I don't seem to be able to say no to you."

"Splendid. I will see you at nine thirty, my dearest."

As Lenora hung up, she began to shake again. What was happening to her? She had never let anyone dominate her like this since she lost her husband. She was the one who gave out orders people followed, not the other way around. She had no intention of going to the doctor when Rodrigo first mentioned it. Now she was committed to see someone—a neurologist she had never heard of—arranged by a man who had irritated her when they met. She was sorry she had admitted to Rodrigo that she couldn't refuse him. What would he ask of her now? What a mess she was making of her orderly life.

No sooner had she sat up in bed and put on her robe than Jeff called with great anxiety in his voice. Jeff's child-like concern for her was like a tonic. His call gave her a grasp on the real world.

"I'm doing all right now, Jeff."

"There must be something wrong. You would never cancel your meeting with the Norwegians otherwise."

"I'm going in for a checkup; that's all. No big deal, Jeff."

"I will come over and take you to the doctor. What time is your appointment?"

"That's not necessary, Jeff, really. I'm fine," Lenora said with a hint of panic in her voice, not wanting to tell Jeff about Rodrigo.

Then Jeff said gently, "Well, call me if you need

anything. I will stay around the office and try to cover for you."

"Thank you, Jeff, you're a dear." Lenora hung up the phone and started to get ready. She was not happy with Rodrigo's persuasive ways but realized her trip to the doctor would put her mind at ease about herself.

Answering the bell on the third ring, Lenora opened the door and looked directly into Rodrigo's broad, warm grin.

"You look absolutely beautiful, my dear. Too pretty to be going to the doctor."

Lenora had planned to be very cool to Rodrigo—she wanted to stay in charge of herself—but he disarmed her completely with his warm manner. He took her arm, and as they approached his limousine, he stepped aside and looked at her.

"Your suit is very becoming."

"Thank you."

"I like you in that color. What is it?"

"Magenta." Lenora felt feminine all over when she was with Rodrigo. He seemed to appreciate every detail of her being. But she couldn't push away that irritation that this same man was trying to take her over.

Seeing the number of runners of all shapes and sizes going in both directions along the special running path of Memorial Drive that led into downtown, she remarked, "I have been neglecting my running lately. After I get a clean of health, I am going to start my routine again."

"I didn't know you liked to run."

"I love it, but lately ..." she said, trailing off as she continued to focus on the runners.

"Lenora, you are going to like Jim Nidert. He is very thorough, very direct and very good at his business," Rodrigo said, dismissing the previous conversation.

"You said he ..." Lenora began, but decided not to continue asking about his mother. Rodrigo seemed not to notice.

The remainder of the trip was in silence with Rodrigo holding Lenora's hand tightly. He guided her out of the limousine, into the building and Nidert's office, introducing her to a tall, thin man with a heavy head of black hair, high cheek bones and large penetrating eyes.

Dr. Nidert picked up his medical record tablet and seated himself next to Lenora, succeeding in putting her at ease. He questioned her about every facet of her health both present and past. Many innocent questions she felt had significance in their answers. He dwelled on her headaches—the location, intensity, time of day, effect of exertion on them, etc. Then, he questioned her at length about the two falls she had experienced recently, asking her to describe how she felt before and after falling and how the fall occurred and how her leg felt.

Dr. Nidert stood and, standing over Lenora, pressed on the area of her head she had described as the location of the pain. He said nothing but kept his eyes on her. Then he had her stand with her eyes closed and move her arms to various positions. He had her touch her toes with her eyes closed.

Finally, he said, "I would like to do a complete physical of you plus X-rays, blood and a urinalysis. It should not take over one hour. I think I have all the information I need now. If you will follow me, I will turn you over to Mrs. Jackson, who will see that you have everything done. I will see you after your tests are completed."

Lenora dutifully followed Dr. Nidert into the internal area of his office complex where she met a handsome, heavy-set woman with gray hair pulled back into a bun. Mrs. Jackson placed Lenora in a small room with instructions to put on the white gown that she furnished.

Dr. Nidert returned to his office and asked his nurse to bring Mr. Caranza in.

Rodrigo rushed in saying, "What do you think, Jim?"

"There are symptoms that could be very serious. It would not be appropriate for me to say anything now, or to you later, for that matter. I am not dealing with your mother this time, my friend. You were right bringing her in right away. Often that makes a tremendous difference."

Rodrigo was beside himself. He jumped to his feet. He hit one fist into the other. "Why is it I have to go through this kind of torture with people I care about?" Rodrigo did not want anyone to answer his question. He paced up and down. He continued, "When will you know something?"

"I want to look at her X-rays and blood tests as soon as they are completed. If necessary, I will arrange a CT scan for tomorrow morning."

"I hope you don't need to do that. I hate that machine."

"I can understand, my friend. Let me ask, when was it you became concerned about Mrs. French?"

"Yesterday. Lenora asked me a question about Switzerland. It made me remember when my mother had a problem with her leg. We all thought she had hurt it skiing. She fell several times in the hotel. The whole nightmare suddenly came back to me. The headaches we attributed to altitude sickness, everything. Mother did not want to fly over the Atlantic, so my dad brought her to New York on the QE2 that last time—that extra time. God, I wish we would have forced her to take the plane."

"Don't blame yourself, Rodrigo."

"I'm not blaming anyone. God knows you did your best. You were right on target."

"There is a neurosurgeon whose reputation now exceeds that of others, Dr. Samuel Butler. Should it come to that, I will recommend him to Lenora."

Rodrigo left Dr. Nidert's office in a state of near

panic.

Lenora was so stressed by the tests and thinking about what could be wrong that she was ready to cry when Mrs. Jackson told her she could put her clothes back on. She asked Mrs. Jackson to show her where she had left them, as the many doors lining the hall looked alike to her. Satisfied she looked as good as she was going to look under the circumstances, she emerged to be taken back to Dr. Nidert's office.

"Please sit down, Mrs. French. I hope it hasn't been too bad."

"No. Everything was fine."

"Mrs. French, I would like to ask you to come in tomorrow for an additional test."

Lenora began to frown. What was this all about? Wasn't the torture she had been through enough? "What kind of test?" she finally asked.

"We want to run a CT scan."

"I have heard of it, but I don't really know what it is."

"It's the best thing we have to X-ray parts of the body to determine if there is any abnormality present."

"What do you mean by abnormality?" Lenora's stomach had a sick feeling. She thought she might faint as she grabbed the arms of the chair more firmly.

"That's a term we use for any difficulty—any growth that might exist." Seeing Lenora's anxiety, he added, "We

266

sometimes run a **CT** scan to be assured there is no problem."

Lenora was ready to accept anything that sounded better than what she was thinking.

"What time do you want me, Doctor?"

"You won't be coming to my office, Mrs. French. My nurse will give you all the particulars. The equipment is on the fourth floor. They will be ready for you at ten o'clock."

Lenora began to cloud up again as she struggled to keep her purse balanced on her knees.

"It's really a series of X-rays run with special equipment. The **CT** means *computed* or *computerized tomography*."

"I see." Lenora did not understand at all and dreaded what was before her.

"It won't hurt a bit." Dr. Nidert smiled warmly, rose and bid her good day.

Lenora walked with unsteady steps out into the waiting room and into the outthrust arms of Rodrigo. She was very glad to see him, even though he had been responsible for arranging the horror she had been through.

Steadied by Rodrigo's strength, they returned to his limousine that was waiting in a special lane of the parking garage reserved for VIPs. Rodrigo, holding both of Lenora's hands to keep her from shaking, told her he would take her home. Lenora was grateful, as she couldn't handle going anywhere else, but she didn't like the way he told her instead of asking her what she preferred.

"Rodrigo, you are too much. I get the feeling my life is slipping away from me and into your hands. You are leading me around like your pet poodle."

"I hope so."

Lenora was bothered by his response but filed it away to deal with it later. She was tired of trying to fight back her thoughts of what Dr. Nidert had told her. Maybe she would wake up and find this whole business was a bad dream. Being around Rodrigo seemed to take away her drive to run her thriving business. She was so overpowered by his lifestyle that her business seemed almost trivial. How could she change so quickly? Just days ago, she was filled with excitement about the prospect of selling Bob McLean and Sam Butler's property. Now she was not in a hurry to return to her office. She would prefer to go home even though she might blow the deal. How could this be? Lenora decided the changes in her were the result of whatever medical problem she had. Lenora was not sure she wanted Dr. Nidert to uncover the problem.

Lenora and Rodrigo headed back to Lenora's townhouse. Noticing she looked chilled, Rodrigo asked if Lenora had any wood. She said she did. Rodrigo stepped into Lenora's living room really looking at it, unlike the first time, and he was surprised by its stunning elegance. The ceiling was two stories, and a huge crystal chandelier hung in the center, giving the room a warm glow. The furniture was primarily early English Sheraton, with scattered tables and chairs of different periods.

"Your house is beautiful, my dear," Rodrigo said as he walked over to her fireplace and began arranging logs to start a fire.

Lenora looked curiously at Rodrigo. His apartment was filled with museum-quality furniture. "Do you really like it?"

"Yes, I do. Of course, I do."

"My mother left me the large pieces. I have collected the rest on my own."

"It is very much you. A combination of beauty and dignity," Rodrigo said as the fire caught the logs and he moved to help Lenora to a large sofa by the fireplace.

Rodrigo sat by Lenora's side and held her hand with both of his. "You are going to be fine, darling. I will be with you tomorrow. Do not worry."

Lenora knew it would be a long night waiting for the tests on Tuesday to determine the course of her future. Every time she let her thoughts drift to the test, a sick feeling in the depth of her stomach developed, and she would feel weak, ready to tremble.

Seated next to the lively fire, Lenora had overcome the chill she was having earlier and was beginning to smile again. Rodrigo had a way of relaxing her with his melodious baritone speaking voice and his charming Italian accent. Lenora felt as though she was being swept along by forces she was powerless to resist. She was sitting enjoying her second hot buttered rum while the opportunity to sell a valuable tract of commercial land was slipping away. Normally, she would be frantically preparing for her meeting. She had not called her office since she arrived at her home.

As the flames flared up before them, Lenora caught Rodrigo staring at her in a strange way. His face had a warm expression, but in his eyes was fear of some kind. She was puzzled. She would not think about tomorrow and the CT scan. She reasoned to herself that she couldn't have anything too serious to feel as good as she did now. Her head didn't hurt at all. There had been no problem with her leg since Sunday evening, and that not a serious problem, no pain, just a little loss of balance, possibly. Still, unease crept in all around her.

Sensing this, Rodrigo said, "My darling, let's have a brandy. Where is your bar? Oh, yes, I see it." Rodrigo returned with two snifters of brandy. "You have good taste in brandy. My family has an interest in the brand." He rotated his glass gently to allow the golden-brown liquid to swirl up the sides of his glass. "I am a lucky man to have found you, *mio caro*," Rodrigo said tenderly as he sat next to Lenora. "It is pure chance I came to Houston, pure chance I got interested in real estate, pure chance I heard about you, pure chance that you allowed me to get to know you. I am truly a lucky man."

Rodrigo sounded serious at times that were not appropriate. Lenora was trying to forget the future and concentrate on the moment. She did not want to think

270

about her relationship with Rodrigo developing into something serious.

"Now relax. You are very tense," he said.

"I guess I am. I have every reason to be."

"I disagree with you, *mi amori*. You have every reason to feel good. You are in good hands, as your television commercial says."

"They are strong hands; I will say that."

Rodrigo took another sip of brandy. "*Amori*, I love to cook Italian food. Anatol will bring everything I need to cook it. You won't need to lift a finger. I know you will enjoy it."

"Rodrigo, I don't use my kitchen that much. You will have a hard time finding things."

"On the contrary. Anatol tells me you have everything I will need. Trust me."

"Don't cook a big meal, please. I am not very hungry."

"You will be, *mi amori*."

Lenora decided to change clothes, so she excused herself while Rodrigo inspected her kitchen. In her bedroom, she couldn't get the bad taste out of her mouth at the way Rodrigo kept taking over her life. First with the events of the weekend, then the doctor and now telling her how hungry she will be. Overwhelmed by what seemed to be a controlling nature, Lenora plopped down on her bed, forehead in her hands. She couldn't do this anymore, she thought. Rodrigo was a caring, yet controlling man. Lenora felt her life slipping into his hands, and she couldn't stomach it. Standing, Lenora walked resolutely to the door of her bedroom and back into the kitchen where Rodrigo was pulling out a pan, presumably to cook with.

"Rodrigo, stop for a moment. Would you come sit by the fire with me and talk?"

"Are you **OK**, *mio caro*? What is wrong?" He took her hand as they sat down on the sofa. Lenora took a deep breath to settle the whirlwind of emotions dancing inside her. This was going to be difficult for them both, but she knew it was the right thing for her to do.

"Rodrigo, you are very caring, generous and handsome, and I appreciate all you have done for me." Rodrigo looked as if he was going to answer, but Lenora continued, "However, I don't think this is going to work between us. I feel like I am losing myself to you, and that isn't how it should feel. It should feel, with the right person, that I am becoming more."

"I don't understand. You don't know what you are saying right now ... I think maybe the day has simply been too overwhelming. You must go lie down, rest. You will see differently in the morning," Rodrigo said with authority, angering Lenora even more.

"No, Rodrigo. There is nothing I *must* do! This is exactly what I am talking about. I am sure that you will find a woman who needs a man to direct her, but I am my own person. I enjoy making my own decisions, having my career. I wasn't looking for someone when I met you, but if I had been, I would want to find a partner to share my life with, not a man who would direct me and turn me into a socialite with nothing better to do than dote on her husband." Lenora got off the sofa and wrung her hands. Rodrigo's face seemed to fall as he took in her words. She had expected him to respond quickly, try to take control of the conversation, but he was unnervingly silent.

Rodrigo rubbed his hands on his knees and then stood up and walked over to Lenora. She turned to face him and hated the hurt that was painted on his handsome features. For just a moment, Lenora began to regret the pain she was causing him. She wanted to take him in her arms and promise him the world. Seconds later, reality sunk back in as he carefully said his next words.

"I am disappointed in you, Lenora. I could give you anything you could ever want; you wouldn't have to work, but I understand." She expected him to say more, but he didn't. Lenora hated not knowing what he was thinking. Rodrigo bent close to her and laid a kiss on her forehead. "I will leave you to rest. When you change your mind about us, you have my number." Lenora wanted to lash out again at his audacity assuming she didn't know her own mind, but held her tongue. No sense in causing more of an argument. He was leaving peacefully.

Rodrigo pulled away from her, pulled out his cell phone and began dialing, and he walked out the door. "Goodbye, Lenora," he said and closed the door behind him.

Lenora was perplexed at how that conversation went. Rodrigo confused and infuriated her, but the moment he walked out the door, she felt a sense of relief flood her. They were over, no matter how he saw it.

She wiped a tear from her eyes. Rodrigo was a dear, sweet man, but he was also authoritative and controlling. Furthermore, he had a lifestyle completely different from her own; she could never adapt to it. She closed her eyes and prayed that tomorrow would bring good news.

CHAPTER
XLVII

Monday morning, Leo found himself in his car letting his instinct work for him. Dr. Butler had been hesitant to tell him about the old building on Lenehan. This seemed to be very specific information—the railroad, Buffalo Bayou. Someone who knew this area had given the doctor this description. Leo doubted the doctor had ever been there or, in fact, had even heard of either of the two streets before receiving the tip. Leo was surprised an employee would give a doctor a tip like this. The employees usually treated the doctors as gods and had little communication of this nature he thought. Also, the doctor's vague explanation puzzled Leo. The doctor would have known the person who gave him the tip, yet he refused to disclose the name or when it was.

Leo pulled up the streets on his **GPS**. The location was barely within the orbit he had drawn and was northeast, the most unlikely direction in his judgment. He noticed on the **GPS** that there were only a few streets with bridges that crossed the bayou. Velasco ended at the bayou, and the railroad blocked the area to the east. He could easily cut off any exit by automobile to Velasco and several streets to the west that were not connected to Lenehan by road. This would be an ingenious place to hide out. Leo began to take the tip seriously.

Leo checked in with headquarters to let them know he was in his car and would be returning within the hour after checking out area "Charley." He proceeded through downtown until he reached Navigation. Velasco connected to Navigation indirectly. This was a low-income neighborhood of small wooden houses surrounding industrial buildings that were in a poor state of repair. There were several groups of men in the street working on their cars and pickups. They stopped and watched Leo drive by. Leo decided to look the target area over from each of the next most westerly streets so as not to alert anyone on Lenehan.

Leo slowly came to a stop at the corner, took out his binoculars from a holder under his seat and surveyed the area to the east. No cars were visible on the street. Leo could see several dilapidated wooden buildings on Lenehan but only one old brick building on the north side and at the end of the street. From some three hundred yards, it looked abandoned. The ground had caved in directly behind the building, and tall weeds surrounded it. Likewise, heavy underbrush covered the eroded bank of Buffalo Bayou.

Leo's heartbeat picked up its pace. He sensed his prey. This would be no ordinary stakeout. It was more like something he had done in war. Leo would risk the embarrassment of chasing a false alarm.

He got on his radio and instructed his dispatcher to assemble four cars with two men, each complete with riot guns, tear gas, walkie-talkies and bulletproof gear, to form a quiet rendezvous on the corner of Live Oak and Engelke, two blocks southwest of the target. He would not call out the SWAT team, as he wanted to handle the operation and would lose control if the SWAT team took over. Leo had not brought his bulletproof gear in his car and asked that Lt. Sparkman bring him a vest and a megaphone.

While waiting for the cars to arrive, Leo thought through his strategy. He had a hunch the brick building was the hideout, but not knowing for certain which building could be housing the terrorists, Leo decided to set a large net, positioning the four marked cars at nearby intersections, including where Velasco intersected Buffalo Bayou, thus blocking escape by auto. Since his was the only unmarked car, he would take someone with him and park close to the brick building. He saw no windows on the south side, so he would be able to reach the protection of the south wall before anyone inside could get a shot at him, provided someone was there to shoot at him. He would then order the occupants out of the building. If there was no response, he would try to put some tear gas canisters through a window on the west side.

Three patrol cars pulled up behind Leo's car in close sequence in less than fifteen minutes. The fourth arrived ten minutes after the last of them. The officers crowded around the hood of Leo's car as he showed the men on his GPS the plan he had devised.

"I am playing a very loose tip and a strong hunch,

men. We may be wasting our time, but I don't want to overlook anything to find these mothers."

His men agreed. Everyone was on station in a position where they could clearly see the building. Lt. Sparkman drove Leo's car to the south side of the building, allowing Leo to jump out and reach the wall without incident. Several of the officers had volunteered to go, but Leo would not hear of it. This was a job he would do himself rather than risk anyone else getting hurt.

"We have you surrounded. Come out with your hands over your heads," Leo shouted into the bullhorn, which amplified it to a near-deafening level.

There was no response. Leo jammed his ear to the brick wall to listen for noise inside. He heard sounds unmistakably made by humans. He motioned Lt. Sparkman to take cover as he was standing near the hood of his car with his riot gun in hand. Just then a crack came from above, and he saw Sparkman jerk backward and fall to the ground. Leo drew his pistol and looked up. The shot had come from the flat roof of the two-story building. He could not see anyone from where he was crouched.

"All units, close in. Sparkman has been hit. Watch the roof."

Leo waited what seemed like an eternity until the two men on Velasco arrived to attend to Sparkman. They found him stunned but not seriously hurt. His outer jacket had a large hole in the middle of his chest, but his flak jacket had saved his life. He was in pain, but he was alive.

Leo barked out orders on his walkie-talkie as the team approached. "Call for the SWAT team. Tell them the route to enter. Get an ambulance. Come on, move it! See that nobody leaves the building."

Leo put his ear against the wall again and continued to hear noises inside. He heard shots and saw one of his men dive for cover or get hit as he approached through the high weeds on the west side of the building. Leo rushed to the southwest corner, pistol in hand, waited a second and then spun around the corner to confront whatever was there. He saw nothing. The shots must have come from one of the windows that appeared boarded up but had cracks between the boards large enough to aim and shoot through.

Leo stayed flush against the building, waiting for another outburst of gunfire to locate the source. Again, there were shots of an automatic weapon from a second-floor window. He knew he must get tear gas into the building before anyone else got hurt. Leo had noticed some glass windows on the east side of the building on the first floor. They were apparently blacked out from the inside but would allow him to hurl in a tear gas canister. Staying close to the building, he positioned himself just to the left of the first window on the east wall. Pulling out a large canister from a pocket in his jacket, he reached up, broke the glass with the butt of his pistol and hurled it inside the building. He could hear it bounce several times then hit something metallic.

Leo moved away from the window to avoid any tear gas fumes. He smelled smoke. Staying close to the east wall, he stopped at the southeast corner and told his men to hold fast where they were in position until the SWAT team arrived.

Now there were shots from an automatic weapon from the second-story windows on the east side. Leo hoped his men had taken cover. They all reported safe. He ordered them to return fire if they got an opportunity but knew it was useless from where they were pinned down. The SWAT team would have a full complement of weapons and more protective gear than his men were wearing.

Now shots were coming from the west side of the building. He could hear them ricochet off the concrete culvert. The occupants in the building were keeping everyone pinned down very effectively. Leo saw no reason to rush the building, as it was now surrounded, and no one could escape without facing his men.

After what seemed hours, the ambulance arrived escorted by two blue and white patrol cars. They clustered the cars in front of the fallen officer to protect against any gunfire from the roof, then the emergency vehicle came up, attended to Lt. Sparkman and quickly got him aboard and headed out of the area. The patrolmen stationed themselves behind their vehicles and listened to Leo on the special channel.

At 2:10 the SWAT team arrived en mass, accompanied by Chief Winslow. He usually did not participate in this kind of operation, but when he heard his chief of homicide was pinned down and Sparkman had been hit, he couldn't restrain himself.

When Leo was satisfied the SWAT team was in position, and the police helicopter was circling overhead, he asked them to cover him while he broke for the cluster of cars on the south side of the building. Over twenty guns were pointed at this end of the building when he dashed across the open area and dived behind the cars.

"You looked like Audie Murphy on that," the chief kidded him.

Leo quickly advised both the chief and Captain Wallace of the SWAT team what had transpired and suggested they play it safe using a heavier dose of tear gas. He mentioned he had smelled smoke from inside the building earlier. Captain Wallace agreed, and his men moved in with large shields to pump tear gas through the windows on the east side. They blasted the boards off the west wall with automatic gunfire then put several tear gas shells through the windows.

Leo commented, "That should drive them up to the roof. The chopper will let us know when they are up there." Soon afterward, a SWAT member with a high-powered rifle picked up movement on the west roof. He squeezed off a round just as a head and gun barrel came into view. Leo could tell the newly visible gunman had gotten hit by the crazy arc of the gun as it fell backward. The helicopter reported a man lying on the roof. No further gunfire came from the building for twenty minutes. Tear gas was issuing from all the openings in the windows.

The SWAT captain ordered the occupants to

surrender, with no response. "We can't stay here all day. I am going to send in four men."

No one objected. The team stormed an overhead industrial door on the east side of the building, but it was well secured and would not budge. They went to a door on the north side that appeared to have been used recently and blasted it open. The men entered with gas masks on to find a large open area with considerable industrial debris strewn around. In one corner of the darkened space, they could make out an old car covered with dust. There was fire in another corner where papers were burning.

The men made their way carefully through the first floor, and then part of the team climbed a metal stairwell to the second floor. They found more industrial debris strewn around. An open trap door to the roof, reached by wooden stairs, allowed them to see clearly in the dark building. No one was evident.

The next move they dreaded but knew it had to be done. The steps were such that anyone emerging from them was completely exposed to anyone on the roof. The only chance the SWAT crew had was to guess at the location of the man on the roof from the helicopter sighting and prepare to return fire in that direction.

The senior officer present, Lt. Mark Storm, adjusted his flak suit, helmet and gas mask, clenched his pistol with both hands, rushed up the stairs, and leaped onto the roof, landing in a crouched position. He saw the gunman lying on his back with the top of his head missing. Storm called for the rest of the crew, and then he announced that the building was secure by walking to the edge of the roof and waving to his fellow officers.

Leo was the first man to go into the building. He rushed to the roof and stood staring at the body. The top of the man's head had been torn off, and his brain was hanging out. He had seen others meet similar fates but would never get accustomed to death. This man resembled one of the composites, but Leo would not be sure until they extracted finger and palm prints from him.

Leo rushed back to the corner where the fire was still smoldering and carefully smothered the remaining fire with an old sack, trying to preserve whatever was left of the papers. He noticed a stack of papers barely touched by the flames and a slightly melted USB drive and bagged them for forensics. He was sure they might get some answers from that. Several large flashlights revealed a corner on the second floor where three men had been living. There were three sleeping bags lined up, a kerosene heater, a charcoal grill, and a stockpile of canned food and empty containers. Judging from the amount of trash, Leo guessed the men had been living in this house for several weeks.

Leo would inspect this area in detail later; however, he got a report on his radio that officers had found tracks leaving the north side of the building and headed toward the bayou. Solis rushed back to the north wall, kicked out the boards of a window, and tried to see some movement through the heavy underbrush leading away from the house.

He barked out orders for two tracking dogs to be brought in and dispatched patrol cars to east and west points on either side of Buffalo Bayou in case the terrorists tried to cross the large railroad yard to the east. If they had gone in that direction, it would be difficult to track them on foot. Leo kicked out a window facing east to observe what might be the terrorists' escape route, now feeling proud that he had uncovered the terrorist hideout.

He asked to be patched directly to the pilot and gave the pilot a description of what he should be looking for. When the dogs arrived, Leo dragged down several of the army-type blankets they had found to give the dogs the scent of their prey. The dogs stuck their noses into the blankets then to the ground and soon started tugging on their leashes in the direction of Buffalo Bayou. Once they were on their way, followed by six members of the SWAT team, Leo climbed back to the roof, this time with binoculars to watch the search from this vantage point.

The dogs went directly through the high weeds past the incinerator and down onto the banks of the bayou, turned east and went under the railroad bridge. Leo lost sight of them at this point but was kept informed by radio from the tracking team and the helicopter. Suddenly, the radio erupted in excited chatter as the two terrorists had been spotted. Leo could hear gunshots in the distance. Confirmation sounded over the radio that one of the terrorists had been shot dead, while one was heavily wounded but captured alive.

CHAPTER
XLVIII

Entering the main hall to the chief's office, a female reporter stuck a microphone in Leo's face and began rattling off questions. A tall, muscular Black cameraman with a TV camera trained on Leo followed her. He brushed her aside and went directly into the chief's office. Winslow had left the scene once the tracking had started, knowing there would be frantic activity back at headquarters regarding the slain gunmen and now the captured terrorist.

The first question Watson asked Leo Solis was, "Where the hell did you get that tip, Leo? I want to know the whole story."

Leo was really on the spot. He didn't want to implicate Dr. Sam Butler, but he also didn't want to withstand the heat from his chief. He finally disclosed that he had picked it up at the hospital. He told the chief that some of the hospital employees lived in the neighborhood and must have known people were hiding in the abandoned brick building. They could have been seen buying food. "It's the kind of neighborhood where everyone knows what is coming down, Chief."

The chief looked hard at Leo and decided to accept this answer for the present. Winslow needed Leo to face the onslaught of the media who would want to know all about the operation and capture. As they prepared their statement, Leo realized he preferred to face the danger of the terrorists over the probing of the reporters who were gathering in the ground-floor conference room for the news conference the chief had scheduled to start in two hours.

There was electricity in the conference room when the chief walked in followed by Leo. The chief started talking before he reached the front of the room that was crowded with local law enforcement, FBI special agents from Washington, and representatives of the CIA who were experts on terrorism and now had the remaining terrorist in custody. Winslow began sharing details from the afternoon as well as the information the CIA techs had uncovered from the melted flash drive. It appeared that there was an international leak in Global leading to the kidnapping of Winrock in order to locate the information they needed to steal his ground-breaking drilling innovations.

Leo watched as the chief completed his statement and patiently answered the media's questions. He was glad that he wasn't the one up there and let his mind wander for a moment. Leo felt a sense of pride but knew that over the years it would continue to bug him that the tip that furthered his career was shrouded in mystery.

Sighing as he watched the chaos of the reporters, Leo couldn't wait to get out of there and take a much-needed spin on the dance floor of the Wild West Western Bar and dance club. He finally felt he had earned a bit of fun.

CHAPTER
XLIX

Rivers Kern was having a quiet lunch with his wife at the River Oaks Country Club when Hillard Tinhauser stopped at their table, greeted the Kerns then invited himself to join them for a short discussion. Rivers put down his fork and gave Hillard a look that meant "I am eating. Say what you have to say and be gone."

Kern was a bottom-line executive. He said little and expected as much from his employees. Rivers frequently interrupted Hillard Tinhauser at the board meetings that Rivers chaired when Hillard shifted the discussion of Global's business into a long, aimless, self-serving discussion.

Hillard Tinhauser pulled his chair closer to Kern, turned his head to both sides to see who was sitting nearby and asked, "What is the latest on Winrock?"

Knowing Tinhauser was almost camping at the hospital, Rivers thought this was a puzzling question. "I'm sure you know more about Rich's condition than I do."

"Oh, I thought Evelyn Winrock might have given you information I couldn't get through the channels," Tinhauser responded immediately.

"Haven't you talked to her at the hospital?" Rivers began eyeing his fork to start eating again.

"I did see her, but she didn't have time to talk," he said, again quick with his answer.

"Hillard, call me at the office if you want to talk about Rich," Rivers said, looking back at his food.

"I think we should have a board meeting as soon as possible to decide what to do about the Winrock situation," Tinhauser said as he rose to leave the table.

Rivers nodded his head, acknowledging he heard the comment, then picked up his fork and pierced the largest new potato on his plate with more vigor than necessary. His fork clinked loudly on the plate as he set it back down.

Mrs. Kern looked up at Rivers, finished chewing a piece a beefsteak and asked, "What's Hillard up to now?"

"I'm not sure. But I am sure we're not going to take any action to remove Rich as president until I see for myself how he is and get his feelings on the matter," Rivers said, his square jaw raised as he watched Tinhauser stop by another table. "I'm going to the hospital tomorrow. I already arranged it with his doctor. There's something going on that doesn't smell good."

289

CHAPTER
L

Rich was delighted at seeing Dr. Paula Wheelas, a fresh, smiling, enthusiastic young neuropsychologist. Most of the nurses were in their fifties and seemed bored with their duties.

Dr. Wheelas opened her briefcase and began to put large cards and answer sheets in order as she explained what they would do.

"The test I'm going to use is called the PALI, the Parker Assessment of Language Impairment. It was developed by someone who is now in the Medical Center."

Richard knew the answer, but he asked innocently, "Who developed the test, may I ask?"

"A Dr. Helen Parker-McLean. Have you heard of her?"

"Yes I have. But not for her test. She is married to one of my close friends."

"Really? How interesting." Dr. Wheelas was

genuinely impressed. She considered Dr. Parker-McLean her idol and followed her various achievements with keen interest. I am surprised she isn't testing you."

"Dr. Butler wanted to keep everything in the family—the hospital family."

Paula Wheelas laughed. "Yes, we are just one big happy family here at St. Matthew's."

Paula proceeded to give Richard a battery of tests on the various facets of language, starting with visual and verbal memory, vocabulary and syntax, non-literal language, nonverbal aspects of intelligence, visual-spatial organization and finally, verbal intelligence.

Paula hadn't intended to give Rich the complete test for each subsection, but his responses were so rapid that she continued until she had done the entire battery of tests.

"I must say, Mr. Winrock, you have established a new record. I have never given the PALI in less than an hour." Rich had completed it in fifty minutes. Thinking that he had guessed at many of the answers since he had taken so little time, she expected the results to be poor. Quickly placing the correct answer grid on her first answer sheet, she looked stunned. Mr. Winrock had done the entire test with no mistakes. The second, third, fourth and fifth sheets were the same. Checking her answer sheet several times, she shook her head and looked up at Richard, who was smiling at her with a twinkle in his eyes.

"How did I do?"

"I'm sure you know how you did, Mr. Winrock. I can't believe it. As many times as I have used this test, I didn't think I could get one hundred percent in even sixty minutes. You are remarkable. We all need to get shot in the head." Paula was sorry she had said that. It just slipped out.

Richard was enjoying himself. "I guess I can go to the head of the class."

"You certainly may. You are fantastic. I am going to give Dr. Butler a report. I know he will be pleased."

Winrock had not really attended to the details of Paula's questions; he just concentrated on the answers, and they were available to him the instant he needed them. In several cases he had almost started his answer before Paula had completed the question. He hoped that she had not noticed. Paula gathered up her papers and hurried off to deliver the exciting news to Dr. Butler, who should be between surgeries.

Paula found Dr. Butler in the doctors' lounge having coffee. She gave Sam a full account of Rich's astounding results and was confused by his reaction. He seemed almost disgruntled by the news.

She asked, "Isn't that wonderful? I see no evidence of any deficit. In fact, he is the most alert man I have ever tested."

Sam mustered some enthusiasm lest he arouse suspicion that apparently it wasn't there to start. "I thought you would find him as you have, but wanted to confirm my observation."

"Doctor, it is a miracle. I have never seen a gunshot patient who didn't have serious deficits in several cognitive categories."

"Yes, Mr. Winrock is doing remarkably well."

"He says he knows Dr. Parker-McLean. Isn't it a small world?"

Sam wondered if Paula Wheelas knew just how small the world was becoming. It seemed to be closing in on Sam from all sides.

"Yes. He knows Dr. McLean. Mr. McLean is on the board of directors of Mr. Winrock's company."

"How interesting."

Everything was fascinating or interesting to Paula Wheelas. She could hardly contain herself as she left to page Dr. Blanchard, who had agreed to meet her in the cafeteria when she was done. Paula went directly there to review the results of Rich's PALI test to be certain that she had administered it correctly and that the answers were perfect. Taking a table next to the wall visible to the entrance, Paula flipped back and forth through her answer sheets, shaking her head. The test had been designed to determine the level of competency on the various tasks involved, from the seriously impaired to well above the normal level. Some patients would score very poorly in a particular area that reflected damage to a specific part of the brain, yet score relatively normally in other areas. Paula Wheelas doubted that even a normal person would score perfectly at the top of each category as Mr. Winrock had done.   Certainly, Winrock would be in a class by himself.

Tim Blanchard was seated at her table before Paula looked up.

"Oh, hi, Dr. Blanchard. Thank you for meeting me. I wanted to tell you what I have found. I still don't believe it." Paula carefully described her administration of the test and the results. "Mr. Winrock not only doesn't show a deficit, he scored perfectly in every category. I would be surprised if he wasn't restrained by the limits of the test!"

"What do you mean, Paula?"

"Just that the test gets more complex and difficult until it is well beyond the abilities of a normal, highly intelligent person with, let's say, an IQ of 150. Winrock's results are off my chart. He could have an IQ of over 200."

"Maybe that's why they wanted to kidnap him," Dr. Blanchard said and then felt foolish at such an inane statement.

Paula let it pass and went on. "Is it possible for someone to receive a brain injury like Mr. Winrock's and not have *any* intellectual evidence?"

"You tell me. You're the expert."

"Well, I've never heard of it if it has happened before. I think I will check with Dr. McLean and see what she says."

"You mean Dr. Parker-McLean? What does she have to do with this?"

"She developed the test. She may know what Mr. Winrock's scores mean."

"Let's don't identify who the patient is. We are supposed to keep a tight lid on everything concerning Richard Winrock."

"I know. I know."

CHAPTER
LI

The news of the shootout with the terrorists had St. Matthew's Hospital throbbing by Monday evening. Having Richard Winrock in the hospital gave all the staff and employees a special interest in the case. Everyone there seemed to feel as though he or she were part of a drama, giving friends and relatives the inside story at every opportunity.

Richard, the central character, did not enjoy his celebrity status. However, his frame of mind was improving. He was now able to move around in his bed, sit up, dangle his legs over the side and lift his arms through their normal range. He was ready to walk, and Sam told him he should be on his feet this week. Sam had arranged for a prominent young neuropsychologist to enter Rich's case to handle his rehabilitation. Sam realized he was taking an incredible risk exposing Rich to neuropsychology to play the dominant role in his treatment. Sam tried to alert Paula Wheelas of Rich's idiosyncrasies, hoping she would accept Richard as an eccentric and not notice the startling statements that slipped out of his mouth.

Instead of being pleased with the news of the shootout with two terrorists dead and one captured, Rich seemed depressed when Evelyn and Lisa rushed to the hospital Monday evening to bring him the news. He listened with little or no emotion showing.

With excitement in her voice, Evelyn said, "Isn't that tremendous, Richard? Not that someone was killed—just that the police found them and their hideout."

"Yes, I am glad to hear the news."

But Rich was not glad. He had known the entire episode. He was trying harder than ever to monitor his words. He would act as if he knew nothing of current events and attempt to refrain from any commentary on the news. He had indirectly told the police exactly where the terrorists were hiding and so was responsible to a degree for the deaths. Even though they were bad men who tried to kill him, their deaths weighed heavily on him.

Lisa was thrilled to see her father again and cried when he demonstrated his newly acquired mobility. "You are going to be out of here in no time, Dad. ... By the way, Mother tells me that you are better informed in the hospital than we are outside. She says you told her about an announcement on the Soviet SS-20 missiles attributed to the chancellor of Germany. You said that was incorrect. Well, my smart dad, you were right. The morning paper had a big spread about this. I didn't realize you were such a student of European politics. Have you met the former chancellor?"

"Well, yes ... I have. Some years ago. At

297

areception."

"I have to pinch myself sometimes to realize I have such a smart, famous dad."

"Nonsense," he abrogated. "A smart dad wouldn't be lying here like this."

"But how could you have done anything about what has happened?" Lisa questioned.

Richard didn't answer. He had difficulty holding back tears. Lisa went on about the exciting events with the terrorists and the phone calls she had gotten from people since the news broke Monday afternoon. Richard continued to look at his daughter with sad eyes. Lisa had always been his favorite. He regretted not having spent more time with his children during their earlier years. Once they had become teenagers, their lives were involved with their school friends. Rich had devoted himself completely to his work and was usually either out of town or exhausted from his rigorous schedule.

He wanted to take Lisa in his arms and hold her, something he had not done in years. Lisa had asked her parents to come for the christening of their latest grandchild, but, typically, it conflicted with a meeting. It seemed that through the years every important event in Lisa's life except her marriage conflicted with work. If only there was time to spend with Lisa, to get to know her. Richard held her hand tightly as he patiently listened.

When their visit was over, Mrs. Winrock and Lisa left Richard's room, allowing him to rest and think about what he should change in his life.

CHAPTER
LII

Dr. Parker-McLean was busy with a patient when she received a phone call from Dr. Wheelas. Since it was described as an emergency, she took the call. She listened attentively then said, "I have not experienced such results. Nor have I heard of them. Are you sure you gave no clues in your administration?"

Dr. Wheelas was indignant. "Why, Dr. McLean, I have administered the PALI to a dozen patients a month. I know the procedure perfectly. No, that's not it. This patient is extraordinary."

"Apparently. When did you test this patient, and what was the medical problem?"

"I can only tell you it was a gunshot wound, and I just finished the test this morning."

"I see," said Helen McLean, knowing she had guessed correctly as to the identity of the patient. "I would be interested in reviewing the results if you will send me a blind copy."

"Of course. I will be anxious to get your comments," Paula answered with genuine enthusiasm.

This conversation left Dr. McLean preoccupied. She was glad that her counseling session was almost over, as her mind kept drifting back to Rich Winrock. She was certain he was the patient Paula had referred to. Completing her session, she went to her library wall, which was lined with books pertaining to her field, and scanned the titles, hoping to remember which of her books contained discussions of the effects of brain injury on extrasensory perception. Realizing this was not the way to find what she was looking for, she notified her secretary she would be out of the office until after lunch and headed for the Medical Center's Jesse Jones Library, three blocks from her office. She would take a quick lunch at the Doctors' Club on the third floor of the same building after visiting the library.

As she searched, Helen first made a list of all the references that discussed parapsychology and then a list of all the references that she judged discussed the effects of brain injury on the psyche and on ESP. The library was overflowing with books on the subject. There was serious research being conducted on the phenomena of the enhancement of ESP powers after brain trauma.

Helen's field was the assessment of brain damage causing aphasias after stroke or brain injury and the rehabilitation of the patients' language capabilities during their convalescence. She had encountered several cases of patients who experienced perceptions that could not be explained. The last case she remembered was a middle-

301

aged woman who told Helen all about her brain operation and being tested for language impairment. Helen was surprised that anyone of the medical staff would discuss with a patient some of the things this woman related. Helen had inquired about this situation and discovered that to the best of the hospital's knowledge, no one had discussed the actual operation with this patient. Helen had researched the phenomenon, commonly known as an out-of-body experience, and discovered there were literally thousands of cases. Typically, the patients imagined themselves looking down on their operation from the ceiling of the operating room.

There were a number of cases in the literature of unexplained perception being enhanced by injury or trauma to the right side of the temporal lobe of the brain. Knowing Rich had been shot on the right side of his head, Helen hoped she would find the same references she had discovered years earlier on the subject. Taking her long list of references, she went to the second floor and collected over one dozen books that she would scan for some information that would throw light on what she now knew about Rich Winrock. Helen did not believe the information Dr. Butler had passed on to her husband.

She also had difficulty accepting that Rich Winrock had answered all the questions on her **PALI** test accurately. She had intentionally designed the test to exceed human ability as the intelligence portion of her test grew more complex. The answers to the final questions were difficult for anyone to answer, even armed with a calculator, paper and pencil, and an exceptional knowledge of logic, mathematics and physics. The fact that Rich completed the entire battery of tests so quickly was also beyond her belief. Perhaps Paula Wheelas made a mistake in the time or somehow gave a clue to the correct answers.

Helen was anxious to actually see the score sheet, as she was certain that a portion of the non-intelligence-related tasks would be difficult for a person with injury to the right temporal lobe. She usually found that recognition with the left hand was affected. For example, people could not identify a common object held in their left hand while their eyes were closed. There were very few exceptions. Rich had been shot in the right side of his head. The bullet passed out the top of his head, according to the lurid newspaper accounts. How could Rich be able to function not only without any evidence of impairment but at a higher level than she had ever recorded? Knowing Rich made accepting these facts even more difficult. He was a very brilliant executive who was known to handle numbers with great facility, but she had never heard of him being referred to as a genius. Scoring off the scale of her test placed him in an intelligence category she did not know existed.

Helen found five books she wished to study in depth, so she checked them out and headed for the Doctors' Club. As she glided to a prominent table to be seated by a smiling maître d' holding her chair, she saw Paula Wheelas seated at a corner table with an attractive young man. Paula looked up just as Helen was about to sit down. Paula waved, then looked nervously at her luncheon partner, then at Helen and excused herself to come speak to Helen.

"Dr. McLean, how are you?" Not waiting to hear the answer, she continued, "I am so excited about what happened yesterday. I don't know quite what to make of it. Are you going to be in your office this afternoon? I would like to come by and drop the test results off. I would really like your comments."

"My, my. You really are excited," Helen said, smiling warmly at Paula. "Yes, come by."

Paula looked over her shoulder and said, "That is Dr. Tim Blanchard. He is a neurology resident. He's new at St. Matthew's. We are working together on a case."

"He's wondering what has happened to you. Better get back. I'll see you this afternoon."

Helen was glad she had placed her coat over her stack of books, because she did not want Paula to know what she was researching. She settled down to eat soup and a salad for lunch. She wondered whether Paula had any idea that she knew the patient Paula was excited about. Perhaps she should decline the information on ethical grounds. Then again, it was important for her to know what the true upper limits of her test should be. She would solve the problem by arranging to see Rich Winrock herself, if possible. Then, and only then, would she believe all the information she was hearing about him. He was a contradiction to the entire twenty years' experience she had in neuropsychology.

When she arrived at her office, Helen called Bob to give him the news about Rich's test results. "I don't know what you have gotten into, Bob. This young neuropsychologist has just tested Rich with my test, and he has literally destroyed my intelligence scale."

"Just what does that mean in plain old layman's language?" Bob asked.

"Don't pull my leg, darling. You know almost as much about my test as I do."

"Not really, but thanks anyway. What does that mean?"

"It means that Rich could not possibly score perfectly on either the intelligence portion of the test or the non-intelligence portion after serious right brain damage. Do you remember how long it took you to work out the answers to the upper limits of the mathematic portion of the PALI?"

"Yes, vaguely."

"Well, Rich did them all, almost instantaneously, in his head, if in fact he is the patient."

"Incredible."

"It's more than that. It's impossible. At least, it is impossible for him to have figured out the answers. He may have given Paula the answers. I just don't know where he got the answers. Listen, darling, I'll be home about six. Let's eat at the club. I want to study some books I checked out as soon as I finish my last appointment."

"Sounds fine, Helen. Drive carefully on the way

home."

Bob turned off the computer. He needed to think through what his wife had told him and did not want to pursue his evaluation of the hotel project further. Bob was much more inclined to believe information that had no rational explanation or proof than Helen was. He had no doubt that there were extraterrestrial crafts that penetrated Earth's atmosphere from time to time, whereas Helen dismissed flying saucers as fantasy. Bob, more a romantic than Helen, wanted to believe such stories as the Loch Ness Monster and the Abominable Snowman. He kept a library shelf for all such books that were published and followed current reports with interest. Helen had finally taught Bob to refrain from discussing such subjects with others, as she assured him it did not improve his professional image.

Having known Richard Winrock for several years made Winrock's current situation fascinating to Bob. He would review all the books Helen brought home and possibly go to the main branch of the Houston Public Library to look up any other references that might shed some light on the Rich phenomenon.

Bob propped his feet on his desk and tried to understand how Rich could now solve problems in his head that were well beyond his former ability. Obviously, if the facts were accepted, his intelligence had been dramatically improved by being shot in the head. The injury must have altered something in his brain. But what? Helen often bemoaned how truly little the medical profession knew about the actual workings of the brain.

The circuitry had billions of connections, as he remembered. Rich must have lost some tissue from the bullet wound. This, in itself, should cause his brain to lose some of the functions, not gain in power. Suppose the circuitry was altered by the bullet wound such that some functions were improved while others might well be impaired? Bob understood Rich was still in bed, so it was not known what motor deficits he might have as the result of his injury.

As far as the information Rich was receiving, Bob had no explanation of the source. He had heard of people predicting disasters and others knowing where to find bodies that were buried and where killers were hiding. Bob did not doubt that some people had abilities of clairvoyance or that messages were occasionally transmitted by telepathy from one person to another. Rich's case was different. He not only seemed to know what was happening in the present in locations remote from his physical powers of perception, but according to Sam Butler, Rich had made some statements about future events. It would be some time before there could be any verification of Rich's prediction; however, the implications of this kind of information being valid were frightening. Bob would be anxious to review what information Helen would bring home. Bob's thoughts made him too restless to return to his economic studies, so he closed up his office and headed for Memorial Park to run the four-mile course.

CHAPTER
LIII

    Lenora sat in Dr. Nidert's office Tuesday afternoon, twisting the gold bracelet on her wrist. She had had the CT scan earlier that day and had been asked to wait in the doctor's office so he could go over the results with her. She looked around at the office, trying to keep her mind from imagining the worst. She fixated on his degrees and certificates lining the wall behind his desk. Briefly, she regretted again breaking up with Rodrigo, as it would have been nice to have someone with her, but quickly pushed those thoughts away. She was a strong and capable woman. No matter what was wrong, she would get through this.

    Dr. Nidert walked in then, disrupting her thoughts. He walked over to the light board on the wall to the right of his desk and hung up a few different images from the CT scan. He placed the rest of the file on his desk and greeted Lenora, "Good afternoon, Lenora. Sorry to keep you waiting."

    "Let's put aside the niceties, Doctor. What is wrong with me?"

Dr. Nidert pointed at the chart on the light wall. "You see this one here? This is your brain. It seems there is a lesion growing on the right hemisphere of your brain that is pressing on your nervous system. It seems to be what is causing your headaches and occasional loss of function in certain nerves—like what happened with your leg on the different occasions you mentioned. On closer analysis, it appears to be a gliomas tumor."

"A tumor?" Lenora felt like she was going to throw up. This was worse than she imagined. She was going to die. She couldn't die, not yet.

"Yes, Lenora. It appears to be benign, but eighty percent of gliomas tumors become malignant and thus should be surgically removed as soon as possible to prevent any further development. It was good that Rodrigo brought you in when he did. Too often, it is diagnosed after it has already spread to the connective tissues in the brain and is inoperable. You are lucky."

Lenora held onto Dr. Nidert's words. She could breathe again. She knew she should ask a dozen questions, but all she could think was that it was benign for now. After a moment, Dr. Nidert continued.

"I know this is a lot to process; however, I must add that it is in your best interest to get the tumor operated on as soon as possible. I took the liberty of calling a friend of mine, Dr. Samuel Butler." Lenora's eyes snapped up at the mention of Sam Butler. Wasn't he the co-owner of that property she had been trying to acquire for Rodrigo, she wondered.

"He has gained quite a reputation for himself over these last few years as one of the best neurosurgeons in the country. His schedule is very tight, but he moved a few things around to get you in to see him on Thursday at nine o'clock. If you are **OK** with this, I will go ahead and confirm the appointment for you and send over all your lab work," Dr. Nidert said as he sat down at his desk, ready to confirm the appointment.

Lenora was stunned. This was all happening so fast. She knew it was in her best interest to accept, so she did. In two days, she would meet with the neurosurgeon, and soon after she would be in surgery. No matter what she did, Lenora still couldn't seem to get a firm grip back on her life. She prayed yet again that everything would go back to the way it was.

CHAPTER
LIV

The rumor mill at Global's offices was working at full speed. Political alignments in the company were already becoming more evident as the executive staff began to regroup to take advantage of the disruption caused by Richard's absence.

Dan London passed Rena's desk in the outer office, and he said in a low mumble without turning his head, "Come on in and close the door."

Rena followed him silently, and they sat facing each other near the windows.

"What have you heard about Winrock?"

Rena's knees almost touched his as she leaned forward to give him an account of what her aunt had told her. "My aunt says that Mr. Winrock said something to his wife that upset her. Something about their grandson's arm. Got broken. Richard knew all about it, but Mrs. Winrock had just heard herself. A friend of my aunt's was on duty with Winrock when this happened, and she filled her in."

"Anything else?"

"Oh yes, Butler did have a session with Winrock last night with the door closed. He came out of Winrock's room in a state of shock. No one knew why then, but Mr. Winrock is recovering very rapidly, I understand, and may be getting out of bed soon if there is no serious paralysis," Rena concluded.

"He is one tough bugger. He astounds me," Dan said with a frown.

"He astounds everyone at St. Matthew," Rena added.

"Uh hum."

"I mean with the things he says," Rena clarified.

"For example?"

"There was a new nurse on the floor yesterday. Winrock could not possibly have known about her, much less her name. She went in to take his blood pressure and pulse or something. Found him half asleep. She says he mumbled under his breath, 'Come in, Mary,' or whatever her name was, without opening his eyes."

"So what did they make of that? It doesn't sound like such a big deal."

"Well, the nurse was really shook up. She wouldn't go back into his room. Apparently, she is superstitious. Thought Richard was some kind of wizard. Had another nurse check on him the rest of her shift."

312

Dan clenched his jaws and said slowly, almost to himself, "That doesn't sound like Richard." Then he said, "Well, thanks, Rena. Tell your aunt to keep her eyes and ears open. Something is going on at that hospital—something strange."

"She will. Don't worry. She'll do anything for me." Rena gave Dan London a knowing smile and went back to her desk.

Dan sat silently in his office for an extended period, turning over the information he had gotten. He must plant the seed with Rivers Kern that Richard is now mentally incompetent to run a large corporation. He thought this may not be too difficult to sell in view of the nature of Richard's injury. Dan would visit with Rivers on other business and drop some damaging comments about Richard under the guise of concern for their president.

Having formulated a strategy, Dan called Andrew Flood rather than visiting the senior vice-president's office down the hall. "Listen to me, Andy. I just got another report on Richard. He is talking now and saying some very strange things. Has people puzzled at the hospital."

"Where did you get this crap?" Andrew answered, impatient at having been disturbed.

"It may not be crap. One of the nurses who cares for Richard told someone he is acting strangely."

"If I was shot in the head, I'm sure I would be acting strangely."

"I'm not sure what all this means yet. But there

may be something to it. One of the nurses refuses to go in his room. He told her something crazy."

"How are you getting hold of this information?"

"Indirectly. From a reliable source."

"I won't comment on that statement."

"What I mean is, I think the information is an accurate assessment of what is observed by a reliable person, this nurse, and she reports what she sees to someone who reports it to me."

"You have quite a network set up. What are you getting at, Dan?"

"If what I hear is true, Richard may have had irreparable damage to his brain that could seriously affect him—certainly his ability to run the company—permanently. I don't think Rivers knows about this yet."

"For Christ's sake, Dan. The man has had only a matter of days to recover, and I read and hear he has made a miraculous recovery. Miraculous!"

"That's just the point. You are not supposed to be so alert and verbal hours after a massive brain surgery."

"Who says so?"

"Well, the doctors at the hospital."

"You said some nurse was feeding you all this crap."

"She's not loose-lipped. She is a serious, experienced registered nurse."

"Get back to the point, Dan."

"Look, let's just say that there is something going on over there we don't know about that may affect the company's future."

"I could apply that statement to nearly everything. Dan, are you sure you didn't get hit in the head during the kidnapping attempt?"

"Be serious for a moment, Andy."

"I'm trying."

"I haven't told you everything, but Richard has said some strange things that have the hospital staff puzzled. Not me, a layman, the medical staff."

"It wouldn't be hard to believe that someone shot in the brain at point-blank range might say something strange."

"For Christ's sake, Andy. I'm trying to tell you that something is wrong with Richard. Don't you understand? One floor nurse won't even go in his room to take his temperature."

"So what do you suggest?"

"I don't suggest a damn thing. I thought you would want to know our leader has lost a couple of cards from his deck. Rivers will have to replace him as soon as he is sure about this."

Both men on opposite ends of the phone connection had more than an electric communication in common. They both wanted Richard's job with Global—knowing they could never achieve a presidency anywhere else. The pursuit of this objective would be deadly earnest for both of them.

Andy responded casually, "Thanks, Dan. I have to go. I have a company to run."

CHAPTER
LV

Rivers Kern arrived early outside Richard Winrock's room and struck up a conversation with the uniformed officer on duty. The officer was uneasy about the conversation and advised Mr. Kern he would need a special pass to see Mr. Winrock.

"I am sure Dr. Butler has arranged that," he said and proceeded to pace up and down in front of the door. At one o'clock sharp, Sam Butler appeared holding a pass for Rivers Kern.

They both entered Rich's room, excusing the nurse during their visit. Rivers gave Rich the best hug he could under the circumstances and sat beside the bed. "It is good to see those bright eyes open, Richard."

"Thank you, Rivers. Glad you could come."

"Hell, this is the first time I have been allowed to visit with you. You have a warden for a doctor," he joked.

Sam didn't bother explaining his no visitors policy; he just smiled at Rich.

"I hear you are doing just great. What I want to know is when you are going to get out of this place," Rivers said with a wry smile.

Rich turned his eyes to Sam for an answer.

"He will be with us for a while, although he is making medical history with his recovery," Sam said.

"At the rate he's improving, how long do you estimate it will take to return Rich Winrock to his original condition?" Rivers asked as if discussing a car repair.

"That is hard to say. We will all know more after a series of tests is completed.

"I will be anxious to hear from you, Doctor."

Having completed his role, Sam left the two men alone and told the duty nurse who was waiting outside not to enter the room until Mr. Kern had left, unless he stayed beyond the agreed time of thirty minutes.

Rivers watched the door close then turned to Rich and said, "You don't know how glad I am to see you and talk to you, my dear friend. It looked pretty bad, you know."

"Yes, I know, Rivers. Thanks for bringing Evelyn over the night I was shot."

"Oh, she told you?"

Rich did not want to lie, so he grunted something that sounded affirmative.

318

Rivers gave Rich a briefing of the overall company activities and was stunned when Rich half interrupted saying, "Rivers, the bidding will be too heavy on Blocks 420 thru 430. The sand is lensing out in this area. Concentrate on 520 through 535—just off Point Conception. The sands should be over one thousand feet thick there. You can probably get the whole fifteen blocks for eighty million."

"Rich, you want us to pass up the 400 blocks?"

"Yes. I know all the big boys are going after them, but they have missed the boat. The big stuff is toward Point Conception."

"I wish I had been involved in our offshore activities more. You know that is not my cup of tea," Rivers said apologetically.

"Nor is it Dan London's double martini."

"Now, Rich, don't get your blood pressure up," Rivers said, trying to soothe Rich.

Rich's voice was getting stronger as he narrowed his eyes and said, "Rivers, listen closely. Don't pay any attention to all the misinformation you get from Dan. Stick to the plan that I developed for the next three years. I have not disclosed all the details of it, only the major points. Linda has the complete program in my safe."

"What have I not seen?"

"The real details. I didn't want to give Dan too much ammunition to use against me."

"I hear what **Dan** is saying, but what is really on his mind? I can't figure him out, **Rich**."

"I hesitate to tell you, **Rivers**, but **Dan** is against the offshore program because he wants our exploration and drilling dollars spent on the onshore program."

"He never has been enthusiastic about our offshore activity, even when we got the big discovery in Galveston Bay."

"**Rivers**, I think **Dan** is too involved with our onshore drilling contractors. You know I have personally handled our offshore commitments."

"What precisely do you mean by his being too involved?"

"I mean he is in bed with several of the drillers. They have him in their pocket."

"**Rich**, those are strong accusations. I hope you are wrong."

"I hope I am too, but I am not."

"Is he being paid off?"

"I don't know if he is getting money," **Rich** said, already knowing **Dan** received ten thousand dollars a month from one contractor, "but he is getting other things that cost a lot of money—like trips to Vegas, hunting trips to Mexico—that sort of thing."

"We have all done that sort of thing, **Rich**."

"Not to the same extent. Dan is under obligations that cloud his judgment."

"Damn, I am sorry to hear that. Are you sure about this? What kind of proof do you have?" Rivers asked.

"Rivers, it is no secret how many pleasure trips he makes. Just match up his trips with his expense accounts. Someone is spending a lot of money on Dan, and it isn't the company."

"Well, I have reviewed our drilling contracts, and we are getting very competitive rates from our two major drilling companies."

Rich decided to drop the subject, knowing Rivers was beginning to question whether Rich was imagining problems with Dan. Rich had never had a similar discussion about a Global executive. Rich realized Rivers did not want to hear one of his top people was being bought off. Rivers had been guilty of similar behavior in his earlier career.

"I'm sorry I brought up Dan's relationship with the contractors, Rivers. Let's drop that subject. I do want you to prepare to bid the 520 blocks."

"Does Linda have the information to back up your recommendation?"

"Well, no. I didn't want that in the file."

Actually, Rich had arranged to participate with two major oil companies in the 400 blocks to reduce the bidding risk and share the exploration and drilling costs.

He was now certain that he had a better course of action available, one that could mean several billion dollars for Global. This information came to him in the same mysterious way that other information concerning the hospital and the terrorists did. Rich did not think through the ethics of using this information for the benefit of his company. He just decided impulsively to tell Rivers of his plans.

"Where is the information on the 520 blocks that has you so confident?"

"It's not in the file as such. The basic seismic work we had done on the whole area is there."

"Rich, I hope you don't expect me to gamble eighty million dollars on your private analysis of some basic data when you have been urging me for months to approve your joint venture plans for the 400 blocks. We have spent a lot of money getting things set up as you wanted them."

"Tell you what, Rivers. Get Andrew Steadman, our geologist, over here with his maps, and I'll educate him. He will be able to convince you. I'm sure."

"I'm not sure Dr. Butler is going to let you do anything like that, Rich."

Rich closed his eyes and clenched his jaw. He knew he would have grave difficulties changing his company's plans to take advantage of the enormous oil reserves offered by the government in the 500-block area off the California coast.

Rich knew Rivers was losing confidence in his

rationality. If Rivers viewed Rich's suggestion as erratic and reckless, that could cause the company serious problems. The joint venture was already formed and prepared to bid on the offshore properties. Withdrawing at this late date would be disastrous for Global's relationship with the two other oil companies. Also, by bidding alone, Global would have no financial support in the exploration and drilling program. The 500-block acreage was in deeper water and therefore more costly to develop.

Rivers was shocked at Rich's behavior. What I have been hearing must have some substance, he thought as he looked down at his fallen president. He knew they would have to keep a close watch on Rich from then on. Rivers left hurriedly, badly shaken.

CHAPTER
LVI

When Kern returned from the hospital after visiting Richard Winrock, he was visibly upset. He went directly into his office without speaking to anyone, closed his door and called Sam Butler. Normally, he had his secretary place his calls, but this one he made himself, and his secretary noticed he was on the line for an extended period. The time he spent on the phone was waiting while the hospital attempted to find Dr. Butler, who was notorious for being out of touch. He finally left an urgent message.

Dan London had an early afternoon meeting scheduled with Rivers, but it was cancelled when Rivers left the building. Dan's secretary had received a call from her aunt, the nurse in the hospital, to advise him that Rivers had shown up outside Rich's room. She called back when everyone at hand noticed how upset Kern was when he left his meeting with Rich. The nurse concluded that Kern must have been upset by their conversation, as Rich was still making historic medical progress. Rena gleefully relayed this to Dan. Armed with this information, Dan rescheduled his meeting to take place immediately upon Rivers's return. Dan was in the process of preparing a presentation to the executive committee on some unresolved questions in the next year's budget and planned to use this as pretense to touch on the subject of the offshore lease acquisition and exploration budget with Rivers when they met.

Walking in with a handful of papers, Dan asked, "Are you all right, Rivers? You don't look yourself."

"I'm fine. Just a little stressed."

"Is there something I can do?"

"No. This problem may be in the Lord's hands."

"What problem?"

Rivers shook his head then stood up and paced around his huge office before answering.

"I am worried about Rich."

"Why? What has happened? Is he having problems?"

"No, nothing like that. He is recovering remarkably. Possibly too remarkably."

"What do you mean, Rivers?"

"I shouldn't let this upset me. Let's drop it. What did you want to discuss?"

"Has Rich upset you, Rivers?" Dan bore in, seeing an opening.

"Yes, he has. I love the guy, but I can't understand

him anymore. I used to agree with everything he wanted to do."

"What's he want to do this time?"

Rivers detected a dig in the inflection of Dan's voice this time. He couldn't hurt Rich intentionally and certainly didn't want to give Rich's major antagonist ammunition while Rich was on his back, helpless, with a hole in his head.

Rivers sidestepped Dan's further questions and finally ended the meeting prematurely from Dan's point of view. Dan had not found out what he was seeking on either the budget or Rich.

Dan left looking grave on the outside but delighted on the inside. He now knew what he had been hearing was valid. Rich was saying things that were reflecting on his sanity or at least his state of mental recovery.

Dan could now start a bona fide rumor campaign that would sweep the company in a matter of days. He realized that the executive vice-president of a major oil company should be above such actions, but Dan had worked his way up through the ranks more by destroying the competition than outdistancing them with performance.

Dan had met his match with Rich and had decided long ago to bide his time until the right opportunity came. Now was his chance to be president. He would play his cards for all they were worth—but carefully. Rivers Kern would not tolerate any dirty tricks. Dan would only have to drop innocent-sounding remarks to just a few people in the company, and they would disseminate the news in all directions. Rena would also be a big help, as she would start the rumors through the secretarial and office service channels.

Rich will never return to this company as president, Dan thought to himself.

Rivers Kern spent the afternoon reviewing information on the forthcoming offshore bidding situation. When he had a strong grasp of it, he called in the company's bidding plans. Rivers was shocked to learn that the company had given only casual consideration to the blocks Rich was recommending. Actually, Steadman felt those blocks might be worthless and had heard by the grapevine that few if any of the companies were interested in them. Rivers asked about BMY Oil. Steadman verified that BMY had done extensive offshore seismic on this area, but he had no information on the results.

"Is there a chance the sand formation could go up, and the oil-bearing sands could thicken in this area?"

"There is always that possibility, but my judgment would indicate the opposite, Mr. Kern."

"That's fine. Thank you, Andrew." Rivers cut their discussion short, leaving Andrew Steadman puzzled.

CHAPTER
LVII

Sam's reverie was broken by his pager, which apparently had been repeated a number of times, as usual. He picked up the phone in the lounge, announced who he was and began talking to Rivers Kern.

"Dr. Butler, I had a long visit with Rich Winrock after you left, and I am worried about him."

"What seems to be the problem?"

Rivers did not want to disclose what was on his mind, but he had decided it was imperative that Rich be insulated from company activities. Rivers was devastated by Rich's suggestions on the offshore lease. After reviewing the secret report and discussing Rich's suggestion with Global's top geologist, he decided Rich was having mental problems and might pose a dangerous threat to Global's future if he began to influence Global's activities.

"Well, Dr. Butler, Rich got excited discussing company business with me, and some of the things he said didn't make sense to me. I have known him for years, and he is acting strange. I don't understand. I thought he was doing so well."

"Mr. Kern, it is not uncommon for a patient who has suffered serious brain trauma to act strangely—change his personality. Most frequently, patients with Rich's general type of injury become more aggressive, more assertive. This sometimes lasts for six months, and then they usually go through a quiet, withdrawn period, and finally return basically to their original self—unless, of course, they have sustained a serious deficit of some kind from the injury."

River's voice began to tense. "I am worried about Rich trying to act as president of Global in the state he is in. I want you to quarantine him if you can—you know, keep people away from him until he comes around. Can you do that?"

"I can maintain the present restriction of visitation by company people. You feel he is getting too involved. He needs rest, not stress."

"I definitely do, Doctor."

"Very well. I will make certain that no one other than his doctors, his family and you can see him for the present. Oh yes, and the detective, Solis."

"Excellent, Doctor, thank you."

Sam rubbed his eyes as he wondered what Rich was up to this time. Sam thought he had better go see Rich right away to get his version of what had just happened with Rivers. Sam was shocked by his own thoughts as he realized he accepted the fact that Rich would know all about the phone call.

Arriving at Rich's room, Sam introduced himself to the patrolman guarding the room and handed him his special identification. Sam had not seen this young officer here and received a careful scrutiny. As he entered Rich's room, he could see Rich smiling.

"OK, Mr. Winrock, what is going on?"

Rich looked from Sam to the nurse and back in obvious fashion to convey to Sam that he would not discuss anything until his attendant nurse had left the room. Sam got the message and excused the nurse, who was glad to have respite from her sitting.

Rich, now sitting up, turned his head to face Sam, who sat next to his bed, and said quizzically, "Sam, I am interested in how you interpret Rivers's phone call."

"You *do* know, right?" countered Sam.

"Of course, why do you ask? Tell me."

"I haven't had much time to think about it, Rich. He is upset with your concern over some business activity he feels you should not be trying to manage. That is the way he came across to me. What are you up to?"

"Sam, I am about to explode over what is happening."

"Let's calm down, Rich. You are not supposed to have any contact with your company business. Don't you know that is not good for your recovery?"

"Yes, I know. I merely am trying to guide Rivers Kern in some highly important business I was handling and he now is handling."

"What kind of business?"

"It is not important."

"The hell it isn't. Let's have it. If I am going to get you back on your feet, I need your complete cooperation."

"Well, Sam, I am trying to ... No, Sam, I had better leave you out of this."

"Why?"

"What I was going to tell you is too heavy a burden to give you. You have enough on your shoulders already."

"Don't you worry about me. Come on."

"Actually, I was trying to change some plans I'd developed concerning our exploration program."

"Why do you want to do that?"

"I have had a change of heart. Want to change the focus of our plans."

"What does that mean?"

"Just that."

"Why do you want to make the changes?"

"The revisions would be incredibly more profitable

to the company."

"When did you decide to recommend the revisions?"

"I don't know."

"Last month?"

"Possibly."

"You didn't talk to Kern about this until yesterday?"

"No."

Sam wrinkled his brow, rubbed his eyes for a long time and then said in a fatherly tone, "Rich, you are not using your ESP to guide your company, are you?"

"Why would you ask that?"

"Because I suspect that is exactly what you are trying to do."

"Sam, you don't understand."

"Don't I? I think I do. Is that it?"

"Not exactly."

"Come now, Rich. Level with me."

"I have merely decided to change the location of our area of interest in our program."

"But why?"

"It is a better area."

"How do you know?"

"I know. I just know."

"But how?"

"What is wrong with using the best information available?" Rich said, realizing for the first time what he had been doing.

"Rich, I don't think there is a precedent for what I think is happening, but I suspect my stockbroker would consider you an insider trading on inside information."

"You know very well that concept doesn't apply. I am not buying or selling my own stock."

"You are using information no one else has to make a 'highly important' decision, aren't you?"

"The data's all out there for anyone to obtain."

"What data?"

"The offshore tract."

"So that's it. You know which tract to acquire, Rich." Sam looked at Rich long and hard.

"What do you expect me to do? Lie here and let Rivers bid the wrong tract?"

"You are sure you know which tract he should bid?"

"Yes."

"You have known this only since your injury?"

"Well yes, actually."

"Rich, I don't know what to tell you, but I am frightened by what you are telling me. Is this really an important decision?"

"Ownership of the right tract will be worth over a billion dollars."

"Rich, I am sorry you have told me this. I have now become an insider. Now, I cannot buy your stock, not morally. Do you realize the significance of what you are telling me?"

"I think so."

"How did Rivers react to your suggestion, as if I didn't know?"

"He didn't buy it. He was angry with me for muddying up the waters. I had a whole plan structured for joint venturing another tract altogether."

"Is your original recommendation good?"

"Oh, yes, there is lots of oil in that area, but not nearly the quantity as in the second tract."

"Rich, I think you should let nature take its course. It frightens me to think you have insights that are worth a billion dollars. God, man!" Sam began to develop a deep-seated fear.

"I understand what you mean," Rich said apologetically, "but I can't lie here and let someone else get that property. The only other bidder will be BMY Oil of El Seguido, California."

"When is this all to take place?" Sam asked.

"In three weeks."

"And you know who is bidding and what they are bidding?"

"I think so. I haven't tested my knowledge to that extent, but everything else I know has proved to be true. Wish you would let me see the newspapers."

Sam closed his eyes and put his head in his hands. He remained silent for a full minute, trying to think through what he should say to Rich. His mind was going blank. He was stiff with fear. His patient was receiving information that had overwhelming importance from some mysterious source. If Rich knew information of this kind, he was both an unbelievable asset to the United States and possibly a devastating threat if the information he was receiving fell into the wrong hands.

Sam had been trying to dismiss, as a bad dream, the entire business of Rich's clairvoyance since it occurred. He hoped that a chemical imbalance in Rich's system or some electrolyte distribution following his injury was causing this strange reaction, and it would go away as his recovery improved. Sam could not completely admit to himself that the whole incident was real, that Rich actually seemed to know everything. Sam would be ridiculed by his medical colleagues if he so much as hinted such a phenomenon was possible. Yet here it was, and Sam seemed to be getting caught up in a most significant occurrence in the business world—the bidding of large offshore tracts—where hundreds of millions would be spent and billions could be earned over a period of time.

He could not, in good conscience, let Rich use this mysterious information for personal and company gain, yet how could he stop him if Rich truly knew everything— everything he wished to know. Sam noticed that Rich had been registering a higher blood pressure since his conversation with Rivers Kern. The pressure of the considerations he was wrestling with could easily kill him. Sam must appeal to Rich's ethics, somehow.

"Rich," Sam said slowly, "this whole situation is completely beyond my knowledge of medicine and equally beyond my judgment of ethics. How can you take advantage of information you are receiving through some freak set of circumstances to benefit yourself and your company? There must be a reason you have these insights into events you focus on. I am quite sure the reason isn't to make Rich or Global rich. You couldn't believe that, could you?"

Rich stared at Sam. Tears welled up in his eyes and ran down both cheeks. "Forgive me, Sam. My instinct is so strong to do what is best for my company, not myself, I hadn't considered what I was doing. My God, what is going to happen to me? I can't live with what I am going through. Can you imagine what it is like to know whatever I wish to know? I have the feeling I am somehow locked into something that is controlling me. Sam, using what I know was sort of a release for me. I felt good about it. Now you make me ashamed."

Rich looked up at Sam with the eyes of a terrified child and said, "I'm sorry, Sam."

"Forget it, Rich. You are putting yourself under a tremendous strain. I should never have let Rivers Kern see you. I will see that no one else gets you upset until you have recovered more completely. My God, man, we haven't even started your assessment and rehabilitation program, and you want to take the helm of a multibillion-dollar vessel."

"Things are not easy for me, Sam. I lie here, and what can I do but think? This flow of unwanted information floods my consciousness constantly. I can't turn it off when I am awake. No one would consider me sane in my present state. What will happen to me?"

"You will get better as your body chemistry stabilizes—as you get stronger."

"I will accept that for now, Sam. I am also frightened. Give me something so I can get some sleep. Please."

"Of course. I will order it immediately."

"Oh, and Sam? Make sure to allow my old friend Bud Hinton to visit. I get the feeling he will be stopping by, and I know what Rivers said about quarantine. You have to make an exception for him. He means no harm." Rich closed his eyes and turned his head away, not accepting no for an answer.

Sam left the room and motioned the nurse to follow him to the nurses' station so he could order a sedative for

Rich and make the allowance for this Bud Hinton. He just hoped there wouldn't be any backlash from Rivers Kern if he found out.

Sam did not want to lower Rich's blood pressure through medication just yet, as its elevation could signify a need for increased blood supply to the brain. Sam was thinking that his patient's brain, which has an autoregulation mechanism, may be manifesting symptoms of a chemical or neurogenic change that he should not override with medication unless his blood pressure became elevated. The next time they talked, Sam wanted to remember to question Rich more specifically about the form of the information he was receiving, whether he was getting whole concepts of information and in what detail. Could Rich somehow be hypersensitive to brain waves of others, thus picking up signals that were normally not detected or decoded?

Sam Butler finished his grand rounds and stopped by the doctors' lounge for coffee and relaxation.

Another doctor in the lounge called out to him, "Sam, you had a call from Dr. Nidert. His number is on the bulletin board. He probably called your office, too."

"He must need to talk to me right away, or he wouldn't have tried so hard to reach me." Sam turned to the messenger and said, "Thank you."

"Jim, how are you? It's been a long time."

"I'm fine Sam. But I have a patient in my office I would like to refer to you. Her name is Lenora French."

"I know of her, and I believe she's the realtor who is doing some land sales work for Bob McLean and me. What's her problem?"

"She has a small tumor in the right hemisphere of her brain. Her symptoms have been headaches, lack of balance and at certain times, a generalized feeling of weakness."

"What do her studies show?"

"They have done the lab work, X-rays and CT scan. I would like you to see her as soon as possible."

"My schedule is full, but if you feel this is urgent, I can make time Thursday, about nine o'clock, and make time for the surgery later the same day."

"Thanks, Sam."

"You're very welcome. Have your nurse send the lab and test results to my office."

CHAPTER
LVIII

At nine o'clock in the morning on Thursday, the nurse brought Lenora French into one of the examining rooms to check her vital signs, weigh her and take a detailed history of her problems.

When she finished, the nurse said, "The doctor will be in shortly."

While she waited, Lenora began nervously twisting her gold bracelet on her wrist. She looked around the office to keep her mind from imagining the worst. The certificates attested to the competency of the doctor who was going to help her, his university background, medical school, hospitals where he practiced as an intern and did his residency. Last, she saw the certificates of awards and honors, which were numerous. The ones she looked at last were the "Top Doc" honors for the past two years.

When the doctor finally walked in, she had calmed down somewhat. What she saw was a tall, handsome fifty-year-old with tousled sandy hair and a twinkle in his eye.

His first words were, "I know you by reputation,

and now I know you in person. What can I do for you?"

"Dr. Nidert says I have a small tumor between the frontal and parietal lobes of the right hemisphere of my brain, and you are the best in the country to take care of it."

"Well, I must say, 'country' is an exaggeration," he paused and said with a smile, "a slight exaggeration." Sam continued, "I have looked over your test reports and concur with Dr. Nidert. You have a small gliomas tumor that needs to be excised. We see these kinds of tumors fairly often in our work, and taking them out is a relatively easy task. Of course, we cannot tell yet how deep it is nor if it is malignant or benign."

When she heard the word *tumor*, Lenora felt as she had in Dr. Nidert's office. She thought she was going to throw up. "I can't die yet," she said halfway aloud.

Sam perceived her concern and tried to calm her by saying, "I know this is a lot to process all at once, but let's talk about what it entails. Let's start with your questions."

"How serious an operation is it?"

"Most brain tumors are serious, more or less so for some tumors than others. Because of that, we must think positively about the entire process. You see, some tumors are superficial, others are deep; some are malignant, and others are benign. Most benign tumors grow slowly and do not invade the surrounding tissue. This is the kind of tumor we hope for."

"Will you cut or shave my hair?"

"We will probably shave at least some of your hair. We might put a good-sized patch on your head to cover where the incision is. If you want, it might be easier to have your entire head shaved; you will then want to wear a wig or scarf. Your head may be bandaged."

"Will I still have headaches?"

"Probably not. Usually the pressure of the tumor causes the pain. You will need someone to take care of you and take you home once you are discharged in a few days. Do you have anyone who can come?" Sam asked.

Lenora took a moment to think and said, "My mother is too far away." She paused, closing her eyes and rubbing her eyes. "My brother can't." Lenora paused again as she remembered someone closer. Someone who would be perfect. "I can call my sister to come for me," Lenora said as she looked up at him with a smile, "and she is a nun."

"She will be perfect," Sam replied with a twinkle in his eye. "We will schedule the surgery for tomorrow."

"Thank you, Dr. Butler."

CHAPTER
LIX

The hospital door opened slowly. A head came in slowly, blocked from view by a large spray of flowers, followed by a large body. Bud said in his big-boy manner, "Can I come in?"

Richard, with a big smile across his face, called out, "Yes, of course. Am I glad to see you, Buddy boy."

"I would have come sooner but was put off every time I called."

"I know. But I think that my improvement has been quicker than expected. In fact, Sam Butler is talking about discharge." He added in a half-whisper, "There is a board meeting of Global in a week, and I plan to be there."

"Well, I have some good news." Bud's face became animated as he began to tell Richard what was happening at the refinery. "The pilot test has been completed, and it is a big success. The new piece of equipment has allowed us to increase production to an unprecedented level, 25% more than usual." Bud's eyes danced as he saw the look of excitement on his boss's face.

"What wonderful news, Bud. We now have a weapon that will take us to the top."

"And how!"

"Bud, were you able to find out about the sabotage?"

Now Bud was even more pleased. "Yes, we found him, a flunky of some of your board members who was trying to make the company look bad so that the stock would go down temporarily, and they could buy additional stock cheaply and then realize a great profit themselves when the stock went back up."

"Do you have the names?" Richard asked, knowing already who did it.

"I do. But I think it is better to come from the culprits themselves who will be at your board meeting. Either they confess, or we will bring criminal charges, and the whole city will know."

"You really are the bearer of good news. And it seems as if the two events had nothing to do with each other. The internal one at the refinery and the external a function of greedy countries who wanted to capitalize on the work of others, and the price of kidnapping and even death. I thank God the event took a turn in our favor, and I survived." As Bud got up to go, Richard said, "Bud, you deserve a vacation. Why don't you take a few days off?"

"I plan to, but I have to give time to the boys at the refinery, you know, to blow off, at least those who worked overtime. I am going to stagger the off-days so that the

344

refinery keeps going at full tilt."

"And how about yourself?"

"When my time comes, Patty and I will take off to our place on the island, where we will rest, watch the games and drink beer. Just sitting on the porch in a lounge chair and letting the cool morning breeze sway us into sleep is enough for me."

As soon as Bud left the room, he began to whistle Charlie Rich's "Sometimes at the End of the Day" quietly. Humming and whistling as he took long steps down the hospital corridor, he waved to nurses and got smiles in return. With a flourish reminiscent of John Wayne, he reached the hospital entrance, and as he went through the door, he let out in a loud baritone voice, "I'm going to back it on up, turn it around, and take it on home."

CHAPTER
LX

A few days later, Dan London went to the Coronado Club to meet Andrew Flood. Dan had become uneasy about discussing private and confidential matters in his office. He had frequently looked for a listening device but hadn't found one. Somehow, he had the instinct his conversations were being monitored. He must be careful. Rivers Kern would not hesitate to fire him if Rivers knew what he was planning.

Andrew Flood was four years older than Richard Winrock, had seniority and had been considered for president when Kern selected Winrock. At the time, Flood stated privately he would not tolerate this treatment, but was unable to find a job equal to the one he had. He decided to wait for an opportunity. When Dan London became executive vice-president to fill the vacancy a retiring executive created, Andrew Flood again privately threatened to quit, but decided otherwise. Dan had never openly solicited Flood's support in corporate politics, but he felt the time was now ripe. Mutual disappointment caused by Richard Winrock would make Andrew and Dan allies, Dan reasoned.

With his angular features and tall, thin frame, Andrew Flood was a distinguished-looking man, although he looked older than sixty-four. He drifted into the lounge area of the Coronado Club, uneasy about the meeting he had agreed to. He did not trust Dan London and would avoid expressing any opinions or feelings that London or others could use against him.

Seeing Flood across the room, Dan motioned to Andrew to join him in a corner, away from the groups that had gathered.

"What's this all about, Dan?" He cocked his head to look over his metal-rimmed glasses as he sat down.

"What would you like to drink, Andy?"

"Bourbon and water. You know what I drink."

"Of course." With the mannerisms of a reigning monarch, Dan motioned to a waiter nearby.

Once Andrew Flood had sipped on his drink and commented on the weather, Dan said, "Andy, what do you think Richard's chances are for returning to Global?"

"You would know that better than I."

"I just wanted your opinion."

"I can't say, Dan. I don't really know how he's doing other than the rumors around the office and what I hear on the news."

"It's still too early to tell what effect the bullet will have on his brain," Dan said confidently. He continued,

"Andy, I don't see how Richard can possibly walk away from this with a full deck. The bullet went clean through his head and came out the top. We don't have that much extra gray stuff up there."

"Speak for yourself, Dan."

Dan was getting angry at Andrew for not taking him seriously. "What happens to that man has a hell of a lot to do with our future. Don't you know that?"

"Of course I know that. Discussing it in the Coronado Club doesn't help that future much, does it, Dan?"

"It may very well do just that. I don't want to sit back and let Rivers Kern screw up our company while Richard recovers or doesn't recover."

"Have you forgotten? Rivers owns this company. He can do whatever he damn well pleases."

"That's just the point. Rivers was not big on the offshore play when he was at the helm. He went after domestic reserves."

"He found one hell of a lot of them, too."

"Of course he did. But he has been out of touch for years. Rivers has told me on several occasions, after a few toddies, that he didn't much like offshore drilling and production. He seemed to think the wells are too vulnerable to tampering or sabotage. There are structures worth one hundred million dollars out there—unmanned."

"I don't know of any cases of sabotage offshore. Do you?" Andrew said, keeping his eyes on the new arrivals.

"There have been some blowouts and fires that have never been explained. Who knows what some crazed bastard will do? You can't discount the possibility. Look what happened to Richard."

"Dan, we don't keep guards on our domestic wells and tank batteries, either. It's much easier to drive by in a pickup and do some damage than climb onto an offshore structure from a boat and risk getting your ass blown up in the process."

"Well, I'm just telling you that Rivers wasn't as sold on offshore as Richard is. You know how I feel. I thought you were more inclined to onshore."

"I hear you, Dan, but don't forget Richard got us into the North Sea play, and that interest contributes twenty-five percent of our total gross revenue every year."

"That egghead has a horseshoe up his ass. Just dumb luck."

"Dan, you better tone that talk down, or you may get a creosote and soda on your next round."

"OK, OK. What I am trying to say is Rivers has a basic dislike for offshore. We should use that knowledge to talk him out of forging ahead on Richard's program. Hell, we have the biggest exploration budget in the company's history facing us—two hundred million dollars—and our fearless leader is flat on his ass with a hole in his head."

349

"It doesn't sound like you have lost much sleep over Richard's condition."

"I am sorry he was hurt, but I'm not sorry he is out of the company."

"Don't sell him short, Dan. Rivers loves the guy. He will keep the slot open indefinitely if he thinks Richard will recover."

"That's the point, Andy. In the meantime, we need to steer the company away from Richard's program. We haven't had an opportunity like this in years."

"What's the real purpose of your little campaign, Dan?"

"It can save the company from a dangerous expenditure at this time." Dan's voice was indurated, tense.

"I see. Dan, suppose you tell me what this campaign is going to do for me." Flood did not take his eyes off Dan as he spoke slowly and deliberately.

Dan began to realize he was talking to someone who resented him as much as they both resented Richard for the same reason.

Avoiding Andrew's question, Dan continued, "Rivers has to rely on us for advice and counsel. I had hoped we thought alike on this issue and could steer him away from the crevice."

"Frankly, I don't agree with Richard either on this

issue, but I am not willing to put my job on the line over it. Rivers knows what is at stake. Since Rivers owns the majority of this company, he can strike out on any program he chooses to increase oil production. Remember, it ultimately becomes my responsibility to produce whatever we find. I'm going to go along with old Rivers. Why should I fight it? I don't have but ten thousand shares of Global. Not enough to make any difference to me at this stage."

"I understand your position, Andy. Let's drop the subject and have another drink."

"Now you're making sense, Dan. Andrew jiggled his glass and looked around for a waiter to refill it.

Apparently, the time was not ripe for a move to change in Andrew's eyes. Dan hoped he had not hurt his own position by sharing his aspirations with Andrew. Dan knew that he would need to tread softly in the weeks ahead.

The day after Dan's discussion with Andrew, the board members of Global received an email from their chairman, Rivers Kern, in which he stated the following:

Board Members of Global Oil and Exploration Company:

Our president has suffered a severe blow that has incapacitated him for over a week. Before he was shot, he communicated to me his evaluation of the possible area for placing our development and expansion money. Richard

Winrock, during his presidency at Global, has provided us with accurate and courageous decisions for increasing revenues and assets. Although I have not always agreed with him, as is true at present, he has never been far from the mark.

So, contrary to the advice of some of the board members, I have decided to support Richard's proposal regarding land expansion and drilling locations. Somehow, I do not think he will let us down now.

Rivers Kern

Chairman of the Board

CHAPTER
LXI

Lenora felt groggy and restless lying in the hospital bed Monday morning. She had been in the hospital a couple of days after her surgery and greatly missed her career. Dr. Butler had been in to see her twice a day since her surgery, and she rather enjoyed the handsome doctor's visits. He had a warm character that was gentle yet strong. Dr. Butler was a better man than her late husband had been or Rodrigo was. He must be married, she thought. Any man—doctor—with such a graceful bedside manner, *definitely* could not be available.

Bethany, Lenora's sister, peeked through the door. She was an embodiment of peace as she walked into the hospital room, her giant cross glinting in the sunlight as her long gray skirt swished as she walked. Bethany had always been at peace. She had joined the convent out of high school, knowing that the path of God was her way.

"How are you feeling, sis?" Bethany said as she walked over to Lenora and laid a kiss on her forehead. Lenora took in the simple serenity and beauty of her sister and sighed; she had missed her. Lenora had been so wrapped up in her career lately, she had not contacted her sister regularly. She realized it had been over two months. Lenora knew when she saw her sister briefly on Friday before the surgery that Bethany was the right person to be here for her.

"I'm doing better. You are just in time for my last inpatient visit from my surgeon," Lenora said.

Sam knocked on the door and entered with his metal clipboard. He greeted them both, noticeably shaken by the resemblance and the presence of someone of God in the room. He felt confident, suddenly, that his decision in the operating room was the right one. He had had the opportunity to possibly do to Lenora what he had done for Rich, but he couldn't, with a good conscience, repeat it without discussing it with men of the cloth. Seeing Bethany gave him a sense of peace that he had made the right decision.

After a few care instructions he gave to Bethany, he scheduled two appointments the following week and a weekly appointment with Lenora for the next six weeks to check her progress and ensure that the tumor didn't return.

Sam smiled at them and thought to himself that although these sisters looked strikingly similar, Lenora was much more becoming. She was a strong and intelligent woman, something he had learned about her over the last couple of days. Sam had known that Carolyn was too young for him, but he had enjoyed being taken care of for once in his life. She had treated him with care and respect, unlike Gladys.

But Lenora—she was the kind of woman he had always dreamed about finding. She wasn't obsessed with fashion like Gladys, and there wasn't as big a generational gap as there had been with Carolyn. No, she was ideal. Lenora would be a life partner for the right man, not a show piece. He scolded himself. He shouldn't be thinking of his patient like that.

He left the room to sign the discharge papers and have a nurse ready a wheelchair, but he couldn't help the tingle of excitement in his chest at the prospect of seeing Lenora again, even if it was only for a check-up.

CHAPTER
LXII

Richard had spent the last two months convalescing; they had passed slowly. He used that time to think about Global, its future and his position. It was one thirty in the afternoon, and Richard was in the office of Dr. David Levine, Sam Butler's associate; Sam was out of town at the moment.

From the window of Levine's office looking northwest, Richard could see his company's marble-skinned office building towering above the others near it. The February sun made the reflective glass of the buildings glow a bright orange. Global seemed so far away from the twenty-second floor of the St. Matthew's medical plaza, yet it would take only ten minutes to traverse the distance.

The view of the downtown Houston skyline excited Richard. He had watched it grow to be the third-largest building complex in the country. The assortment of geometric shapes made the buildings seem unreal—like a play city built with colored blocks.

The awareness of his physical and mental

conditions during his stay in St. Matthew's Hospital had changed his feelings for this sparkling city. It was more a living organism than a pile of bricks, mortar and glass. The lifeblood of Houston was oil, which coursed through the most elaborate pipeline complex in the world in the same way blood courses through the vascular system. Houston's heartbeat was the throb of the pumps and compressors that forced natural gas and petroleum products to market. The muscles of the city were the collection of refineries and petrochemical plants that translated the raw oil and gas into the needs of the country. Then the brain—yes, the brain—was made up of the thousands of small office cubicles occupied by scientists, lawyers, engineers, executives, bankers, accountants—all communicating with each other by e-mail, phone and fax. Yes! Houston had a brain.

The part of this living city Richard appreciated most was the medical center that kept the city healthy, monitoring and managing it like the endocrine system of the body, which tempers every moment of life by constantly modifying our feelings, thoughts, behavior and reactions.

Houston had been financially sick for over twenty years, starting in the early 1980s, resulting from the lower crude prices and loss of tax benefits from producers. But just as the body uses creative means to heal itself, Houston changed its oil-dominated focus to petrochemicals and high-tech developments, particularly in computers and health care. Richard realized he would not be sitting in Dr. Levine's chair if he had not gotten extraordinary medical attention from one of the largest medical centers in the world.

David Levine had scheduled the meeting with Rich to allow himself time to complete his grand rounds. As Richard sat quietly in the office, he reflected on the bizarre events that had occurred in his life. He was strangely not surprised that the hospital staff, particularly Dr. Levine, considered him a medical miracle. Except for a slight impairment of his left arm and leg, Richard had regained normal motor functions. Richard wasn't certain Levine fully understood the consequences of the information that Richard received when he had the flashes, flashes that Levine had named *MVBs* for *molecular vision bursts.* Rich knew already what Levine would say about his plans to return to Global, but he made up his mind that he must return to his company if it was to survive.

Bursting into the office, Dr. David Levine went directly to Richard, shook his hand vigorously and said, "Sorry I'm late. We discussed your case today, which could have gone on for the rest of the day. After my office called on my beeper to say you were here, I told the group I had an emergency."

"No problem. I plan to go to a company board meeting at three this afternoon; we're fine."

"Richard, you don't seem to understand that you have been through a serious trauma. Very few people recover from a brain injury. You cannot get back to work yet. It's been only two months since your surgery."

"Levine, let's don't debate this again. I don't entirely accept the fact that I am endangering my life by doing what I not only enjoy but must do."

"That doesn't make sense. There is nothing you must do if it could kill you."

"I don't believe that," Rich said.

"Have you received any *information* about this decision?" the doctor asked.

"Not actually. I get very few flashes about myself, but some of the MVBs that I do get take me into the immediate future. You said yourself that the danger of an aneurism or clot will lessen with time. I should be out of danger soon."

"What am I going to do with you, Richard? I feel like I helped Butler save your life, but I am powerless to preserve it."

Richard laughed out loud. "You have some Indian philosophy, there. I won't hold you responsible for me."

"Let me tell you again. Because you have said that you are walking into a den of vipers if you go back to your company, the vipers might bite you, and the stress could kill you. You don't need money. Why don't you go take a trip around the world? You should be thrilled you're still alive."

As if talking to one of his children, Richard said, pitching his voice lower, "You know I appreciate what you did and are trying to do."

"Why don't you listen to me? I am not exaggerating

the risk."

"If I don't go to this meeting today, some things will happen that I may not be able to reverse."

"So?"

"Too many of my friends and family have invested in my company. We have over six hundred shareholders all over the country. I can't let them all get taken by sheer greed. You have twenty thousand shares, don't you?"

"I'm not concerned about those shares; I'm concerned about you."

Realizing further discussion was useless, Levine walked to his bookcase and slipped out several MRI films. He walked to the window to hold them up to the glass.

"These two disks are wired in to cover the entry and exit of the bullet. The real miracle is how the small caliber bullet could go through your brain without doing more damage than it did."

"Well, it did, and here I am. And I will attend the board meeting this afternoon. I have some news for them, and hopefully, they will have some good news for me."

Richard got up to leave, knowing that Levine would not prevent him from going to the board meeting.

CHAPTER
LXIII

At two thirty in the afternoon, Daryl White came to Richard's house to pick him up for the board meeting at Global Tower. Earlier, Evelyn had bought him a suit and tie and white shirt and dressed him for the occasion, his first outing since his brain injury.

When he spotted Daryl, he called out, "I'm ready."
"Everyone is waiting for you," answered Daryl, "board members and staff."

Rich swallowed hard and said, "Let's go." He had opted for a wheelchair because he was still not fully himself in the energy department, not to mention that the Global hallways were long and slick.

As the limo with Richard and Daryl approached Global, it made a U-turn and parked right at the front door. There were flags on each side of the main entrance and a large number of people on each side of the door.

"What's going on?" asked Richard. "It looks like the Academy Awards."

"Well, bro, I think they're here to welcome you home. The entire staff wanted to share in the homecoming."

Richard was flabbergasted. His face lit up as he greeted the men and women who had been a part of his business and a part of his life for so long.

Once inside the building, the crowds continued. Daryl guided him to the tower elevator and went with him to the top floor.

When he exited the elevator, he again saw friends, but this time they were board members and the executive staff.

"What a welcome this is," cried Richard. "A million thanks to all of you."

After about thirty minutes of chatter from excited voices, Rivers Kern called the meeting to order. Linda called the names of the board members and staff who were present. Answers came from the board members—Moore, McLean, Tinnhauser, Slizer and Finley—and from the staff—London, Hood, Payton, Sledman and Richard Winrock.

The minutes from the last meeting were read and approved. Then Kern stood up and said, "We have some serious business to take care of first."

He looked around the large table and said in a solemn voice, "Over the past few months, there has been a significant amount of unrest in the company. Richard and I have tried numerous times, sometimes with other board members, to determine the cause of the disturbance. At the refinery in Texas City, there appears to have been deliberate efforts to sabotage the efficiency of the refining process. Fortunately, Bud was aware of what was happening, found the culprit and remedied the problems.

"At the administrative office downtown, there was a campaign to undermine the decisions of Richard Winrock, our president, and encourage an attitude of pessimism about our future. Some of this was communicated to outside competitors and to the media. The latter problem, leaked to the press, has been identified and remedied.

"I've given considerable thought to the reasons why. There are a number of possible reasons someone might jeopardize his job by that action. Number one, if the stock goes down, outsiders will sell it, and the insiders will buy it low, knowing that Global really is a strong company.

"Second, if someone is in collusion with another American company or foreign group, it will allow the prospective buyers to buy it cheap and give the individual making this possible a large commission. Third, by blaming the president for the company's travails, there is a possibility for him to be fired and for someone else in the company to take over the role of president. There may be more reasons, but I don't see any value in reviewing them here.

"Two competent individuals who guard our company's resources and personnel, Clyde Warner and Arnie Anderson, have identified the sources of the problems. But, instead of making it public, we have decided it is better for the company—and the individuals concerned—if those in the wrong would simply stand up and leave the building, no words or questions spoken. The names of the board members who leave will be sealed. Therefore, this matter won't hinder Global's reputation. We will leave it to the civil courts to provide appropriate punishment for your crimes against the company, against the stockholders and against the colleagues who were once your friends."

First, Slizer stood up, pulled together his papers and walked out. He was followed by Tinnhauser and Finley. After they left, there was a pause during which no one moved. Slowly, Dan London stood and walked out.

The staff, who had been unaware of the efforts to undermine the company, were stunned.

Kern said in a firm voice, "We will now continue the agenda. In case you or President Winrock haven't heard the good news, the lot that Richard recommended to test our new drilling techniques was the right one. It looks like it will compare to Spindletop. Second, the pilot test we were conducting at the refinery under Bud's supervision has proven to be successful; we now have a twelve percent increase in production capacity. Our thanks to everyone involved under the leadership of Richard Winrock."

There was wild clapping in response to these announcements. In fact, most of the staff and board members went to congratulate Winrock. The secretary then reported on the remaining tasks for the board, which included nominating individuals to fill the board vacancies and replacing Richard Winrock temporarily while he had a chance to fully recuperate.

"I nominate Rivers Kern to be interim president until determinations are made regarding the company administration," called out Bob McLean.

"I second the motion," called Thad Moore, "and ask for a unanimous vote."

The board then accomplished all their business, and the meeting was adjourned.

CHAPTER
LXIV

"Hello," a soft raspy voice responded to the phone's ring.

"Lenora, this is Bethany. Your voice sounds like one from outer space."

Lenora laughed, "Well I am coming out of a deep sleep. Is everything OK at home?"

"Everything is fine. You have been on my mind since I returned home. I am afraid I have become attached to Houston, to the Medical Center and reattached to my sister."

"That's good news! Maybe you will come back to Houston for a visit soon? The past month you were here went by so fast; we were so busy with our trips to the hospital. Besides, I miss your good cooking."

"Tell me, how are you feeling? Have you recovered your stamina? Have you gone back to work?"

"I am better and have more energy. I go to the office

only part time. The staff has been great and helpful. Also, I have tried to broaden my focus on life. I actually go out and am trying to make new friends outside of my professional colleagues."

"That sounds great! Who?"

"Someone you met when I was going to the hospital for my check-ups, Dr. Helen McLean. You may remember her as the neuropsychologist, the wife of Bob McLean? Bob and Sam—Dr. Butler—were partners in the real estate deal I was involved with.

"Well anyway, Helen was interested in the tests that were used in my case. And so, we became friends and luncheon partners. I like her because she has managed to be successful in her home life as well as in her professional life."

"I'm so glad you have found someone like Helen for a friend. I'm curious, have you seen Dr. Butler outside of the clinical evaluations? I really do like him."

"Now that you mention it, we bumped into each other at the nursery. We were both looking for plants for next season. On the spot, he invited me for coffee. This was followed by an hour conversation about the Medical Center. He is dedicated to making it the leading provider of hospital care in the country."

"No personal chit-chat?" Bethany asked, her voice a bit disappointed.

"No. And I'm not sure I want that, nor does he. However, I do admire him."

"By the way, do you think you can get away from Houston in a few months? Mother has been wanting to see you, as have I. My recent time with you was wonderful but short."

"Maybe. That might be fun and helpful to me too; you and Mother would be like medicine."

"Well, think about it and take care of yourself. Let's pray for each other."

"I will, and thank you for call, Bethany. I love you."

"I love you too, sis."

CHAPTER
LXV

Six men and a woman sat at a table in Bob McLean's library, somber and silent. Bob stood up and introduced himself and everyone in the group to each other. "I will introduce each of you by first name only. Thus, each person's point of view will be interpreted without the influence of his or her reputation or professional position. On my right is Richard. Next to him is Sam, followed by Donald, Paul and David." Each man bowed his head at the mention of his name. Bob turned to the other side of the table saying, "To my left is my wife, Helen, and to her side is her special guest, Michael.

"Dr. Samuel Butler," Bob said as he pointed to Sam, "is a neurosurgeon at St. Matthew's Hospital. I mention his title as it will help us to validate a medical issue that might have far-reaching implications and consequences and for which we will request your advice."

Sam remained seated, looked about the room and began his story: "Two months ago, I was called into the emergency room at St. Matthew's to attend an adult patient with a gunshot wound in the head. The patient needed surgery immediately and was taken to the operating room, where for two hours, I surgically repaired the area of the brain that had been injured. Because every injury is unique, I had to improvise my procedure, keeping careful account of each step that I took.

"The post-surgical response by the patient was good, particularly his communication skills. To the surprise of the nursing staff, the patient began to repeat information about the surgical details and other events to which he had not been exposed. After a period of four to five days and after subsequent similar behavior exhibited by the patient, I and numerous other doctors and nurses concluded the patient was experiencing something like extrasensory perception. Being highly educated and experienced, the patient became aware, himself, of his ability to know events before or during their occurrence; the psychological reactions of the patient to his problem were noted by the medical staff.

"Now, as a result of what happened, I find myself in a moral and ethical dilemma and need help resolving it. The problem is that through extensive reading of research on the clairvoyant-type effects of injury to the brain and by reviewing my own procedures in tissue repairs, I believe I know what may have caused the effects and my role in causing them during exploration and repair.

"The dilemma is, what do I do with the information? Do I share it with the medical world, provide the population with significant information about the brain and a new communication method? Or do I guard the information so that no one will ever use it again?"

"I've never heard anything so preposterous in my life!" The words exploded from a single voice in the group of listeners.

Bob interrupted, "Wait a minute, David. You need to hear the rest now. Rich, why don't you pick up the story?"

Richard stood up and for few seconds did not say a word as he looked around the group. He began, "I am Richard Winrock, and I am the patient. I am a chemical engineer by education, and I serve as president of a major oil company." At these words, the faces of David, Paul and Donald began to show some recognition.

Richard continued, "Two months ago, I was shot in the head, taken to St. Matthew's hospital and operated on to repair a bullet hole. Dr. Sam Butler, well-respected neurosurgeon, used his excellent skills to put my brain tissues and skull back in working order. When I woke from surgery, I felt good and immediately ready to communicate with those around me. I was surprised that I knew so much about what had transpired during my emergency ride to the hospital and my surgery. What really scared me was that I knew what had happened at work and at home during the ordeal as well. I began making comments to that effect, frightening the nurses who immediately called the doctor."

David interrupted, "Are you trying to tell me that you are clairvoyant? Do you expect us to believe this?"

371

At that moment Bob stood up to take control of the meeting. "Not without some follow-up information. I know this seems like a stretch of the imagination at the moment. Helen, please introduce our next speaker. His presentation will help you understand the broader picture."

Helen stood and said, "It is my pleasure to introduce Dr. Michael Miller—to his friends, Mike—who is a neurophysiologist and director of the Center for Brain Studies at Hollman University in Boston. Mike has been a colleague of mine and of Dr. Butler's for many years, and both of us respect his knowledge of the brain as well as his scientific research. We have asked him to be here today to present an overview of ESP and to lead our discussion on the events of the past two months that have occurred at St. Matthew's Hospital." Helen paused and said, "Dr. Miller."

Miller began, "You have brought me here to address the topic of extra sensory perception, ESP. The debate about acquiring knowledge of events in humans without sensory input is centuries old. To date, the scientists have refused to accept such a phenomenon as truly existing and refer to the studies of ESP as pseudoscience. These scientists refer to ESP studies as investigations of anecdotes and refer to those who believe and study ESP as parapsychologists. ESP, most scientists say, does not exist.

"*True* scientists, as they call themselves, use instruments such as the electroencephalogram and neuro-imaging measures to examine the brain waves for evidence of **ESP.** According to these true scientists, the parapsychologists have no evidence to support their claims, because **ESP** behavior cannot be measured in a laboratory, nor can specific experiments be repeated.

"Most legitimate scientists recognize that different areas of the brain are specialized for different functions in man. These modules have different roles in cognition. To some extent, the modules are sensory, but the complex behaviors, such as reading and understanding conversation, are connected to areas of the brain other than the primary ones. According to these scientists, there is no evidence to support any function that is not space or time oriented.

"The opposite point of view is presented as the theory called *Experiment with Time,* Dunne's theory of *serial time*, which proposes that time exists in layers on dimensions, and the different layers are viewed in different perspectives. Dunne concluded that the origins of all layers is *absolute time*, created by God. To the believers of ESP, the ability to have connection without space or time, as is exhibited in cognition without sensory perception, indicates there is a *first cause* that creates the human reality as opposed to the position that the development of humans is a function of adaptation and is caused by the environment in the form of evolution. The *First Cause Theory* proposes a God that creates reality as opposed to the evolution theory that describes the evolution of reality."

After pausing for a few seconds, Mike concluded with his presentation. "Now, let's get down to a discussion of our particular case. I'd like to ask Dr. Butler about the specific occurrences in the hospital considered to be ESP. First, do you have an opinion on the type of ESP that Rich has been exhibiting?" asked Mike.

"We know it's not telepathy or retrogression. But neither are we sure if it's clairvoyance or precognition or both," answered Sam.

Mike continued, "Do you have any data on the co-occurrence in time of the episodes of ESP with the events that they portray? Did the ESP precede or follow the expression by the patient of his knowledge?"

Sam responded, "Unfortunately, we did not keep those kinds of records, not knowing, at the time, that such information would be relevant to our understanding of the problem."

Mike paused, then said, "I guess it really doesn't matter unless we are to do a research study. For research, we would need to know if it was precognition—knowledge before the event—or clairvoyance—the ability to see events happening somewhere else. They both involve a disassociation of general time and space from the dimensions of time and space in which the individual finds himself."

Bob interrupted, "We must accept that the witnesses, who were numerous, the patient and Sam, the surgeon, are reporting accurately."

"Right!" said Mike. "And now we move onto the question: What was the phenomenon that did occur? The scientist would say that this is an example of the evolution of the human brain in the manner that other sensory aspects of the brain have developed in response to the needs of the culture."

David broke in, "Evolution doesn't take place in one day after a gunshot wound. That idea is preposterous."

"Besides, how does evolution know where it is going in the future? The culture has not developed that far," added Donald.

"The point is," Sam said, deliberately and with gravitas, "my dilemma is what to do with the information I have. Ethically and morally considering this information, what are my actions from here on?"

Bob picked up the discussion. "Sam is asking how to find the answer to a significant problem: What does he do with the information that he has discerned? Is there a place or a gate in the brain that can be opened to another level of cognition, like a side gate to another dimension? Is it available to be communicated? And should Sam reveal this to humanity? Knowledge about existing and future events could prevent serious bellicose exchanges among nations and would help prepare for national disasters."

"Well," commented Paul, "knowledge of the working of the brain could help individuals who have some type of brain malfunction. Using it may lead to cures for numerous perception, memory and cognitive disabilities."

"On the other hand," said Donald, "such a procedure could have significant negative consequences on society. Who would be allowed to execute the surgery? What price would people pay for the ability to change brains in that manner? What would happen if the wrong people could get ahold of secret information? Would only the rich be able to afford it? Could those who have the surgery become the powerful and our society become rebellious?"

Paul answered, "It appears that all actions have both beneficial and detrimental consequences. What else do we need to take into consideration that could close the door to our brain to prevent the catastrophes that might follow?"

"Frankly, speaking from experience, it is not a pleasant situation for the person who has what we are calling ESP." Richard commented, "I really didn't want to know everything about everybody."

"We could talk about this for days and not arrive at an overriding conclusion." Bob McLean closed his eyes and put his head on the back of the chair.

"Is there not one conclusion that we could all agree on as being the determining factor?" offered Rich.

"Before trying to reach a conclusion, let me introduce the three members of the group who have not yet been identified." Bob turned to David on the end and said, "This is Rabbi David Kohen, of the Congregation of Emanuel," as he pointed to David. "In the middle is Paul Kinser, pastor of St. Luke's Methodist Church, and this is

Monsignor Donald Flynn." He indicated the next person. "He is the priest at St. Francis who also teaches at the seminary. Now, Monsignor Donald, would you add to what has been said?"

"I have listened with great interest and a significant amount of fear to what has been recounted here today. I understand the moral and ethical dimensions of the 'postern' and the seriousness of the determination we are trying to specify. There is one dimension that we have not yet spoken of, and that is the spiritual dimension. Hopefully, we will see that the spiritual dimension is going to provide the answer to Sam's dilemma.

"The Catholic Catechism reminds us that we are created in the image and likeness of God. Taken literally, it means that we are like God, but we have limitations that are not God-like. Catholics believe that these are a result of original sin. The issue here is that the human being is what God wants it to be. They have abilities and limitations that are ordained by God. There are likely many things that our brain has the inherent capacity to do, but the 'postern door' is closed for us as humans. My belief is that we should not open it. Instead, I think we should thank God for allowing us to learn one of the secrets of the brain. However, because it was learned accidentally, we should let it remain hidden until it may be released, later, in God's time."

Rabbi David Kohan added, "I too can see no ultimate human value to moving on with the surgery you describe. In fact, I believe we should forget that it exists. Sam, I admire the excellence of your work in surgery, but I also admire your wisdom to ask for help in finding the moral and ethical considerations."

Sam responded, "Thank you, Rabbi, Pastor, and Monsignor. This burden has been lifted off my shoulders, as well as those of Bob and Rich. Now it is carried by the five of us. I think the decision to close the 'postern door' is the right one."

CHAPTER
LXVI

Lenora was in the garden watering her plants when the telephone rang. She was surprised to hear Bob McLean say, "I know this is short notice, but Helen and I would like to invite you on a short jaunt to New Orleans this weekend. After your medical ordeal, you need to get away for a few days. Helen has become fond of you and would like to get to know you better."

Lenora gasped, but quickly regained her composure. "You mean, this weekend, starting today?"

"Have you been to New Orleans before?" he asked Lenora.

"No, but I've heard and read about it. I am most eager to roam through the French Quarter."

"So is that a yes?" Bob asked.

"We would pick you up about ten for a noon flight. Helen is going to attend a neuropsychological conference and must be there by four o'clock. The plane will be ready by eleven. And, by the way, Sam Butler is also going. It's a good chance for you two to get to know each other better."

"Well," there followed a long pause before Lenora answered, "it sounds like a great trip, but it might be awkward for Sam and me."

"A trip to New Orleans would remove the awkwardness. Say yes."

"It would be exciting. Yes, I will be ready."

Lenora hung up the phone and began to pack.

"What should I take?" said Lenora aloud. "I am going to take a trip to New Orleans, one of the entertainment capitals of the world." She danced around the bedroom, pulling out clothes and packing as rapidly as she could. She stopped and wondered, "Whose plane is it?"

Promptly at ten o'clock the doorbell rang. She ran around the room tucking into her bag the last few items she might need. Arriving at Hobby Airport, the limousine circled through a series of gates and finally parked next to a large white 727 near a private hanger. Bob's pilot and co-pilot approached the limousine, opening the door for the passengers. Bob gave both pilots warm handshakes then introduced them to Mrs. Lenora French and Dr. Samuel Butler as they helped Lenora into the plane.

The plane's interior stunned Lenora. It had the same type of elegance as the McLean home. The upholstery on the sofas and lounge chairs was done in exquisite Bargello. Oriental rugs were on the floor, and heavy leather chairs surrounding a large mahogany table swiveled in a full circle. A matching large mahogany bar stood against the wall separating the central lounge area from a large stateroom and bath.

Bob seated Lenora in a large lounge chair next to Sam then disappeared into the cockpit area with the pilots. Because Helen was busy going over notes, Lenora sat quietly in her chair trying to take in the luxury to which she was being exposed.

Sam was attentive during the flight and answered a number of Lenora's questions about the airplane and the countryside that they were traveling over at six hundred fifty miles per hour.

Just then, Lenora looked out the window and saw a long river. "That must be the Mississippi River." She could not believe they were already approaching the New Orleans International Airport when the captain suggested they fasten their seat belts. The plane taxied to a spot at the far end of one of the terminal buildings. Workers pushed a portable staircase to the plane, and the passengers disembarked and entered another limousine, this time a huge gray Cadillac with heavily tinted windows. As the limousine moved toward town, Lenora thought that she really had changed: She was with friends she knew little about, in a city unfamiliar to her.

Lenora had not visited New Orleans and was amazed at the difference between it and Houston. It seemed to Lenora that, from the air, the countryside was primarily covered with water; dry land was the exception. The buildings they passed on the highway into town seemed to Lenora to be built in congested construction, mostly of wood. The neatness and cleanliness of Houston was not present. It was an old city; the streets were lined with statues and crypts. She could see the water damage that must be a remainder of Hurricane Katrina. The city had recovered a lot, but not totally.

They entered a residential area consisting of large stucco houses set high in the air to protect against the flooding that often occurred. Proceeding down Napoleon Avenue, which originally had a wide neutral ground and was the path of the electric streetcars in both directions, they stopped in front of an old house that had been converted into a restaurant. This was not at all what Lenora had pictured in her mind.

The foursome exited the limousine. Lenora, who had been chattering all the way into town, asked, "What is this? Where are we going?"

Sam chuckled and answered, "It's not the French Quarter, I assure you."

They walked through an open area with an old-fashioned white marble tile floor, a long wooden bar lining one wall, and a small oyster bar in another corner. People were crowded around both bars several layers deep, and the conversation was almost deafening as it reverberated off the wood-paneled walls. The management of the restaurant greeted Bob with a wide smile then led them into a private dining area at the front of the restaurant.

Pascal's Manale had three servers to hover over them the entire meal. They placed a tray of seafood in front of each of them. Bob said, "This place is known for its barbeque shrimp."

"I cannot get the shells off the crab or shrimp without spilling the sauce, but they are delicious," laughed Lenora.

After lunch, they went to the house on Walnut Street where they were staying and rested for a while until they began dressing for dinner.

"My, it seems that all you do in New Orleans is eat," said Lenora.

Helen said, "We thought you would enjoy a quiet, elegant dinner."

It was Friday night, and the foursome opted for dinner and dancing at the New Orleans Country Club. The jazz band on the second-floor ballroom and the New Orleanians were in full swing. Few places on earth could compete with the dancers in the Crescent City.

After dinner and a waltz around the floor, Sam and Lenora slipped out to sit under the giant oak tree downstairs at the back of the club. They began exchanging stories about growing up and college days and then began communicating their dreams and opinions about religion, politics and other important things in life. They realized how alike they were. Then, noticing the time, they joined Helen and Bob for a last brandy.

The house they occupied on Walnut belonged to a friend of Bob and Helen and was free for the weekend. It was a lovely French house lined with internal balconies around a garden patio. The excitement of the night did not prevent a sound sleep.

On the way to the lake the next morning, Lenora began to recognize some landmarks she had seen as they entered the city earlier. Finally, they arrived at the lakefront and parked by an imposing yacht in a canal. Bob advised his guests that they would have a short cruise and brunch on Lake Pontchartrain. The crew of the yacht was expecting them and greeted them warmly. This Saturday was a beautiful, brisk day with bright sunshine and a gentle wind. Lenora declined to sit outside, preferring the large enclosed bridge above the main lounge.

The yacht cruised past several large groups of boats that were engaged in races and soon was nearly out of sight of land. Lenora did not realize Lake Pontchartrain was so large. She sat back sipping wine and thoroughly enjoying herself.

The crew nested the yacht gently back into its berth just after sundown. The lakefront had become a fairyland of lights. Lenora found the cruise restful and was excited about touring the French Quarter with Sam.

The French Quarter was an exciting place to be on a Saturday night. Couples and groups of revelers roamed up and down the narrow streets. Lenora and Sam joined them listening to the music coming from the bars and looking through the store windows of antique shops scattered through the Quarter. They laughed and sang along with other visitors.

By eight o'clock they were hungry, so they stopped in at Arnoud's, where luckily, they were able to get a table upstairs on the balcony. When they returned to the house, they found Helen and Bob were fast asleep. Lenora and Sam were not sleepy. Sam suggested the possibility of staying up and talking some more. Would you be willing to continue our discussion from this evening?"

"I would love it."

"If it gets too late, and we get hungry, we can go to Camelia Grill down by the end of St. Charles, near Carrollton. It's open all night, and we can get great omelets." They talked until one o'clock the next morning.

Sunday morning, after a cup of coffee and a beignet at Café du Monde, they returned to the airport for the flight home. The trip to the airport seemed a long one for Lenora. She was tired and anxious, an anxiety caused by her feelings about Sam. He had been a perfect gentleman during the entire weekend and that made her realize that the feelings were one-sided. This was no time to lose control and start imagining that something existed between them.

Once everyone was on board, Lenora quickly announced that she was very tired and would spend the airborne time asleep. She was actually tired, happy and sad.

Sam was also pensive, moving quickly to the back of the plane. For a while, the only noise in the plane was the engine itself.

Then it happened. Lenora felt someone move into the seat next to hers. It was Sam, she knew. She felt his hand searching for hers. He found it and held it. The grip was warm and caressing. Without a word between them, they held hands all the way back to Houston.

EPILOGUE

The story is over, and I hope you enjoyed reading about *The Postern* and the people who served as characters. You may want to know what is happening in their lives now, so I will end this book by telling you about each one.

The first is Bud and his wife Patty. They decided to take a month off and spend it down in Galveston by the bay. (Galveston has always been a place to rest, and so that is what Bud and Patty hoped to do.) They went fishing this morning and caught a mess of fish. This afternoon Patty is in the kitchen frying up the fish with the hopes of sharing them with others in the neighborhood. While Patty is in the kitchen, Bud is in a lounge chair on the wrap-around porch on the second floor of the house. His boots are on the rail, a beer is in his hand, Charlie Rich is on the radio, and Bud is sound asleep. This is what he hopes to do every day for the rest of his month off.

The second person we will look for is Leo Solis. Because he lives a stressful life in Houston as chief detective, his relaxation takes him to Fredericksburg, Texas, in the Hill Country, where he grew up. Just now he is driving up to the favorite haunt of the young people and getting out of his car. Within five minutes he is surrounded by the youth of the community calling out, "Hey champ! Hi, how are you? Have you come back to live with us?" This adulation comes from the young people because Leo was the champion quarterback for the Fredericksburg football team and won many medals and gold stars in his time.

Then, together with the teenagers, he spends the afternoon chatting and looking up friends.

"Why don't you come to the community center? We are having a big bash, a big hoopla. I know the people from Fredericksburg would love to see you," says Jack, one of his old friends.

"OK, I'll do that," Leo says.

Leo gets spiffed up in his jeans and boots—like all the Fredericksburg cowboys like to dress. He goes over to the hall where two bands are playing alternately. His favorite is country western, so when he gets up and starts dancing, everyone in the room stops, and all eyes follow him as he escorts the pretty girls around the dance floor. He is really good. If he is good in detective work, he is good at football; and if he is good at football, he is the best country dancer in the neighborhood. So, I think we will find him on the dance floor practically every night of his vacation.

The couple we are looking for next we find on a cruise ship on the rivers feeding into the Mediterranean Sea. Rich and Evelyn Winrock left Houston, got on the cruise ship in Florida, and have been on the ship ever since. They have seen everything, done everything, invited their children along, and some actually joined them for a little while. They have learned how to relax, and they have enjoyed it so much more than anything they have enjoyed in a long time. It's funny, how when you have a brush with death, you appreciate what you have so much more, and you learn how to enjoy it.

We find Bob McLean and his wife, Helen, still in Houston. They enjoy their city so much that they don't like to leave. Helen has her work in the Neuropsychology Center at Baylor, and there she is so involved in studying, reading and seeing patients that she really relishes every day of her life helping people.

Bob, on the other hand, enjoys sitting in his chair, feet up on the ottoman, reading the *Wall Street Journal* and other financial journals of the U.S., selecting stocks he wants to buy and sell—having the greatest time in the world. He will probably have lunch at the River Oaks Country Club and share a good war talk with his friends. So, Bob and Helen don't need to go out of town to relax and have a good time. They can do it at home.

The final couple we will enjoy seeing are the newly married couple, Sam Butler and Lenora French. They had gotten to know each other very well over the last few months of her convalescence. He got to know not only her but also her sister and the rest of her family as well. They fell in love and married, knowing it was the right thing. For their honeymoon, they decided to take a month-long visit to Puerto Vallarta, Mexico.

They rented a three-bedroom villa up on a cliff where they can look out and see the bay that leads out to the Pacific Ocean. It's exciting to be there, especially when you have full-time maid service and a cook. In having a native cook in residence, you are able to relish the tasty Mexican dishes and authentic food of Mexico. No wonder their friends are going to visit.

So, you see that almost everyone is happy in what they are doing—all except for the wrongdoers who tried to take over the company. They are all caught up in court because of the many witnesses who reported their malfeasance. Who knows what punishment they will receive?

It has been a long trip from the shooting at Global to where everyone is now. At least for the moment, they are in good shape. We don't know if we will see them again, but it has been fun.

Hope you enjoyed the journey, and thank you for reading the book.

ABOUT THE AUTHOR

Robert Woolfolk graduated from Tulane University in 1947 with a B.E. in Chemical Engineering and started his professional work with a major oil company, creating new technologies in offshore gas technology and petroleum processing, which are still used today. After many successes and a merger, Woolfolk became a foreign venture manager, a private consultant and finally he formed his own international oil company. He traveled the world through work and his time in the Navy.

Woolfolk was a star athlete qualifying for the National U.S. Olympic Tryouts. His sports were: diving, pole vault, high hurdles, discus, javelin and running. He also won hundreds of medals in the Senior Olympics.

Robert Woolfolk was born in New Orleans, Louisiana in 1923 and lives in Houston with his wife and daughter. He has also written *Little Slices of the Big Easy.*